Are you going to SKOWHEGAN FAIR?

Robert Wesley Clement

20 Twenty
Literary Group

ISBN
978-1-962868-82-2 (Paperback)
978-1-962868-83-9 (eBook)
978-1-962868-81-5 (Hardcover)

This story is dedicated to all the men and women who have done their part to make America the most generous country on earth. Most of us came from modest means and have used the gifts that our creator supplied us with to build successful, fulfilling lives. Along the way we offered a hand to the oppressed, the afflicted, the trodden down. I refuse to get drawn into political discourse I will simply say this— when we sit down at the table to break bread whether we use our right hand or our left, we are all brothers and sisters.

TABLE OF CONTENTS

INTRODUCTION

When the most anticipated event in town, the Skowhegan fair offers up more than the smells of hot dogs, fried onions and peppers and French fries our world is thrown off balance. When the night sky offers a light show that has nothing to do with the moon and stars we must find true north on our own.

When in fact our entire world as we know it, is thrown what seems an un-hittable big old sweeping curve ball, as a town and a nation we have to stand in there and trust our instincts.

The characters in this story are composites of people I have known and loved throughout my life. If you think you recognize them, walk up and shake their hand they made this a better world.

The summer of 1963 was filled with hope. Carl Yastrzemski was having a season that had New Englanders believing their Red Sox might emerge from the middle of the pack and challenge the dreaded Yankees. If John Glenn could circle the earth then surely the bean-towners could do better.

With a young energetic President in office teenagers were beginning to follow national events. John F. Kennedy was our President he was our hope for a brighter future. We were being asked to make the world a better place by volunteering around the globe.

Rachel Carson was asking us to examine the way we treated our world. Words like Pesticides and DDT became part of our vocabulary.

A conflict in Southeast Asia was beginning to challenge our knowledge of geography—an undeclared war more and more becoming the lead-in on nightly broadcasts. We looked to Walter Cronkite to make sense of it. He was the most trusted man in America.

We let our parents handle the heavy lifting, we teenagers remained insulated by the comedies and game shows that filled our living rooms. TV was our entertainment medium.

Some things we couldn't ignore. Older guys we remembered from recent football and other sports teams were suddenly commanding attention for an entirely different reason.

The first funeral attended by members of the class of 1964 for an older former sports star who was now being hailed as a hero for a very different reason— he died for his country.

And still we refused to believe our innocence was lost. Surely this conflict would not last— we were after-all the most powerful nation on earth.

Music was changing, the Beatles arrived. But just below the surface a different lyric with a common theme; the collective voice of protest. Bob Dylan sang of it. Glenn Campbell sang of it. Joan Baez sang of it. Simon and Garfunkel sang of it. We heard the words, but still— it was a different world this side of the Kittery Bridge.

In the little Central Maine town of Skowhegan in the county of Somerset none of it seemed real. What was real was Ma Beane's hamburgers, hot dogs, and fries served up by local beauties— feeding our evenings.

Adults stopped in for some of Ma's famous fried clams and shook their heads at our actions as we danced on the outdoor concrete pad. The outdoor juke box lived on hard earned quarters— no protest songs for us just good old rock and roll. We sat in our cars telling tall tales or planning the evening's mischief which usually entailed enticing one of the girls who served us food to a ride home.

Spinning tires— would on the hour it seemed— send squeals and blue smoke into the night, Ma Beane hurriedly trying to catch a glimpse so she could chastise the culprit when they returned— as they always did.

Route 201, the north–south spine that ran right past Ma Beane's, carried heavily laden trucks that seemed to be trying to catch their breath from the long uphill climb as they passed one of our two watering holes. Trucks coming south were just as noisy as they downshifted from a steep hill they had just descended.

Just up that hill was the Drive-In Theatre. Friday and Saturday night we'd load two or three of us into the trunk of a car, park next to the woods and when darkness arrived emerge to watch the night's double feature. If we were fortunate enough to have a girlfriend we might get to borrow the family auto and actually pay for the opportunity to hold hands and make out.

Directly across the road from Ma Beane's was a shoe factory and a Drapery factory where many of our parents toiled away for minimum wage, or sweat through eight hours of piece work.

The little elementary school many of us had attended was just across the parking lot from the shoe factory. A little league field with benches that the factory workers sat on eating their bag lunch was a playground for us when we were little.

On the other side of town Barry's Pizza was the hangout for us guys. It was our man cave. We played pinball, planned our battles, Swigged bottles of RC Cola and Nehi Grape soda. Some of us even worked there. On weekend nights our poker games sometimes took place in the back room after the place closed. Gossip, half-truths, and just plain bragging bounced off the walls with the same regularity as the steel balls working their magic on the chosen pinball machine. From planning hayrides to stealing apples and corn Barry's was our headquarters.

We weren't little kids anymore. There were new girls moving to town, some working in those shoe factories— some housed nightly in the woman's reformatory just outside town. In the past the reformatory had loomed as a silent fortress. A prison we were told, with all the ramifications that term implied.

With a new warden and a new approach young women were being allowed to leave the grounds to work during the day and in some cases attend high school.

I had grown three inches in the last year and had actually gained ten pounds. Just tonight at Ma Beane's I met a girl recently returned to our town. She's awfully pretty, Sheila, is her name. She will be a sophomore at Skowhegan High School this year— if she stays. She's traveling with the fair but hopes to find a place to live back in her hometown— I hope to get to know her. She was sitting at the one little table next to the Juke box with a former running-mate. He has been gone for two years as well, left when he was a sophomore. I thought I had changed— this former Cross Country runner now looked like he could better help our football team. Gregg Croteau says he won't be here long he's traveling with the fair for the long term.

Killings, robberies, and race riots were still something our parent's read about or viewed on television screens. It wasn't happening here. What was happening here was summer— school vacation.

1963 was the last summer of freedom for our graduating class of 1964. Our senior year promised to be filled with fun, new friends, just one more year of stuffy classrooms—even that tolerable when you're top dogs. Yup, it should be memorable.

❁

Indeed it would be memorable both locally and World-wide but for reasons none of us could have imagined. I am telling this story but everything that follows was either told to me, I saw for myself, or read about in the local paper. I am a watcher, my name is Myron. First though, Sheila the girl I just met has the floor. When she told me all that had happened to her in the past year— I said you ought to write a book. She said just give me the first few chapters.

❀

This story is being told fifty-two years after it happened. Two years ago my fiftieth reunion took place and that evening I was reminded of what a remarkable class I had been part of. As athletes we were nothing spectacular, scholars there might have been one or two.

Hard workers—that might best define the people I shared that evening with. Hard work also defined the heart and soul of the town we grew up in. We made that town our own— at least in our own minds— at least for that year. When I look back it is clear, innocence was lost during our senior year not only for our town but throughout the nation. The music that echoed all that happened that year surfaced in the form of both protest and downright defiance. Enduring musical artists provided the lyrics for a cultural revolution that even today is listened to, paid attention to, and referred back to.

Anyway, say hello to Sheila for me.

PART ONE

HOPES AND DREAMS

- SHEILA

- FLAGLER COUNTY FLORIDA

- JUNE 1962

Sheila reached across the table for another biscuit to sop up the remaining juice from a canned baked bean dinner. Her hand never landed as a huge hand covered her own and squeezed. The voice at the end of that hairy paw sounded like it had been squeezed out of that same can of beans.

"Always ask first Missy, that's the way we operate here ain't that right, Mother?"

Heads nodded in unison, nervous snickers giving those heads voice. Three food stained mouths painted in bean brown flecked with biscuit crumbs broke the tension; Sheila looking at the three tousled little boys had to smile. The smile righted the boat and she kept her temper in check. Even the dog sliding from chair leg to chair leg beneath the table, begging for a scrap or finding a dropped morsel, perked up his ears when Albert had the floor.

Sheila's Aunt Terry mostly nodded in agreement no matter the topic or perceived indiscretion. Clearly this live-in boyfriend was in charge, though Sheila hadn't seen where he offered anything but monetary support for the family of Six—her included.

Still holding onto Sheila's hand while making the circuit with his eyes, Albert James Brown continued, "You been here more than a month now, you ain't one of them slow learning short bus individuals are yuh? Seems like we might already have one in your youngest Terry, he don't say a word, just grunts."

Terry nodded her head but was clearly not happy with this conversation.

Sheila looked directly at the hand covering her own, "Sorry Uncle Albert my mind was wanderin' I guess." She tugged her hand loose, placing both hands in her lap, determined not to cry; her face feeling as pinched as her hand.

Fifteen years old and fifteen hundred miles from where she wanted to be, Sheila was feeling a little sorry for herself this evening. She took a deep breath and managed a smile. "That was a good meal Aunt Terry, can I help with the dishes?"

Albert gave the girl one last look, grunted, scraped back his chair from the table and took the five steps he needed to reach the television grabbing a can of Pabst Blue Ribbon from the fridge on his way. The three children ages 5, 8 and 10 all boys, all born of Terry none of Albert, slipped out into the twilight to join friends.

A semi-circle of trailers that might have been dropped from the sky into the middle of nowhere was their playground. A dirt drive fringed by junk and jungle passed in front of the trailers, the exit resembling the stick end of a long fudgicle. The rural roadway unseen from here remained quiet a quarter mile away.

Sheila looked out the kitchen window while both hands remained busy scrubbing the bean pot. Rectangles of light seeped from the half circle of tin cans this small community of people claimed as their own. She raised her eyes to a moon just now appearing above the canopy of vegetation–refusing to be strangled by the jungle. The evening's first visible stars were clamoring for attention while Sheila herself reflected on how different her life might be if she were gazing from a window in her former life— she sighed. It actually seemed she had died and been born into another time and place.

Florida, shaped like a wounded thumb— the keys explained as little drops of blood— a description her mother had used when showing Sheila a map of where they might move after Mom got her nursing degree.

Sheila had made the trip minus her mother after a tragic accident, complicated by a hit and run driver who had not been found. It had been a journey no young girl would have wished for or imagined.

Aunt Terry spoke, causing Sheila to fall away from the moon and her mind to land like a dropped dish.

"What did you say Aunt Terry, I was just wanderin' again I guess."

Before Aunt Terry could repeat her question, Albert spoke up from his battered recliner. "I really can make arrangements for that little bus to stop roadside if you think you could navigate the quarter mile stretch, Missy," Albert snickered into his beer. *How does he even hear us, he has that damn TV cranked up to screech,* Sheila thought.

Aunt Terry put her hand on Sheila's shoulder and asked, "I was asking if you planned to go in to Sunday service tomorrow morning, you've missed the last two weeks. We miss your voice in the choir."

"Honestly, I'm finding what I need right out in the morning light," answered Sheila. "There's a little pond just through those trees and wildlife like you can't imagine—it's peaceful there. Besides the other girls in church don't seem to like me much, they say I talk different and act different."

Aunt Terry nodded her head, she understood the hard time her niece had in finding her way to rural Florida from in-town Skowhegan, Maine.

Sheila had been a star in every way— Jr. High Academics, Soccer and the voice of an angel to boot. Since joining Aunt Terry and her three hellion boys, combined with the constant snide comments from Albert and the teasing of the girls on Sundays, Sheila seemed to be melting further into herself with each passing day. Not much music touching the girls lips these days.

Maybe high school would give the girl a new start. Of course new starts were hard to come by.

Terry realized her own situation indicated a long haul might be the reality— a life sentence maybe.

Albert was mean, verbally but not physically abusive to her or the boys. He worked hard, drank hard, spent hours watching television, rode his beat up cycle and occasionally when the mood struck him— took Terry dancing.

Shaking her head as muted threats and promises of payback bounced back and forth from the trailers on either side of hers she realized comparatively she probably got a first round draft pick in old Albert. Nervously laughing to herself and nodding her head she thought, *holy shit if my gun sight was aimed any lower I'd be shooting myself in the foot.* Her eyes grew wide, *HELL I ALREADY HAVE!*

Sheila looked at her Aunt for an explanation. Aunt Terry just looked bemused and shook her head, a conditioned response to most everything it seemed.

Albert was laughing like a hyena at some chauvinist remark being beamed to millions of households confirming the superiority of men. Sheila folded the dish towel and went out to watch the young people gathered in the dusk like a swarm of mosquitos. Navigating with the only light left for their recreation— the moon, stars, and leaky light from the windows of a dozen trailers.

Sitting on the rickety metal steps smelling recent eatings—not so recent eatings— and genuine neglect, Sheila focused instead on the sounds of the night. She tuned out human voices from outside and muted the sounds from televisions from within; what she had come to think of as, *the din from the tin.* Constant barking of half a dozen dogs, laughter, squeals, and slapping of mosquitoes all evaporated as Sheila focused on the blackness of the jungle edge and beyond. The youngest boy Jeffery came to sit with her, Sheila rubbed his head.

The birds would be roosting by now hanging from limbs. Rabbits were silently nibbling around the edges of this nothingness. Utter blackness like a pulled curtain, stood just a foot away from the meager penetration of light. Sounds from the dark began competing with the children playing and the TV.'s blaring. Frogs provided the chorus while one wild animal after another took umbrage preparing to recite their lines on center stage— for after all they owned the night.

Sheila heard it all and yet none of it as she floated high above the ground retracing every foot of her journey along the Atlantic Coast. She could recite chapter and verse of where she'd been, name the states she'd stopped in and what moved the journey forward to this final destination, Bunnell, in Flagler County, Florida. Staring up at the stars, the earliest source of night time navigation, she began trying to map a path back north.

Jeffery leaned into her, his head laid on her shoulder.

A rubber ball struck the bottom step with a thunk startling Sheila into what is called a fight or flight mode. Pure reaction and muscle memory had the ball in Sheila's hand and thrown back into the darkness, Jeffery with his head now on her lap was startled by the sudden movement. The thrower— the oldest and tallest boy in the group— went down as if shot.

Not hurt but shocked, the boy came up wiping the dirt from his hands sputtering, "What hit me?"

Sheila aware now of what she'd done, gently removed Jeffery, pushed off the step and ran to the boy. In the eerie light of a nine-thirty night Sheila entered the group of boys and girls and put out her hand. Peering into the half-light the boy was not someone she recognized— even in the dim— Sheila was sure she had never seen this kid before.

Addison Williams wiped his hands again on his pantleg took her hand and like a true southern gentlemen bowed and introduced himself. His voice was mature and his grammar correct, his clothing relaxed but not ragged or filthy, hair long but neat. Sheila knew in that first twenty seconds this boy was as foreign to this place as she.

"Well Addison Williams, I apologize if I hurt you— just my natural reaction to a threat I guess— my name is Sheila, Sheila Thompson. You aren't from here are you?"

One of the boys from the last trailer on the left facing the road spoke up. "He's my cousin on my Daddy's side, Right AW," like a dog seeking approval he looked at Addison Williams beseechingly.

"I am Jed's cousin for sure and I sure am pleased to meet you Sheila Thompson," his eyes never leaving Sheila's. "I live in Orlando, my parents have a little cottage in Flagler Beach. Have you been there, Jed said you weren't from around here?"

Sheila flinched slightly, "So you have been discussing me even before we met and did I hear Jed call you

AW?"

Sheila could see Jed's sheepish grin even in the dim light.

"Jed said there was a beautiful girl who had moved into the neighborhood and he calls me AW because the first and last letters of my name form the initials A.W."

"That explains it." Sheila sighed aloud, "so are you going to just hold that rubber ball or are we going play a game?"

From that moment the two teenagers became a team—this team would experience an unforgettable season.

The summer was a flurry of mornings and evenings and several days at the beach with her new friend.

From eleven 0'clock morning till six in the late afternoon it was dog-dirty hot. One small air conditioner and several portable fans kept the boys,

Aunt Terry, and Sheila in the living room during the heat of the day— every day. The boys claimed the cartoon channels early while Sheila and Aunt Terry bonded over soap operas after one pm. The soaps seemed a million miles away from these tin houses sporting horizontal prongs that beamed tragedy, despair, and despondency to those actually living it— without the frills.

Sheila walked and jogged in the early mornings while it was cool enough to catch your breath. She found animal paths in the piney forest navigating around swamps discovering small ponds with birds of all description— birds that were much larger and more colorful than the Sparrows, Robins, Crows, Ravens, and Blackbirds she had grown up with. This was Sheila's favorite time of day. Well at least until Addison began showing her the beach at Flagler.

• SEPTEMBER 1962

School started and Sheila joined three other high schoolers from the trailer park on a full sized yellow bus that stopped a dozen times picking up kids who all seemed to wear the same expression, clothes, and resignation needed to survive a day in high school.

Staying invisible was the best defense from rumors, teasing, or being called upon in class.

Sheila had no intention of standing out in any way. She had signed up for a middle level program that included mostly business subjects. She actually enjoyed the Typing and Business Math classes which seemed to make sense. She went through the motions in Physical Education class, even throwing like a girl. She wore her hair cut short and used no make-up. Her plans did not include four years at Bunnell High School.

Her General Science teacher seemed more interested in trying to impress the girls who dominated the front row than in teaching anything. Workbook pages filled out ad nauseam— not even corrected— passed in every two weeks for teacher perusal constituted most of the grade. Open book tests— the class was told to applause— would be the visible justification for a nine week grade on the report card sent home.

Sheila was learning a lot. Not a lot to do with education but scads of useful information on how easy it was to get by if you flew beneath the branches. Not all teachers lived by this philosophy but four of Sheila's instructors never raised a pulse in their instruction.

Sheila couldn't fake her ability to read though and even in the first week her English teacher Mrs.

Boardman, had her figured out. At the end of class in the second week she asked Sheila to stay a minute after class.

"Sheila I can't help but notice how well you read, are you sure you are at the right English level?"

"I am satisfied with what I'm doing if that's what you're asking?"

"Sheila, you seem a lot more capable than your class mates, I could get you into a more challenging group."

"To be honest I don't plan to be here long Mrs. Boardman, I hope to go back to Maine soon."

"Well ok, I won't push but let me give you some more challenging reading to do at home. I won't grade you on the books but you will enjoy the stories I think— deal?"

"I don't have a lot of extra time, my Aunt needs a lot of help with three boys"

"Just try this one— Charles Dickens— he has a lot to say about overcoming obstacles, *Great Expectations,* one of my favorites."

Sheila accepted the book nodding her head like Aunt Terry, thinking '*I hope this doesn't become a habit.*'

School days were a blur of sameness, the one point in the day Sheila looked forward to, the double doors of the bus opening in the afternoon. The cloud of dust that trailed them to and from school caught up and enveloped their exit then moved past like a fog bank. Holding her breath till the dust dissipated, she approached the row of mailboxes standing roadside. Their closed mouths mute witnesses to the contents of what an empty mail box might mean to the owner. A slow shake of a head in resignation, or occasionally a shriek of delight signaling the arrival of money or word from a relative.

Sheila had asked Aunt Terry if she might bring in the mail every day.

"It's that boy in Orlando isn't it? Well I'm happy you're happy about something. I thought I was gonna have to get a crutch to hold that chin of yours up," she kidded.

"He's coming up this weekend— I'm going to meet his parents at their cottage."

Aunt Terry studied Sheila briefly, "We need to do something with your hair. I'm going to treat you for all the work you do around here. Let's get your hair and nails done Friday afternoon. You have to quit disguising yourself as a boy. I'll make an appointment in Bunnell."

Sheila beamed, "Thanks Aunt Terry I would appreciate that."

"Don't say a word to the boys, they tell Albert everything— well two of them anyway—he gives them nickels to narc," Terry nodded her head.

"Donna next door will come over to stay with the boys, we'll combine the trip with getting some groceries and nobody will be the wiser." She whispered, "I've got a little bean-can money stashed away," She smiled. "You can say if asked— which you will be, that man misses nothing— that one of the girls at school gave you a do-over. We can use

Donna's car too. She's the one friend I have in this hole."

Sheila gave Aunt Terry a big hug and went out on the steps to read the letter. She held it reverently, she smelled his splash on scent— *my dad's, Old Spice* he had told her. Addison's letter was written as a poet. The two knew one another's thought's by now so Addison playfully described his days since his, *last sighting of Sheila,* as he termed them, in dramatic form:

> *Oh withered morn finds me wilted still*
> *I gaze from bedroom window sill.*
> *Curtains drawn that pale the sun*

Life's only solace a heart I've won.

Fair damsel but I an iron steed

Nae jungle, river, nor swamp impede.

Precious starlight with nod and wink

Trumpets my arrival high above your sink.

The letter wasn't signed. Neither teenager signed their correspondence. The words expressed their signature. Sheila committed the words immediately to memory and ripped the letter as lovingly as possible.

The two had conspired to leave no trail. No perceived contraband Uncle Albert or Addison's parents might use against them. The letters the two exchanged used their own language and the emotion expressed filled the very air. She had told Addison how she wistfully watched the moon rise out the little kitchen window and now he had included it in verse.

Completely satisfied— that at least something positive had entered her life— she rose and entered the trailer ready to attack those damn potatoes.

Friday arrived just as it always does but this one had Sheila actually smiling as she entered the bus. Before she could sit down, the bus lurched forward sending her like a pinball to a seat three rows back. She landed on the outside edge of a seat occupied by two senior girls she had not been introduced to. "Sorry about that, that damn driver doesn't give a person time to sit before he gits," she kidded.

If looks could kill— "That damn driver is my Uncle, Missy and that bag you landed on is my lunch."

Sheila was dumbfounded but determined not to have any trouble, *especially today*, she thought. Her next thought brought Uncle Albert to mind just as the girl grabbed her arm. It had just occurred to Sheila that down here being called Missy was not a term of endearment and she smiled in spite of herself. Seeing Sheila smile, the girl grabbed her by her sweatshirt. "You think I'm fooling here?"

Just as her introduction to Addison had begun with an involuntary response, grabbing the older girls arm and bending it backward without thinking began a whole new relationship.

The girl uttered, "Don't think this is funny, I'll" she screamed, "OW," as her arm was twisted.

Sheila re-entered the moment and tried to smooth things. "I am truly sorry, I don't think any of this is funny, all I want to do is get to school and get home." From the front, "Well you won't be getting to school on this bus," bellowed the driver who was already pulling over to the side of the road. "I saw what you did to that girls arm, I'll be writing a report. Now get off the bus."

Sheila, about to answer back stood up to glare but a girl sitting next to the window in the seat one row to the front and across the aisle touched her hand and signaled her— putting her finger to her lips.

The girl stood up. "I'm getting off too Red and I'd be a little hesitant to write up that report if I was you, I watched how this all happened– and **My** uncle is the bus supervisor."

Staring angrily in the mirror at what he determined were two trouble-makers he nevertheless realized this could end badly for him. He managed, "Never mind girls, just sit down nobody is going anywhere except to school. And you Missy sit in that seat with your new found friend and keep your hands to yourself."

Everyone on the bus was watching this unfold and all eyes seemed to be on Sheila. *So much for flying beneath the branches, eh Missy,* thought Sheila trying on what appeared to be her new name.

As she settled into her seat beside her rescuer she let a minute pass before she spoke. The bus was back on the highway and the noise level of both bus and passengers was loud enough to cover normal conversation. She offered her hand, "I'm Sheila and thank you for helping me out. I would have been in deep junkyard dog doo-doo if my pretend uncle heard I was kicked off the bus– he already thinks I'm on a bus that's way too long."

The girl innocently took her hand, "my name is Dana, and you're new here aren't you?"

"It's my first year of high school and first fall in Bunnell, though it still seems like summer compared to where I came from in Maine."

"I have watched you get on— so you live in that trailer park in the woods?"

"With my Aunt Terry, three boys, a dog, and a son of a bitch pretend uncle. That is my story and I'm sticking to it," Sheila smiled with resignation.

"I've never been down in there but I hear stories," offered Dana without elaborating.

Sheila didn't reply, remembering the number of times flashing lights and sirens had turned into the gravel drive since she had arrived here. Both girls rode the next several miles in silence studying the floor and the seatback in front of them. Through the window the impenetrable jungle-like landscape— broken only occasionally by a dirt path, building or small farm— seemed as silent as the girls.

The bus smelled of fuel, over heated engine oil, rubber, and flatulent kids— an occasional giggle announcing the next wave of stink. Sheila finally asked Dana what grade she was in.

"It's my junior year, I'm already gone though if you know what I mean. I want to go to college in St. Augustine. It's the neatest city, the oldest in America too. When I get my license I'll take you there. What about you?'"

"I'm a lowly freshman. I am tall for my age though, Aunt Terry says. I really want to get back to Maine, that's where I'm from, all my friends are there— no disrespect to you."

"None taken, I will be your friend for the time you are here though, it looks like you could use one." Dana whispered, "Don't worry about that girl you just had a run in with, she's a bully and you stood up to her, that will be enough to discourage her."

"Where do you live? You are on the bus when it gets to my stop."

Dana hesitated briefly as if weighing her answer, "My father drops me off at the first bus stop in Flagler County, just north of the Volusia County line. We live on a large horse farm with parts in both counties so he made the choice for me to attend a rural high school opposed to one in Daytona."

"Do you ride?"

"Like the wind! It's my passion, I draw them too and I want to become an illustrator of children's books using horses to help tell the stories."

Sheila found herself nodding her head like Aunt Terry. "Would you teach me to ride?" She reddened slightly, "I met this boy and he rides too, he lives in Orlando on a horse farm." Sheila smiled, "I would love to learn."

As the bus pulled into the drive in front of Bunnell High School and stopped, the two girls sat waiting for the bus to empty. The offended girl glared at Sheila but said nothing as she exited the bus. Sheila was feeling so good about the ending to what could have been a disastrous Friday morning that she apologized to the bus driver, leaving him speechless and defenseless.

Sheila sat with Dana on the way home and the girls discussed plans to get together in the near future. Dana said she was testing for her license at the end of the month and then would be driving to school, would Sheila care to change her mode of transportation?

'*Those stars are lining up,* smiled Sheila nodding again, *Aunt Terry what are you doing to me?*' The skies had darkened and the first drops of rain began to settle the dust as Sheila exited the bus. She didn't think much about it until she opened the letter that had been lying in the dark enclosure all day— a prelude to the weekend. Sheila couldn't wait, she settled herself on the trailer steps and opened the letter. Drops of rain, little teasers accompanied the torrent of despair.

Cleverly couched in terms of endearment the message was nevertheless disappointing.

Three days of gloom or so I'm told, No beach to walk

Or hand to hold.

Shades of gray,

Heavens tears

Drumming on leafy jungle

The world weeps I fear.

Deserted beaches

Deaf to waves pounding

Mirror my racing heart

That outward reaches.

Oh Sun return that I might start

With parchment crisp and dry

Signaling all is well and in seven days,

We'll risk another try.

By midnight the pounding Sheila heard was accompanied by long jagged shards of lightning suggesting a welding of the entire community. Sheila looked out the small bathroom window and watched strobe-like flashes— revealing what in Maine they termed a gully washer. Water was snaking under, around and over scattered debris; toys and engine parts– anything that could float was floating. The ground so level here that the deluge of water enlarged what was quickly becoming a pond. The area of the dozen trailers now resembled stranded lifeboats floating on a sea of brown.

Newspapers were not required reading in this house and Uncle Albert refused to watch the local news and weather on TV. Sheila had no prior knowledge of what was to be a washed out weekend.

Sheila witnessed thunder and lightning that left her feeling as threatened as when one of the junkyard dogs broke free and menaced the neighborhood. She retired to her small fold-away cot in the hallway at the entrance to the boys' bedroom. She had closed all the windows earlier.

Uncle Albert and Aunt Terry had retreated to their room early in the evening with Uncle Albert clutching a small bag. Sheila put the boys down closed all the shades and opened the book her English teacher had offered— Great Expectations. Sheila's own great expectations had been put on hold including the trip to town for a do-over. The hallway light flickered almost in tune with the sound and light show going on just through the thin wall. Sheila let her eyes fall to the first chapter. The beginning was a little unsettling to Sheila, what with lightning and thunder and the drumming of rain on the tin roof. Reading about tombstones in a graveyard and little children dying in infancy had her tucking her single blanket up around her shoulders. The man in the graveyard sounded too much like Uncle Albert to be comforting. Sheila looked at the closed door to her aunt's room still curious about that brown bag.

When a giant bolt of lightning trembled the trailer, she trembled herself, deciding to postpone this story till well past daylight. She closed her eyes and dreamed of Addison.

Sheila was first up, she made a pot of coffee and studied the swirling mess out the kitchen window. The fresh coffee she had just added a little milk to matched the color on the palette just beyond the glass. She was drinking her second cup and watching cartoons— two of her nephews having joined her on the couch all huddled under a blanket— when Uncle Albert stumbled out to go to the bathroom. His hair was a mess of greasy tangles, clothed in just his briefs, his hairy chest and ever growing gut turning his belly button into a long drooping frown. Sheila noticed all this with just a glance and went back to watching Bugs Bunny and Elmer Fudd, feud.

Albert went to the fridge, farted as he bent to grab a beer. He chuckled to himself trying not to look at least a little sheepish. His head at a slant he voiced a cockeyed "good morning Missy I see you're doing your homework," he snickered. "And feed those yung-uns, I think your Aunt and I will be sleeping late on a rainy morning." He disappeared back into the bedroom leaving only a black cloud of ill will and a stale fart in his wake. Sheila thought, *'he's like that damn dust cloud that follows the bus he just leaves a bad taste in your mouth. Where's Elmer Fudd with his shotgun when you need him?'*

• OCTOBER 1962

Sheila stood by the road. The bus had come and gone. Dana should be here any minute in her 5 year old fifty-seven Chevrolet. Cherry-Red with white side accents it rode like a dream. *'Here she comes now,'* Sheila mouthed to herself. The girls had gotten close over the past month and the ride to school—a seven mile trip—had given the girls time to really get to know one another. With the radio up just enough to provide background music the girls chatted, "So you let your aunt know you're spending the weekend at my house, right?"

"She's going to clear it with Uncle Albert but she's fine with it. I do most everything around the place all week long."

"What the hell has Uncle Albert got to say about it?" Sheila was forming her answer when Dana suddenly stomped on the brakes nearly putting Sheila into the windshield.

"What just happened?" stammered a shaken Sheila.

Dana was already out of the car and looking to see if she had missed the creature.

"There was an alligator in the road I swear, but I missed him—he must have gone into the swale."

Settled back in the vehicle, both girls suddenly giggled and Sheila answered the question that seemed hung in the air. "Uncle Albert thinks he's running the whole show cause he brings home a very meager check every week, then spends most of it on his own perceived needs. Left-overs that's what Aunt Terry and the boys get and I get left-overs from them. But to hear Albert talk he is our salvation. I can't stand the creep. So come hell or high water I will be staying with you this weekend."

Dana looked across the seat with admiration; *'this girl has guts she'll get by alright.'*

"I have a favor to ask about this weekend," voiced Sheila.

Dana looked at Sheila quizzically, "ok ask."

"The boy I told you about, Addison, he's coming over from Orlando this weekend do you think he could join us for a horse ride?" Dana thought for a minute saying nothing, keeping Sheila in suspense. "Does he have a horse riding friend he could bring," she paused for effect. "Just kidding, of course he can join us."

• NOVEMBER 1962

The weather was still warm while the nights began to cool down to comfortable. Sheila had no way of contacting her friends in the North. She had been hustled away so quickly she had no addresses, and Aunt Terry didn't have a phone. The only friendships she had developed here were with Dana– and Addison of course. Uncle Albert was his same old mean self but it seemed even he realized they had all learned to tune him out so he vented most often these days into his ever present can of beer.

The boys had come to respect Sheila. She played games with them, washed behind their ears, joined them outside, read stories at night and tucked them in. She especially loved the youngest, Jeffery and was forming an opinion on what was wrong with the boy. She planned to try a little test with him before speaking to Aunt Terry about it though. Aunt Terry seemed to be relinquishing all responsibility for the boys to Sheila.

The little brown paper bag was making more and more guest appearances, though the performance remained behind a closed bedroom door.

Sheila was finding she actually enjoyed the added duties. The days and nights were flying by, Thanksgiving only two weeks away. School was bearable, nobody bothered her, Dana was her friend, she didn't have to ride the bus and she was in love— a little worried but in love.

Four days off coming right up had Sheila making plans with Dana. "I told Aunt Terry I would get everything ready for the

Thanksgiving meal but I wouldn't be there. She knows I plan to spend the four days with you."

"You mean Addison and me don't you?"

"Well yeah if that works for you."

"Just kidding, I have my own reason for wanting Addison to join us now don't I?"

"A damn good-looking reason at that," laughed Sheila. What had started out as kiddingly asking Addison if he had a friend who might be interested in meeting someone, had turned into a romantic interest for Dana.

Both couples were now riding horses, sometimes together but lately following separate trails. Sheila waved goodbye to Dana Wednesday afternoon then watched the quickly moving vehicle disappear in a cloud of dust. She checked the mailbox and found nothing but circulars advertising holiday specials. Kicking pinecones as if they were soccer balls she managed to keep three of them moving on the dusty gravel road all the way into the trailer park. Singing to herself Sheila was looking forward to the four days with Addison, Dana, and Wyatt– Dana's new best friend. Sliding left and right as the pine cones rolled end to end Sheila looked like the soccer player she had been in Maine, dodging defenders while matching her foot work to the rhythm of song. In fact she was humming to herself as she pulled the trailer door open.

She could tell immediately something was off. First of all the TV was not on. Aunt Terry wasn't sitting on the couch watching a soap opera, waiting—patiently waiting— she was forever reminding Sheila— to watch over the boys so she could go have an afternoon cup of coffee with her best friend Donna. Oddly, the boys were not fussing or fighting either.

Sheila had reminded Aunt Terry that with the boys in school all day she could have coffee with Donna anytime. Aunt Terry had reminded Sheila that it wasn't afternoon just any time, besides she was busy most of the day doing housework and such. "You aren't going to begrudge me a little quiet time with my friend are you, it gets lonely here with all you kids gone you know."

Sheila could have debated sentence for sentence the holes in Aunt Terry's reasoning but let it all slide, for after-all she was a guest here as Uncle Albert so often reminded her.

Donna was seated at the kitchen table the boys weren't visible and it was quiet. "Hi Donna, where's Aunt Terry and the boys?"

"You might want to sit for this Sheila, want a cup of coffee, I made some?"

Sheila got a funny feeling in her stomach— the same kind of feeling that had brought major changes to her life in the last year or so. "I don't want coffee, what's happened to Aunt Terry?"

Donna took a sip of coffee looked Sheila in the eyes and put the cup down as softly as she could. She began in a voice barely audible, "The boys are in Bunnell, I asked Old Bill Wacome, you've met him haven't yah all? Asked him if he'd take them for an ice cream and some fried chicken and fries?" She took another sip of coffee. Like a pump, it seemed she was going to need some priming.

"Where is Aunt Terry, what's happened— did Uncle Albert hurt her in some way?"

Donna sighed like she was reaching for air way down in her socks, "Your Aunt Terry is in the hospital. I came over shortly after lunch and she didn't answer my knock. I found her unconscious." Her eyes widened, "I ran to my place and called the Sheriff's dept. They sent an ambulance."

She twisted her hands back and forth rubbing them as if ridding herself of some unseen debris.

Sheila was on her feet her eyes wide, "Well we need to get over there. She's at the hospital, right?"

"I've been waiting for you, let's go— and just for the record I had nothing to do with what's wrong with your aunt."

Sheila looked at Donna strangely but made no further comment. They rode the seven miles in silence, Sheila wringing her hands and sighing nearly as deeply as Donna had. Keeping her head on the window glass she could see nothing, but imagining the worst.

Donna had the radio tuned to a country station and seemed content to hum along with Willie and not have to explain anything.

The worst turned out to be a reality but not for the reason Sheila had imagined.

Sitting in the waiting room, smells you can't find anywhere else adding confusion to the sounds that accompany illness or accident, Sheila found herself thinking about the story she was well into. In the book Great Expectations, Pips Aunt, Mrs. Joe had been brained senseless. If it were Uncle Albert that was lying in the next room Sheila could almost applaud the similarity of situation. Sheila had lately been finding many parts of the book that seemed to parallel her own life. Her friend Dana was a little like Pips Uncle, Joe Gargery— many times putting Sheila's wants and requests before her own. She was a true friend just as Joe was to Pip. Now just as it seemed Sheila might imagine her own expectations being raised a little she felt in her bones someone was about to step on her fingers.

The Doctor finally came into the waiting area. "Do we have a relative here I can speak to privately?"

"I am the closest relative that I know of," offered Sheila. "What is wrong with my Aunt Terry?"

"I am Dr. Woodruff, I was on duty when your aunt was brought in six hours ago. She is still unconscious from what appears as an overdose of some stimulant that we are checking her blood for. I think she will recover, her vital signs are returning to the normal range."

This man sounds like a Dr. that's for sure, thought Sheila.

"Thank you Sir. How soon before she can come home?"

"Well there's more to this than her present condition I'm afraid."

"What do you mean sir, what's going on with my aunt?"

"Your Aunt has a heart condition that has nothing to do with whatever she took. We need to do some more testing but it appears the heart itself is not healthy."

Sheila tried to take all this in while her mind jumped from possibility to possibility. The only firm landing for her thoughts was the reality that her next four days would not go as she had hoped.

"What does that mean? Is she going to be able to come home when she wakes up?"

"I think it's safe to say your aunt won't be coming home for at least five days. With the holiday some of the tests we need to run won't be completed until early next week. I'll be watching her closely and bringing in a heart specialist as soon as we know a little more. I am very sorry young lady if I am frightening you but this is very serious."

A Dr. for sure. Sheila looked down at her feet suddenly very conscious of how selfish her thinking had been directed. Sheila trudged into the lounge carrying the weight of the world.

Donna was waiting and Sheila gave her the news along with asking a question. Is this stuff Aunt Terry overdosed on from that little brown bag Uncle Albert has been bringing home lately?"

Donna squirmed but answered, "Probably so, I think its high grade Marijuana dipped in something, it provides quite the buzz. I have tried it myself I confess but hallucinated the first time so I haven't done it since– scared the bejeesus out of me. Your Aunt loves it, says she tries to keep a little buzz going most of the morning time now. She must have used more than she was supposed to, and now you're saying her heart is bad? I'm no Dr. but I think the two are not connected except maybe her heart freaked out or something."

"Damn that Albert he's just trouble in a three scoop cone, I hate him so much."

"Well you might want that to be a quiet hate for now, you're going to be the only adult in that trailer for the time-being. Be polite and helpful with the boys and stay out of his way–that's my advice. I'm just a rock throw away, if it hits any of that tin I'll come running."

Uncle Albert arrived shortly after dark unaware of any of what had happened. He was expecting a rare extended holiday himself and Sheila was sure after she told him what was going on he'd be arming himself with the supplies he would need to make it through four days. Sheila heard his Harley as it entered the park– Albert wasn't one to tone down the window rattling bike until he turned it off.

Sheila looked out and watched him empty his saddlebags. He put his groceries– as he termed his beer— in a cloth sack and climbed the three squawking steps whistling— Albert was on vacation.

Sheila was alone, the boys were not back yet and she so truly did not want to begin this conversation.

Uncle Albert continued to whistle while he put three six packs of beer in the fridge. When he finished he looked back from the door before closing it and acknowledged Sheila's presence for the first time. "Well Missy where is everybody? I see old Tom Turkey laying in here looking as down at the mouth as you— at least he has a reason, or am I missing something here?"

Sheila took what was to be the first of many long breaths— she thought of Donna having to dig down deep— and began. "Aunt Terry is in the hospital, she's really sick, something to do with her heart the Dr. said."

Sheila was not going to mention the brown bag, let somebody else sing that woeful song. Albert's eyes widened but his mouth stayed closed. "Donna found her unconscious and an ambulance took her to the hospital in Bunnell." Albert's mouth began to open but Sheila beat him to it. "The boys are with Mr. Wacome, he took them as soon as they got home from school." She held up one finger like a teacher asking for the floor, "Donna said there was no way to contact you, I'm really scared for Aunt Terry," Sheila was in tears.

Uncle Albert's mouth re-closed— he opened the refrigerator though— he peeled a Pabst from a rack opened it and took a long pull without ever taking his eyes off Sheila. He walked into the living room turned on the TV and pulled out a cigarette. Uncle Albert didn't normally smoke in the house which had always struck Sheila as odd. Sheila knew one thing, his reason didn't have anything to do with subjecting the family to second hand smoke. This evening though Albert seemed to be breaking his own rules— whatever they were.

Sheila had prepared a tuna sandwich and left it wrapped in the fridge. She told Albert about the sandwich and said she was going to Donna's for a bit. She would watch for the boys and get them ready for bed. Albert gave her an odd unfocused look but said nothing.

In the few steps it took to reach Donna's place Sheila had already planned what she would tell Addison and Dana. She would down-play what had happened but beg off for the weekend. *Let's see what next week brings I have to talk with Addison— alone.*

Albert was gone when Sheila arrived back at the trailer to herd the boys inside. She thanked Mr. Wacome for taking the boys and rubbed the head of each of the boys as they reached the top step. Uncle

Albert must have walked his bike out to the park entrance then babied it from there. She was glad he was gone, sneaky or not. She cleaned the boys up and put them to bed. They were still excited about the treat they had for supper and didn't say anything about their missing mother. They were tired and didn't even ask for a story. Sheila kissed their foreheads and closed their door. The tuna sandwich hadn't been touched and Sheila realized she hadn't eaten since noon herself. She polished it off with the last glass of milk from a gallon jug.

She sat at the kitchen table making mental notes between bites. I am not going to be the mother here if Aunt Terry can't come home—she made a check mark in the direction of the light—number one. She rummaged through her notebook trying to find the phone number of the Mom in Skowhegan who helped her through her Mother's sudden death in the hit and run accident— Norma Gray. Her daughter Ethel had been her best friend. She couldn't find the number and felt guilty even looking for it

Unlike Aunt Terry, her own mother had been an athlete– a single mom but a committed one— who was taking evening classes to get an accounting degree. Her death while crossing a street with an armful of groceries had struck Sheila hard and there had been no family around to help Sheila through it. Mrs. Gray had taken her in during the worst of it and Sheila would be forever grateful. Beyond the woman's name and her memories of Ethel there was little left to remind Sheila of what she would be going back to– if indeed she could go back. She just knew she would not be able to stay here, especially if Aunt Terry was not going to be capable of taking care of her boys. Sheila loved them all but knew better than to think she could provide care in the long term. And Uncle Albert, she sure as hell did not want to be around him when he rediscovered his voice.

But what about Addison and Dana, the two were responsible for the bounce in her step she had been experiencing lately. *What could she do where could she go? Could she stay with Dana there was plenty of room but it was a big leap from friend to roommate. And she was in love with Addison, how could she leave him? Especially now!* Without realizing she had left the table, she had cleaned the counters, turned off the kitchen light, washed her face and brushed her teeth. She had been brushing her teeth a lot more often as of late. Sheila sighed, unfolded her cot and crawled beneath the covers. As warm a night as it was, she still shivered herself to sleep— she had no room for *Great Expectations*— not tonight.

Thanksgiving morning Sheila woke to the sound of Albert's Harley approaching the trailer. It was still early, still bleaky black outside. His headlight reached directly into the living room window as if snapping on a lamp, the windows rattled. Sheila hastily put on sweats and moved to the kitchen to make coffee. She peeked out. Albert was still sitting on his bike seemingly lost in thought, the bike continuing its guttural idle. He finally looked up when the kitchen lights caught him in his reverie. The motor went silent and a short time later the steps announced his entrance. He looked like he'd been up all night, his greasy hair hand wiped back past his ears. His eyes were red and the stubble on his face ashen. Sheila suddenly thought of the skeleton bikers that graced posters Albert had hung in the living room. In that moment Albert could have made money posing with his haunting visage— then he spoke.

"We're gonna lose her– they didn't say it like that but I could tell," his voice trailed off sounding like one of the little boys still asleep.

"I'm making coffee Uncle Albert, you want I should make you a cup?"

"That would be nice, I've been drinking out of that hospital vending machine all night and it sure didn't taste like coffee." Albert walked to the kitchen table sat down and put his head in his hands.

He sat like that a long time his hands telling a story to his head. When he got his lines straight he spoke, "Missy– I'm sorry, I mean I" he trailed off momentarily then got it right. "Sheila, last night gave me cause to think on stuff, a lot of stuff. I watched my Momma die with the cancer, watched my father drink himself to death," he looked up then. "I watched my brother hauled off to the slammer for life," sighing deeply he continued, "I got a sister who won't have nothing to do with me cause of the way I've been. It's all connected you know." He was wrestling with this new way of thinking. "Sheila I'm not into self-pity but last night I realized what a good woman your Aunt Terry is," his eyes watered. "Her laying there being all quiet like, it hit me, if I lose her, the only good thing in my life is gone." Albert looked up, the red in his eyes reflecting off tears, genuine and the first Sheila had ever witnessed from the man." Sheila poured a black cup for Albert, added the sugar and milk she needed for her own and placed the steaming brew in front of Albert and sat across from him. She studied the mop of hair that faced her.

Albert was not being Albert. He wasn't cussing or being disrespectful. He had called her Sheila. He looked defeated.

The mop of hair spoke. "She woke up just before I left but she's still too out of it to talk. I'm going back in around noon." Albert was still looking deep into his cup but ignoring the contents.

Finally he raised his head, "I'm gonna try to get some sleep." He rose, his knees creaked audibly as he shuffled to his bedroom door. He stood there as if waiting to be beckoned in then sighing deeply opened the door, shook his head then disappeared.

Sheila sipped her cup and thought *that was as close to a conversation as we've had since I turned up here.*

She returned to the mental notes and check marks of last night while grabbing her notebook. She wrote down several realities she was now facing. The boys wandered out to the kitchen demanding breakfast, Sheila swept her notebook off the table and planted a smile on her face, a smile being held in place by sheer willpower. "Well let me get right to it gentlemen and while you're eating you can tell me about the fun you had with Mr. Wacome." Jeffery immediately glued himself to her leg and together they pulled out plates and the frying pan.

• DECEMBER 3, 1962.

Aunt Terry arrived back at the trailer on a morning in early December with weather that in Maine would have been mid-summer like. Uncle Albert had traded in his Harley, buying a six year old four door mud brown ford sedan with high mileage and a permanent crease in the passenger side fender. Aunt Terry was pleased– not so much for the vehicle itself but rather the message Albert seemed to be sending. Terry was weak and would remain so. Her heart was failing but with close attention and a quiet lifestyle she could possibly live another ten years. She had accepted the news in the typical Aunt Terry fashion— nodding her head— hoping she could at least see her boys into adulthood. Albert and Terry talked things through and with Sheila's help after school and Donna's commitment to stop in daily, Albert could keep on working. They would talk with Sheila about this plan this afternoon. Albert would take care of Terry and the boys on weekends and let Sheila be with her friends.

Sheila heard of this grand plan a week after Terry had come home— following a corn chowder chow down. The boys slurped, slopped and sopped their biscuits spilling their way to a holding of bellies while complaining they were filled up. The dog licked the floor clean, moving strategically from chair leg to chair leg beneath the table. The youngest boy copied the next to youngest who copied the oldest as they held their bellies moaned and continued to plead for release.

"Go for god's sake," muttered Albert

Sheila cleared their bowls and was ready to start the dishes.

Aunt Terry asked her to come sit back down.

After listening without comment Sheila took a deep breath and gave Aunt Terry her own look into the future. Albert had followed on the heels of the boys leaving the sharing of this plan to Aunt Terry. What was apparent after the two hugged and cried together was that Sheila's immediate future seemed very much up in the air— maybe she'd have some answers within the week?

❀

Sheila left the house at 10:10 pm. She had so much to think about. She needed the solace she could find only in the darkness and the night sounds that signaled she was not alone. The metal steps echoed her exit through the back door. Sounds loom large in the jungle, especially at night. That term— jungle— was a fair assessment of where the girl found herself, navigating thru a series of back yards in the dark. Various odors creeped from garbage cans and open windows. She thought of the smells she'd just left behind in her aunt's house— Corn Chowder and biscuits— comfort food. From the trailer next door overpowering smells of boiled cabbage and pork chops fried in lard, wafted in the stillness. Subtle smells of families added an odor of comfort and normalcy that merely masked the smell of hopelessness that Sheila was feeling this evening. Even the stars refused to comment. The moon, well he was a little under the weather it appeared— thin and wan.

Wrecked cars, old appliances, broken toys and nearly impenetrable vegetation forced her to move slowly using her hands to guide her progress. Just as her eyes seemed to adjust, a rectangle of light from a living room would throw her back into total darkness. Dogs chained in back yards ran up to sniff her, scaring the bejesus out of her straining against their chains. They snarled and stretched, choking themselves as they lunged. Growls challenged her at every turn. Her hands were her eyes, feeling her way. The news she had shared with her aunt hours ago would be translated as softly as possible when the man of the house returned from his new three to eleven shift.

Can't even imagine how that will go, thought Sheila.

Sheila mentally counted the darkened exteriors with rectangles of light sending out flashes of illumination, drama both on screen and off mimicking the barrage of thoughts going through her own head. She slowly made her way to a place that would allow her to contemplate her own next episode. There was no need for quiet, dogs barked at all hours in this little neighborhood. She got past the last trailer, breathing a sigh of relief as her feet found gravel. The dirt track directed her towards the road. Her eyes adjusted to the new constant blackness and a row of mail boxes standing empty of the news took form. Sheila counted her way to Aunt Terry's mail box reimagining the joy that had filled her afternoons over the past few months. Tonight it was just a black hole, as empty as she was feeling. She could hear the real owners of the jungle everywhere in the overgrowth. She stood hugging the mailbox and revisited the conversation she'd had with her Aunt.

"I 'm sorry Aunt Terry but I can't stay here. I honestly wish I could. Uncle Albert is really trying and I love you and the boys."

Aunt Terry with tears in her eyes nodded her head. "Where will you go, there's nobody left for family?" "I'll have a better idea after tomorrow, Dana is going to take me to see Addison."

• FEBRUARY 1963

Four months with child Sheila found herself being summoned to the office. Sitting in a plastic chair just inside the main office, a chest high counter hiding her from the activity of the secretaries. Sheila held her breath. Her head back against the office wall she closed her eyes. A long sigh left her lips.

It seemed she'd been holding her breath and sighing for the past three months. Since the first of several long conversations with Dana and Addison way back in late November.

The first meeting with Addison had seemed hopeful. He took full responsibility for the unplanned, poorly thought out dilemma Sheila and he were facing. The first meeting was at Dana's home. She had picked Sheila up on that November night in the usual spot next to the mailboxes. Aunt Terry's mailbox which had carried messages of hope and affection shrunk away into the dark when Dana pulled up, headlights seemingly aimed directly at it accusing—as if it had played a living part in this new drama.

Addison, in that first meeting, was certain his family would accept Sheila. They had spent time at the cottage over the summer in Flagler Beach his parents warming to Sheila and the first serious relationship their son was experiencing.

Dana was having her own problems– caught speeding, her father was threatening to take away her driving privileges. Dana on a shortened leash could not offer Sheila a way to Orlando to meet with Addison's parents so Sheila had convinced Aunt Terry's friend Donna to take her.

❀

It seemed Donna welcomed a road-trip. This was her first opportunity to counsel Sheila and she used the drive to expound at length on the unfairness of the world. A world that allowed men to do their damnedest and always emerge un-blemished while the woman ended up with a face full of pimples in society's eyes. A whole life time of regrets and recrimination left her lips as she named names, dates, detailed offenses, and her non-traditional responses. A past that included four previous husbands and two live-in boyfriends– she was actually married now to what had been husband number three. "Prob'ly shouldn't have let him go in the first place, he's the best of what's been a poor lot, so that's in his favor."

Sheila, hearing the buzzing of Donna's constant attack on quiet found herself nodding her head again and again. Hearing but not letting the sound penetrate, Sheila realized Aunt Terry probably used nodding as a way to ward off mosquito bites of complaint and sarcasm that if not warded off would raise great welts of doubt about ones' self-worth. Sheila had learned a great deal from her Aunt without a word spoken. Sheila was trying to keep a positive attitude but Donna wasn't helping any. And still the mouth moved.

Orlando emerged from the jungle and occasional farm just as Donna was finally winding down. "Well now we made it in good time don't you think?"

Just in time, Sheila was thinking, *thank god she didn't have any more husbands to disembowel.*

They reached the horse farm around 11:30-ish. Addison's dad was standing in the entrance to a huge barn. He saw Sheila, didn't wave but turned and disappeared into the semi-darkness.

Donna pulled into a circular drive just as Addison opened the door to a white brick fronted Colonialstyle two story home. Screened-in farmer's porches one on each end, stuck out like ears— hearing all conversations, formal and informal. Addison came to the car smiled in the window, opened her door and took Sheila's hand.

Though Addison asked politely, Donna insisted on staying in her car. She tuned to a country station and smiled a smile that indicated she intended to stay in the car— *so don't even ask again.* "I'll just catch up with my cowboys."

Walking up the thirty foot bricked path to the house Sheila noted the path had three exits. Straight ahead took you into the main house a large door and three steps to mount, a paved path on the left seemed like an extension of the formal living room side of the house—the shaded side— the pulled shade— curtains drawn— dark side. Trees seemed to stand sentinel here, keeping the porch bathed in half light. To the right, Sheila saw in one glance a sunny porch that allowed your eyes to reach right in and get comfortable— in butternut yellow leather chairs and a sofa. Her eyes would be the only occupant of this porch off the kitchen. They exited left, bad sign her mind registered, *that other porch is off the kitchen, early morning every day is a new beginning side— where normal living smells exit— good food smells, coffee smells and fresh from the shower smells— Addison smells.*

Addison opened the screen door and held it for Sheila. It was like entering a room where you'd hold a viewing, the furniture stiff and unyielding, offering a squeak of complaint to Sheila's intrusion as she sat. *Formal side for sure. Addison probably doesn't even realize how this is all being staged, I sure hope not.*

When Mrs. Williams edged her way through the door from the house carrying a pitcher of lemonade and a bowl of sliced fruit and vegetables, the waxed smile on her face matched the bowl of waxed fruit that was serving as centerpiece on a low table. The dark-wood sofa and chairs lining the wall offered all the comfort of a war room. There was background instrumental music being piped in that offered a sound track for this little performance. The selection wasn't mournful but it definitely was somber.

"How nice of you to come visit our home Sheila, a far different look than the dreamy ocean shore offers, wouldn't you agree?" Her gaze suddenly turned away from Sheila— her whole body rotating— examining her vast property. She sighed contentedly,

"Unlike the ocean— Paul and I built all this out of Jungle and forest." She studied her hands. The smile hadn't revealed teeth yet. "Would you like some lemonade?" Mrs. Williams seemed impressed by her own effort to be civil, "I just now picked and squeezed the lemons and the veggies are from our garden."

Sheila noted that Mrs. Williams' lips moved but the waxen smile never left her face.

"No thank you, I'm fine."

"Addison?"

Addison shook his head no.

"Paul will join us after a time, he is cooling down the horses– just finished a long ride with your dad didn't you Addison?"

Addison didn't respond he simply nodded his head. *Shades of Aunt Terry,* Sheila sighed.

Mrs. Williams dressed in a dark blue suit jacket and matching skirt looked to be hosting a business luncheon— with Sheila the agenda. *All we need is a chalk board and a pointer,* Sheila could even envision the headings on the chalk board.

Mrs. Williams cleared her throat took a sip of lemonade and tried unsuccessfully to look sympathetic. "Addison has shared your condition with us, most unfortunate and untimely," a short pause, "I think we can all agree on that."

No melting that wax even in the heat of summer, thought Sheila.

A mere moment passed—but in reality a lifetime.

"Paul being a veterinarian obviously sees your situation through the eyes of one who witnesses the result of nature's most normal response to stimulation." She let that sink in. "He's probably right." She sighed. "BUT, when it concerns your own offspring and the hopes and fears for their future it does take on new meaning, don't you think?"

What the hell did she just say? Sheila's head felt like it had just been attacked by the same swarm of mosquitos that had made the trip down from Bunnell. *Did she just compare her and Addison's relationship to two animals rutting?'*

Addison remained silent. *He obviously is not driving this vehicle, probably isn't even a passenger.*

The silence was deafening. Sheila looked out through the screen and tried to see the issue from Addison's parents' perspective. All this effort to build a home and a life as they viewed it, was being challenged by a little heartbeat that had no way of knowing the angst, fear, and maneuvering it was causing. Sheila watched Mr. Williams walk across the lawn from the barn. He walked like Addison, assured and comfortable in his own skin.

Paul Williams dressed in denim and a cowboy hat and boots entered the screen door, his cowboy boots providing the only sound. He nodded to Sheila reached for the pitcher and poured a glass of lemonade. He removed his hat placed it reverently on an empty chair then took a long slow drink nearly emptying the glass. He sighed, then he sat.

Addison favored his father in size and shape. A shade over six feet Mr. Williams looked a little like that Marlboro man in all the magazines and in the TV commercials. Coming down off his horse this cowboy was handed the pointer without a word exchanged. Using the sky beyond the porch as his chalkboard he voiced what Sheila had been thinking just a few moments ago.

"Let me fill in any blank spaces. Winnie and I are native Floridians, came up from the Miami area twenty years ago. Winnie earned her credentials to work with animals at the same university I attended." He smiled warmly at his wife. "She joined me six months after I opened my practice here. We built this horse farm together from a plan," a sweeping hand embracing the property. "She designed this house from a plan, Addison was planned– he joined us when we could afford to let Winnie become a full time mother."

Paul continued to look out over the fields never making eye contact with Sheila. Then he stood and looked down at her, "You have to have a plan Sheila, or things just happen. Do you have a plan?" Sheila's mind had left this conversation while Mrs. Williams had been speaking and only heard Mr. Williams' final question.

Sheila suddenly felt forty years old. She folded her hands in her lap to keep them from screaming. Sheila asked if she might use the bathroom. The long ride to Orlando and the stress she was feeling begged a time out. Addison showed her the way and waited outside the door while Sheila relieved herself and composed herself. When she returned she noted the parents remained on their designated chalk lines— this scene had been rehearsed. Sheila sat, sighed, looked up directly into Mr. William's eyes and began in a hushed voice, "My mom and I had a plan once– It was working too." Thinking of her mother gave her strength, her voice gained timbre.

"Funny how plans can change without you having any say in the matter. One stranger having no regard for another person's plan can change everything."

Sheila's voice now strong and certain of what these people had in mind continued, "So no Mr. Williams I guess I don't have what you'd call a plan, I just have a little seed growing inside me that brought me to your porch hoping Addison might help me make a plan," a small pause, "there's no space left in my head right now to construct one by myself." Sheila looked directly at Addison then lowered her head to study the formal throw rug beneath her feet. Her hands, wanting to dart out in all directions quietly clenched, squeezing the life out of one another— not betraying the fury she was feeling toward this family— especially Addison, who remained voiceless.

Mrs. Williams seemingly startled, cleared her throat again. Sheila raised her head, *maybe she's as nervous about all this as I am and when does Addison take up that pointer anyway?*

Her eyes wider, teeth showing through a different smile she began anew, "I am sorry dear if I sounded unfeeling earlier. Certainly you both are too young to be dealing with this alone so Paul and I do actually have a plan, would you care to hear what we decided we will do?"

Sheila, looked around at the setting once more, her eyes and head clear now. "Can I ask where you were when you planned this plan, I'd really like to know?"

Mrs. Williams looked at Sheila strangely but answered, "Why right on this porch just two nights ago."

Sheila stood up unfolded her hands and began walking the length of the porch toward the screen door. She sighed as the door closed behind her. Donna's car sat quiet on the circular drive. A country song offered sound from her open windows. Johnny Cash was telling anyone who would listen that he, *could hear a train a-coming.* Those damn mosquitoes buzzing from the porch steps barely reaching Sheila's ears as she lowered herself into the seat and Donna turned the ignition.

Sheila looked back at mouths still moving, carrying shocked expressions. The teacher looking at a student leaving a lecture without permission.

As soon as the car moved forward Donna began. "Went as I expected it would I'm assuming, yep been there done that."

If a tape could be played in reverse— just as the car churned the miles on the return trip— Donna repeated— word for word— her own trials and tribulations.

At least one mosquito had made it into the car, chuckled Sheila without humor. Sheila heard none of the nuggets of wisdom being shared on the return trip, not even bothering to nod occasionally. Getting home was filled with sounds of country fried pain and sorrow that took a break only to hear commercials promising a fresh start from every known malady and new transportation to celebrate.

Just as light began to fade, taking with it the foolish dreams of a school girl they pulled into a very different drive. Sheila sat in the car thinking the setting might be different but people fall into one of two categories no matter their circumstance— they are either givers or takers. Aunt Terry one of those givers was looking out the window and greeted the slow ascent of discouraged feet with a hug that produced the first tears Sheila had shed all day. In the end it was decided that Sheila would stay through the school year, have her baby and then plan for her future.

Sheila, lost in reflection didn't hear the secretary call her name, coming back to the present when she was touched on the shoulder.

"Are you okay young lady, I've been calling your name, the principal will see you now.

Principal Walter Simmons was standing behind his massive desk. His office looked out over the playing fields. A physical education class was being conducted. Students in gym clothes were playing what appeared to be flag football. Sheila heard a muffled whistle and some hollering. He turned as Sheila closed the door behind her.

A southern drawl so pronounced Sheila didn't understand the words at first reached her ears. She waited for a follow-up.

The principal lost in his own importance read Sheila's quizzical look as a sign that he was speaking to a dullard. Any pretense at being cordial evaporated. "Missy I'm a busy man and it sure looks like you've been busy too," a smirk reached his lips but his eyes weren't smiling. "You're sending the wrong message Missy," He looked down at his notes. "Sheila, is it?

Sheila nodded her head. *Obviously being labeled Missy down here was not an informal greeting, but rather a callous put-down that seemed to take up residence in people trying to make you ill at ease.*

"Not from down here I see, a freshman, hmm, and you live in that trailer park out there that ." He threw up his hands, "No matter, I've had to go out there several times over the years." He shook his head in disgust. "Never a fun trip. You live with your Aunt, is that right?"

Another nod of the head.

"Do you have an idea why I might have asked you to come to my office?"

Affirmative nod. Downcast eyes.

"No reason for emotion or getting all sentimental here, Missy. Simply put, in your condition you can't continue your education here at Bunnell High school."

Sheila cleared her throat to respond but the principal put up his hand ready to bat even the slightest response aside.

"You do have an advocate here however. I met with all your teachers and it seems one of them actually believes you are capable— if not terribly motivated. Your English teacher, Mrs. Boardman has volunteered to tutor you at your home." He sat up straight, this conversation with himself going as well as he had planned it.

Sheila thought briefly of that fateful screen porch conversation and just had to get two cents worth in, "You don't have any relatives in Orlando do you?" Sheila couldn't help herself, she smiled.

Obviously responding to anything Sheila might have said was not part of the script and the principal ignored her.

"You can receive all your credits for the year and you may return to the school for your sophomore classes. How does that sound?"

No sense speaking now, the deciders have decided, Sheila nodded again.

As Sheila rose to go the Principal gave direction to what going would look like.

"Your books are in the office, there is a bus driver waiting to transport you, we'll be in touch, good luck Missy."

As Sheila left the office the secretary gave her a sympathetic look knowing what Sheila had just gone through. "All business that one," she uttered looking to the door with the brass nameplate.

❀

Mrs. Boardman came once a week on Wednesday afternoons at exactly four pm. Lots of those days they sat on the rickety steps just talking. Sheila was being given more Charles Dickens to read. A lot of the hopelessness and helplessness the author wrote of seemed very personal now. Sheila read *David Copperfield,* and *A*

Christmas Carol, which she read aloud to the boys. Softening some of the ghostly passages she had the boys mesmerized. Sheila had to admit she looked forward to Mrs. Boardman's visits, talking with someone who allowed her to just be herself.

Just when it seemed at least the school year could be salvaged an epidemic of deadly Influenza struck from sea to shining sea. If Sheila had access to a newspaper or Albert had watched the evening news she would have learned that over 45,000 Americans would die from the epidemic this flu season.

Aunt Terry her heart already weakened by disease was struck down in mid-February. She was in the hospital for a week nearly dying twice. Bed ridden when she returned, Sheila became nurse and head of house-hold. Mrs. Boardman herself had taken ill and the tutoring stopped.

❁

Suddenly Sheila found herself going back to school— elementary school. When the letter came from the elementary school it was Sheila who went to conference.

"I think Jeffery has a hearing problem. I probably should have picked up on it up earlier but with twenty-two other children in the class." the teacher Miss Prince, sighed. "Jeffery's a smart little bugger he's reading lips and stays quiet, nods a lot, he's a watcher."

Sheila thought, *I know how that goes.*

"I would like to have him tested. Informally I did a little testing myself and he can hear sounds but not well enough to process all the words. He reads lips and body language so well he understands most everything. If I'm right it could be a simple fix."

"I noticed things myself but I didn't know what to do. If you need papers signed I can get them to his Mom. Is this going to cost anything? There is no money I can guarantee you that."

"The testing is free let's get that done and see what they find, we'll go from there. He's a neat little kid. He deserves a chance."

❀

Jeffery got his hearing aid— provided by the local Kiwanis club— on his birthday, his eyes lighting up like it was Christmas morning. Jeffery looked up into Sheila's face and his look added the final line from the story Sheila had read nightly; "God bless us everyone."

• APRIL 1963

When the fair arrived in town it was Sheila giving the boys the laundry list of admonitions guaranteed to keep a smile on their faces and not a quick exit. "We need to stay together, Brian you are the oldest so I'm depending on you to help me today. You each have five dollars to spend on rides and food. Let's make a day of it, so don't spend all your money at once."

Every sense filled to overload with sounds of rides zooming, smells of french-fries beckoning, midway barkers grabbing your arm as you passed their booth.

Sheila, still a kid herself simply loved the fair. When Brian promised Sheila the boys would stay in the penny arcade while she did a once around she let herself breathe in the atmosphere. Her head on a swivel she remembered the times she walked the midway in a different place. *It was mid-August when the fair arrived in Skowhegan. With a group of junior high friends she'd devoured cotton candy, caramel coated apples, fried dough and of course French Fries. They had sat at the top of the world on the Ferris-Wheel trying to locate their own streets and houses.* Sheila continued to walk the midway in Bunnell with her mind fifteen hundred miles to the north.

She didn't recognize a single kid from Bunnell High School as she wandered the dirt circle of tents and booths. Almost exactly like the midway in Skowhegan— nothing much changed from year to year but something different to do once a year never-the-less. When her name was called from the basketball shooting booth she didn't react at first. When her name was called again she was startled. She located the voice but did not recognize the tall long haired young man passing the ball from hand to hand while grinning ear to ear.

"You are Sheila Thompson aren't you?"

Sheila approached the counter, "Do I know you from school?"

The young man standing across the counter wearing a Boston Celtics t-shirt and a big smile wore his long blond hair beneath a Boston Red Sox baseball hat.

"You might not recognize me but in fact I lived three houses down from you on Hanover Street in Skowhegan, Maine. My name is Gregg Croteau."

Sheila once more was transported back in time and place to the town she was born in. *She was sitting on the porch watching a young guy in sneakers and shorts and a baseball hat pass by her house as he began a long run. He was a high schooler, older so they didn't speak but she'd had a secret crush on him.* Two years had passed and he was taller and sturdier now but just as good looking.

"I remember you Gregg, you were the only boy with long hair in the whole town as I recall?"

"I'm afraid so, long hair wasn't highly regarded either— at home or school—one of the many reasons I'm standing in front of you today." Gregg sat the ball aside, removed his hat and bowed.

Sheila thought briefly of Addison then shook him out of her mind. "What are you doing way down here Gregg?"

"Do you remember the movie, *Toby Tyler?*" Sheila nodded. "Well I was a freshman in high school and had just finished my first year of Cross Country running. I came in fifth in States and my coach was filling my head with what my future might look like— I was feeling pretty puffed up." Gregg smiled, "Do you remember my Mom? Probably not, she never came out of the house except to go to work. Well she filled up my head with a different vision of what my future might look like if I didn't get my hair cut, or quit school and get a job to help out." Gregg smiled. "I did get suspended several times for my hair."

Sheila watched Greggs face alter from story teller to combatant.

"She had and probably still has, a drinking problem, smoking problem too— oh and let me add yelling. My dad he drove truck for a long distance hauler, not home much, tired out when he was." Gregg paused, "You still with me?"

Sheila thinking of her early days with Uncle Albert could see where this might going.

"Anyway I saw that movie with this little kid going off to join the circus and I was hooked, went around singing that *Biddle Dee Dee* song and on veterans day two years ago I asked the old man to let me ride along on his way south with a load. We had a layover in North Carolina and there was a fair in town. Suddenly that song re-entered my head. I wandered the midway allowing my head to fill back up with a future I could plan myself. I remembered parking cars at the Skowhegan State Fair with a couple of friends and the fun we had. I told my dad I wasn't going back home. He raised his eyebrows but knew what I was dealing with all week— every week at home— so when I told him I'd landed a job with a traveling fair, he just chuckled and asked if there was room for him. Then he opened his wallet and gave me a hundred bucks."

Sheila nodded, *what's there to say, everybody has a story.*

Gregg sighed, "So I re-named myself Toby, it's not the circus but I've met some really nice people the last two years. And that's why I'm not at home ready to start my senior year at good old Skowhegan High. So Sheila Thompson what's your story?"

Sheila, said "let me get you a coke, I'll be right back." When she returned Gregg was explaining to a player why the prize he'd won was just a trinket. "You have to sink three in a row to get the bear, sorry." The man left grumbling to his kid that all the games were rigged. Sheila overhearing the conversation had to chuckle. "I would have to agree with that guy Gregg and I'm not talking about the fair." She handed Gregg a coke, "You were already gone when my Mom died," she paused, and checked her Aunt Terry's watch. "Let me round up my nephews and I'll come back and tell you why I'm not in school at all."

❁

When the fair moved to its next venue, Gregg Croteau had a new old friend bunking in a sleeping bag in a small camp trailer. A ten ton truck loaded with canvas fronts and wooden stalls pulled the little trailer behind. The journey north would see the equipment loaded and unloaded on midways in three dozen towns and cities along the Eastern Sea Board.

Sheila had talked well into the night with Aunt Terry, Albert, and their friend Donna. No one wanted to see her go but they all understood. Donna agreed to be the caregiver for Terry and with Uncle Albert's promised help they would make it work. The hardest part of goodbye was holding Jeffery in her arms as he cried and cried. They were sitting on the metal trailer steps in the early evening his head on her shoulder, Sheila patting his back and ruffling his hair.

"I promise I will come back, maybe with the fair next year if I'm still with them. You have to promise me you'll work hard with that speech teacher. Jeffery you are such a good little boy, I'll never forget you. By the way I bought you a little gift. Follow me. Sheila went back into the trailer and put the record, *Biddle Dee Dee* on to play. I'm going on a little adventure just like the boy in the song. Play it and think of me.

❃

Sheila and Gregg became best friends during the stop-start-set up-satisfy the crowds need to throw away a little money— then tear down and move on and do it all over again.

By May the fair was in Rhode Island and Sheila was having difficulty disguising her condition. Greggs boss and now Sheila's, stopped at the balloon breaking booth and called her to the counter. A wise-ass but a pretty good guy he broached the subject in the only way he knew how—by being a wise-ass. "Sheila if a wayward dart should pop that balloon you're wearing under your sweater, would I have to hand over a teddy bear?"

She looked at her boss waiting for the shoe to drop.

"So I'm thinking maybe until that balloon pops without anyone's help maybe you can work in the office, help with a million things I have to do."

Sheila smiled, *a grownup who was not judging or looking to make things more difficult, what a novel idea.*

"Thank you so much it does tire my legs and back standing for ten hours a day."

"Well Gregg's a good kid and he vouches for you and you have held your own the past few months, besides maybe you'll bless me by giving the kid my first name," then he chuckled. "My first name is Hiram— so don't punish the kid with that moniker. Just treat him better than I was treated which won't take a lot—deal?"

They shook hands. Sheila was left with a smidgen of hope that maybe just maybe this might all just work out.

Gregg was working in the animal barns this week in Rhode Island. Calling himself Toby to everyone but Sheila, he was enjoying the change from standing in a booth for hours at a time. He found that he loved the animals and this week was sleeping in the baby animal barns with mother and offspring. His boss approached, with a new offer. "The guy who normally manages the race horse stables just got fired for being drunk on the job. These are high profile horses worth a lot of money. You will get an extra two bucks an hour if you want the job." He became serious, "I personally recommended you so don't let me down Toby. I'm not a smart-ass around these people so make sure you treat this seriously too." His eyes widened, "Big money people, some with less than sterling backgrounds," he whispered, "possibly Mob money."

The same nucleus of horses along with a smattering of local horses at every stop would compete during the late spring, summer and fall in all the New England States. It was when the fair hit Massachusetts that Toby, (Gregg) met the Gambino Brothers.

Sheila worked diligently in the little trailer that was the office for her boss. She had no trouble learning to type and she had good money managing skills. She thought back briefly to the two classes she had taken that made even more sense now. Her mind was all over the place. She wondered if Gregg would become more than a friend, but neither seemed ready to even discuss it yet. As she gazed into the mirror in the mini toilet in the little pull-along home, her growing baby kicking madly she dismissed the idea entirely. *What good looking guy in his right mind is going to want to be saddled with this responsibility?*

Gregg introduced Joe and Eddie Gambino to Sheila one afternoon as she was sitting on a bale of hay eating a sandwich and sipping on a coke. The two brothers entered through a rectangle of light. Their silhouettes offering wild gestures accompanied with heated sound.

Sheila sat quietly in the shadows hearing but not focusing. She heard swearing and what sounded like a dirty joke being tossed about.

By the time the two young men noticed Sheila, Toby, the name the men knew Gregg by had moved to her side. "Hey guys this is my friend Sheila, she works for Hiram in the office.

Eddie ever the smart mouth noticed Sheila's condition and suggested with a swallowed giggle, "Looks like she's been taking her work home with her— working nights?"

Joe the older of the two brothers cuffed him up-side the head and followed up, "Don't pay any attention to him, he got dropped on his head as a kid and has never been right."

Eddie glared at his brother but stayed silent.

"We actually came to see Toby here to offer him a job permanently if he's interested." After an hour of banter and ballast being thrown around the two brothers left the barn. Eddie made one more wiseass comment about Sheila and his brother cuffed him again and shoved him out into the sunlight.

Sheila had heard the proposal and said nothing. Toby had asked if he could think about it for a day or so. He didn't want to leave Hiram high and dry.

When Toby showed up for supper in their little trailer Sheila gave him her opinion. "I have never seen two more spoiled acting guys in my life. They act as young as the nephews I left behind in Florida. I didn't like them Gregg, something fishy about them, they don't look at you, they look through you."

"You may be right but they are offering three bucks an hour more than Hiram and I'm not getting into a bidding war. The only difference is I will have to sleep in the stable every night with lights out by eleven. Their family has a lot of money tied up in horses so I understand the need for extra security. On the upside I get from nine am till after the races end every day to myself."

Sheila nodded, letting Gregg find whatever balance he was seeking before deciding.

"We'll be following the same circuit so we'll still be able to hang out. I know Hiram is going to be pissed though. He has kind of alluded to what some of these horse owners are into."

PART TWO

A RIVER RUNS THROUGH IT

- MYRON

- THURSDAY, AUGUST 15, 1963

Skowhegan, Maine is a medium sized town that evolved from a river that runs right through its heart. Tucked half way between the Atlantic Ocean and the Canadian border there would seem to be little to distinguish it from a hundred other towns in the grand state of Maine. For most of the year that would be true, but for two weeks in mid-summer Skowhegan changes. For two weeks in August things happen in Skowhegan that just wouldn't, some say couldn't, happen at any other time. As you may know from personal experience or perhaps have heard, Maine tries to pack a heap of living into its two summer months. Summer starts on whatever day July Fourth falls and Labor Day is the last hurrah for most folks. July and August in Skowhegan includes State Fair time. It is the big social event of the summer for kids. For the older crowd it's a brief respite from the mundane day to day make a living— feed the kids—clean the house—go to bed and start all over sameness of life. In Skowhegan the fair takes on a life of its own and for eight or nine days the State Fair draws young and old together.

❀

We gathered at the entrance to the mid-way. Seniors all, we have worked the Skowhegan Fair parking cars since our freshman year. As soon as the fair ends preseason for fall sports will begin. September will usher in our last physical effort on the field or on the wooded trail—last year of parking cars too, I hope.

Larry and John both play football on a team that has had a good deal of success the past two years. Now it's their turn and things don't look very promising.

My name is Myron Therrian, I run Cross Country, an obscure sport that barely garnishes the attention of even the rabbits and game birds we scatter on our wooded hilly course that skirts the town.

In our school and in our town if you aren't a runner yourself or possibly the parent of a runner you have no appreciation for the sport— or the runner. One of those runners would be me, my name is Myron. Yes I know I told you my name earlier, my name is Myron and wow do the kids— both friend and foe— boys and girls, have fun with that name tag, kinda like the sport I run—no respect. (Just think Myron and Urine.)

Anyway, good thing I have thick skin and a slight frame that doesn't invite physical confrontation. I am however blessed with a biting wit which disperses targeted sarcasm— I do not lose in a war of words.

Our job during fair week—which we do well I might add—is simple: get as many cars as we can into as little space as possible, while leaving enough space so the fair-goer can exit whenever they wish. There are eight of us in all and we each carry a flag and whistle that we use to signal the driver to— follow that flag. Over the course of a twelve hour day with one hour off for lunch and another for dinner, we will park over a thousand cars— seamlessly.

If our football team follows our car parking model maybe they can make playoffs this year. I look at Larry and John—I don't see it happening.

Our cross country season looks hopeful though.

Coach Stroud the fearless leader of us flag wavers also serves as the Cross Country coach, he says a new boy will be joining us this year— the missing piece he called him.

The second part of our daily effort is a little more personal. After dark with the cars all parked for the grandstand shows, we are to keep scoundrels— our boss's name for them— from slipping under, over, or through the cyclone fence that circles the entire fairgrounds.

Not sure we'll be able to top last year in the laugh till you puke funny things that happen at the fairgrounds. Great story I gotta tell it.

So it's a Tuesday night and Larry, John, and I, we have been a team within the team for fair week every year since we started our freshman year of high school.

Had another team member for a while, Gregg, but he's been gone for two years. Anyway we are walking the perimeter of the grounds when I spy with my little eye a movement just outside the fence. We decide to linger and watch, it was a quiet night and nothing of note had happened since the fair opened on the previous Thursday. Sure enough the movement begins to take form— a wheezing of expended energy and whispered swearing. The scene was taking on the image of Pigpen, the character in Peanuts who never emerges from a cloud of dust.

The form becomes more definite as the minutes pass, lights from the spinning Tilt- O- Whirl dispersing darts of light followed by shadow. A very large girl is trying her best to squeeze through a very small breach in the fence. We counsel and quietly make a decision. Another ten minutes produces a sweat and dirt covered girl of high school age— one of our own maybe. She rolls over, lies there quieting her breathing. Slowly she makes it to her knees with another round of heavy breathing clearly audible— her head tucked into her chest. She pushes upward with one leg, brushing dirt and debris from her sweat soaked tee-shirt and jeans as she rises. Larry the biggest of us three, yells, halt! The girl is looking directly into the bright lights that ring the Tilt-O-Whirl which is producing flashing lights and screams from the riders. She squints— we all have our badges out and look as official as three kids can look. "You just broke the law young lady," Larry informs her then pauses for effect, "but you know, this is your lucky day."

Still trying to catch her breath, the girl, still squinting, hands still moving on her sweatshirt. Sweat is forming little rivulets of dirt while she paints her clothes a muddy brown.

"We have been watching you for quite some time and we all decided if a girl can actually get through that wire she doesn't deserve to be brought to the fair office— no siree she should go free."

The girl sighs then nods her head in thanks— saved by compassion. She smiles then, having no idea what going free will look like.

Larry smiles back, "You just turn right around and get back the same way you came miss and you're home free," his smile turning into the devil smile we had come to love and hate since we all began paling around years ago.

When what had just been said sinks in, the light comes on and the girl glares at each of us in turn. Sweat still glistening on her brow and a new fire in her eyes— a different nod appears— she still doesn't speak. We throw up our hands in a-what- can-we- do manner and watch the girl return to the fence. She squares her shoulders assumes the position. The wheezing seems louder and the swearing just barely discernible— somehow seems a little more directed.

When you're a cop you can't take these things personal though. We didn't hear a lot of the swearing anyway, we were too busy falling all over ourselves laughing— true story. We didn't recognize her from our school so didn't expect any payback in our *near future.*

With our extensive experience as guardians of the midway we wander away feeling the world is at our command.

Nothing exciting to report this year as yet.

• PAUL

• THURSDAY, AUGUST 15, 1963

My name is Paul Leland and I am about to enter my senior year of high school which would signal the beginning and the end of this town's influence on who I would become. I didn't grow up in this town but came from a much bigger town in Massachusetts. When I graduate I will leave this state and go to college in Massachusetts. My Dad retired early and bought a place in East Madison, Maine on the lake. We are one of the few families living year round on a dirt road my Dad has to keep plowed all winter. Before this year I spent two years in a smaller high school seven miles from my home, Madison High. I was never a particularly popular kid there, in fact to be honest I felt rather invisible. My mother is worried about me so now in my senior year I am changing schools from Madison to a larger high school in Skowhegan. My family is only adding to my invisibility by sending me to school in Skowhegan– at least that's how I view it.

Either Mom or Dad will drive me the six miles every morning and pick me up at the end of the day. Some of those days will be late since I am going to run on a Cross Country team for the first time. On the lake I had no access to kids my age so the woods became both my playground and my playmate. I have found I can run really fast and seemingly cover long distances. My Mother says running on a team will help me find some friends. She found out who coaches the team and I am going to do a trial run for him and he told her if I can help the team he'll get me a job parking cars at the fair. His number one runner works for him and he wants me to pal up. On this morning I am still mad at my Mom for making me change schools in my senior year.

• GREGG (TOBY)

• THURSDAY, AUGUST 15, 1963

Gregg Croteau had been awake for hours, the fog that had rolled in overnight wafting in and settling on his blankets. Open on all four sides the barn offered little protection from the elements and Gregg found himself shivering. Though he had spent a few nights in barns like these he still had not gotten used to all the sounds emanating from the animals throughout the night. Gregg was not exactly a city boy but sleeping in the animal barn at the Skowhegan State Fair might take a little getting used to. He worked in the racing stable in the afternoons and evenings and thought he was through with all this. In the horse barn he had a nice little sleeping space, with four walls. Another guy not showing up for work had him spending last night with the baby animals and their mothers.

As he lay there hands behind his head the gray light of dawn allowed shadows to emerge. Thoughts, like those shadows, entered his mind. *'I'm back in my own home town, wonder who will notice?*

Born and raised for the first sixteen years in Skowhegan he left home riding shotgun in his Dad's 18 wheeler. On that trip he made the decision not to return to his Mother's mental abuse. On a whim he found a job with a traveling fair in Holly Springs, North Carolina. He had been around fairs before. At fourteen he spent a summer parking cars at the Fair which annually spent two nearly weeks in Skowhegan. A sudden thought, *I wonder if those guys are still working here*

The sucking sounds of baby animals getting fed had him realizing he was hungry as well. He rose from under the covers and stretched, easing the stiffness in his back. Exercising the crick in his neck, his head moving like a windshield wiper the shadows in the barn began to take shape. Gregg could see the baby calves jockeying for position. The mother animals were patient and Gregg noted at least one mother he knew who could take a lesson or two. He got up and added water to some troughs, his own stomach growling. He pictured how good an omelet would taste about an hour from now. His mind wandered as he moved along the pen enclosures. He grabbed a bale of hay in each hand and walked the twenty yards necessary to begin feeding the critters. Gregg was a big guy now and strong, but he hadn't been in high school. He was a Cross Country runner back then. Easily handling the 50 pound bales, he chuckled at how average he had been in school; average height, average weight, just an average student. The only thing he shined in was running back then. *Still running,* he mused. He had grown 5 inches and gained forty pounds of muscle since then. *If they could see me now,* then a thought reached his lips, *I might actually run into one or two of the old crew while I'm here.*

Gregg, warmed now stripped down to his tee shirt and threw his sweatshirt onto his bed role. He began to whistle and it seemed as if all the animals in the barn joined in. Gregg suddenly thought of Sheila with her own baby tucked in a little travel trailer with the fortune teller behind the big tents. He smiled to himself thinking, *after the fair closes I'd like to have a serious talk with that girl, probably not realistic but, who knows.*

Planning to bring back a breakfast sandwich for Sheila, Gregg put his sweatshirt back on and began the trip into town to get fed.

• NORMA, ANNA, AND ETHEL GRAY

• THURSDAY, AUGUST 15, 1963

The fog shrouded Skowhegan in a blanket of quiet on this early morning. Just as the children of Norma Gray would rise and flex their youthful muscles soon, so to would the fog rise to let the sun flex its might for a few more days.

Norma rolled from side to side and stretched out to her full length, wiggled her toes and hugged herself. Norma was well aware that her queen sized bed allowed her plenty of freedom of movement but for one painful moment she wished there was someone to bump into, someone who might just recognize all she had to offer a relationship. Sighing aloud her thoughts turned to what the day might bring. Norma had asked for one day off and she got to take the girls to the fair— yippee!

She closed her eyes, the thought of her two girls, Anna and Ethel, brought a smile to her face. She looked at the bedside clock 7:14 am. Normally she would be at work by now. The ladies at work would have shared the latest town gossip and any jokes their husbands or boyfriends had found fit to tell a woman. She smiled again. She actually enjoyed her work at the Drapery factory— if only they paid a decent wage.

Norma was forced to work a six day week and the over-time helped but didn't give her the time with her daughters she would have liked. She had asked for the day off to take her girls to the fair— and for another very special personal reason. She hugged herself once more as she thought of surprising the girls.

So stop whining, she said to herself, rolled out of bed and headed toward the bathroom. After a longer than usual shower, thinking of her girls overhead, Norma toweled off and made the bed.

Sitting in her kitchen waiting for the first cup of the day to finish perking she tried to fashion what would be a suitable punishment for her oldest daughter, Anna. The past few days had been hell as she had gone through every emotion possible. Terror first, then outright panic— followed by frantic calls, then the call that ended those emotions but raised others. The emotions that emerged from the supposed kidnapping and missing overnights, coupled with the official line that not enough time had passed to be a missing person investigation. Her frustration with the local police department had been wasted energy. Then the reality that it was all an effort on her daughter's and her friends part to cover up a damn party gone wrong at Lake St. George, eight miles away had her angry, embarrassed, and determined to discipline.

Let me get through today and we'll sit down and discuss this rationally, right now she would only aggravate the situation, she was too angry for words. She couldn't even ground the girl—yet. Today was about the mother, she wanted her daughters to see what hard work and perseverance looked like.

She hollered up the stairs for the girls to rise and shine. That's once she thought, knowing that too would be a longer than usual process this morning. Oldest daughter Anna had her best friend in the world, at least for this week, staying overnight. This girl had not been party to the party and seemed a calming influence on her volatile daughter so she had let her stay. Norma had heard the three girls well into the darkness laughing and gushing about who knows what. Fifteen year old daughter Ethel had been banished to her room sometime after eleven— the slamming of her door had quieted the volume. The two remaining teenagers whispered important stuff back and forth— things an about to be sophomore would never understand according to Anna.

Norma smiled to herself as she poured her first cup of coffee and turned on the radio. Seventeen year old Anna, a senior this year thought she had all the answers now. She had fallen in and out of love several times since school let out in June. With emotions that moved from laughter to tears on a daily basis Norma felt like she was living through an ongoing episode of *The Secret Storm*. Kid sister Ethel was no help in the romance department unless one can truly have feelings for a soccer ball.

Anna would come home crying about this guy or that guy and Ethel, never without her soccer ball would tease her sister— yelling *'kick 'em that's what I would do, just kick 'em.'* She would then proceed to demonstrate with her soccer ball threatening to destroy anything in its path. Anna would shout to her mother to get this crazy person away from her and Norma would rush to rescue not Anna but her few good possessions from destruction. This latest incident though brought alcohol into the family dynamics for the first time. Sure she knew kids felt the need to experiment with adult pastimes, but this past week went way over the top.

Norma turned to get up from the table to call the girls once again. Before she could rise daughter Ethel appeared in the doorway stretching and yawning, her beloved soccer ball balanced on her head. In one motion she dropped the ball to the floor, dribbled over to her mother planted a kiss on her forehead and said, "Mmmm you smell excellent mother dear!"

Norma turned down the radio, gave Ethel's beloved ball a little kick that sent it into the living room, grabbed her daughter and gave her a big hug. Moving back toward the coffee pot Norma offered to cook breakfast—something she didn't normally get to do.

"All I want is juice and toast mom, I plan to chow down at the fair."

"Well at least let me put the toast in for you and pour your juice. I don't get to play mom with you guys in the morning very often. I'm sure you don't plan to hang around with me at the fair so humor me, ok." Noticing just a hint of sadness in her mother's voice, Ethel showed sensitivity beyond her years. "Maybe I will have a scrambled egg with that toast mom I am pretty hungry this morning."

Norma smiled and went to the head of the stairs.

"You two girls better rise even if you aren't going to shine, this train is leaving soon," she hollered to the staircase. They had all agreed last evening they wanted to be at the fair by eleven. The hour before the midway opened would give the girls the time to check out exhibits and not miss any time on the rides. In the seconds it had taken Norma to get to the head of the stairs and back an ungodly noise had taken over the kitchen. Ethel seemed oblivious to this assault on the ears as she wielded a yard stick over her head in an attempt to measure any growth spurt that might have arrived overnight.

"Here let me help you with that," said Norma as she deftly changed the station back to her golden oldies and reached for the yardstick. Moving to the doorway where earlier milestones were clearly visible, she looked her daughter straight in the eye. *Fifteen going on twenty-three*, she thought to herself— *young but painfully wise.*

Now that older sister Anna was '*looking for love in all the wrong places,*' according to Ethel, mom and her youngest daughter spent most of their evenings alone. Looking into her eyes she thought, *I believe she can see right into my soul.* Norma held the measure on the crown of her daughter's head and when the new mark was measured she stood at 5'4." The youngest, wisest, and soon to be tallest. Ethel seeing this new mark grabbed her soccer ball and began dribbling around the furniture pumping her fist shouting, "ALL-RIGHT!"

Norma watched this young graceful athlete and thought of her own ambitions that had been short circuited by a lack of healthy activities for girls when she was in school. It seemed girls gained recognition in her day by who they dated and parents who thought getting their girl married off signaled they had done their job well— a mindset that had led to an early pregnancy and hurried marriage. The relationship— you couldn't really call it a marriage— ended after six stormy years of unsuccessfully playing house. Her high school memories were limited to that senior year when she had to be home schooled. Well her girls were not going to have their dreams short circuited. *I've got to think of a consequence that will show Anna just what awaits her if she doesn't think before she acts. And poor John her latest boyfriend— that is obviously over as well, I liked John,* mused Norma.

Outside, the fog began lifting and rays of filtered sunlight seemed to be following Ethel around the room. Norma brightened realizing she had two wonderful healthy daughters to be thankful for, and a day off. *Think positive,* she chided herself.

"ALL-RIGHT" she shouted, pumping her fist and laughing out loud.

Ethel looked at her mom and said, "You are really weird." Then they both started laughing.

"Why don't you go get your sister and her buddy, you can take your soccer ball with you," smiled Norma.

Ethel caught the meaning in her mother's smile and started dribbling toward the stairs, "ALL-RIGHT," she yelled as she managed to switch stations in one motion then headed up the steps two at a time.

The Beatles were breaking into their rendition of, *Help* on the radio when older sister Anna and her friend Shellee began shouting their version of help— without the music.

"Mom call off your dog," shouted Anna.

"Mrs. Gray she's dribbling that ball off my head, help please"

We're going to have such a fun day, thought Norma sipping a last peaceful cup of coffee of the day.

- REBECCA

- WHITTEMORE'S RESTAURANT

- THURSDAY, AUGUST 15, 1963

"Good morning," was more than a hollow greeting for Rebecca, she genuinely enjoyed meeting people, always attempting to raise at least a smile— most of the time it worked. Rebecca was in her last summer at Whittemore's Family Restaurant, a popular breakfast spot located on the busiest thoroughfare of town.

Depending on your starting point Route 201 enters the town from the Southeast and exits to the North, all the way to the Canadian border if you've a mind to. Trucks travel this highway following the mighty Kennebec River through Somerset County with the towns of Fairfield, Skowhegan, Solon, Bingham, Jackman and finally into the Province of Quebec. The river leaves route 201 and sneaks in the back door of towns to the west, Madison, Anson, and North Anson. On route 201 those trucks, traveling North with engines revving as they begin the climb out of Skowhegan rattle the windows of Whittemore's.

Trucks traveling south produce a different but equally disturbing noise as they back off their engines descending the steep pitch into the heart of Skowhegan. The regulars sit eating and talking— their conversation automatically moving to pause— as trucks roar by. Those trucks will be joined by hundreds of cars during the days the fair is in town. Route 201 travels directly past the fairgrounds and serves as a conduit for fair goers from a number of those towns east and west of Skowhegan as well as those north and south.

Rebecca knew all this because she was born and raised here. Rebecca also knew this was perhaps the last summer she would be working these tables, kidding with the regulars— and hearing those damn trucks. She had just gotten her senior proofs back yesterday and was blushing as her boss showed a picture of a smiling young woman to a table of old guys who were now oohing and ahhhing— knowing it would make her uncomfortable. Rebecca had come to love these guys though during the last two summers. Wendal James, the owner liked Rebecca and even managed to get her some hours on weekends during the school year.

❧

Gregg Croteau entered Whittemore's, studied the dining room, pointed and asked to join a customer already seated. The restaurant was busy— popular enough without the fair in town— this morning it was standing room only. The regulars could be heard muttering among themselves about how glad they would be when— the *big show*— they called it, left and they could get their regular tables back.

Rebecca loved the extra business though. The extra tips she was pocketing would help her life plan, a senior year with lots of expenses attached—plus her travel plans would take money.

Rebecca's travel plans involved being in love. It wasn't a boy she loved, it was a man— a very important man! Her bedroom walls were plastered with magazine photos of this man. Rebecca knew she couldn't share this man's life but she could share his dream. Rebecca fully intended to make this man's dream her own. Rebecca intended to join the Peace Corp. She could see the dashing red haired man smiling down at her even now. Her boss brought her out of her daydream but she was still smiling to herself as she refilled her customers' cups and asked the newcomer if he would like some.

"Yes thank you," answered Gregg.

"Would you like a menu or are you ready to order?"

"Give us just a minute. Bring Toby a cup of coffee and we'll be ready, we don't need a menu we've eaten in here before."

Gregg thought, *I really should let these guys know my real name, this could become confusing.*

Rebecca moved away refilling cups as she made her way to get a cup for this big handsome newcomer. She thought she might have seen the men in here before but had not waited on them.

"Nice ass huh," Joe Gambino expressed with a smile and a wink.

"I didn't notice, I was noticing how well she moved, she's comfortable with herself."

"What are you talking about," said Joe, "man you are one strange dude. Those animals must be affecting your mind. By the way how did you sleep last night?" Joe Gambino Jr. was the nephew of a state representative who also happened to chair the Agricultural Committee for the State Fairs that made the circuit in Maine every summer. Joe had been given the cushy job of over-seeing the livestock for the next ten days. That made him Gregg's boss even though he was barely twenty. Joe had appeared from time to time since Gregg was hired several month ago in Massachusetts. Gregg normally just attended the race horses but did other jobs as needed. Joe had invited Gregg to breakfast the past two mornings. He would be a junior at University of Maine in the fall and the three thousand bucks he was receiving from his Uncle would buy a lot of kegs over the course of the year.

Gregg was about to respond to Joe's question when Rebecca returned with that same smile and friendly manner.

"I've seen you two guys in here before but I've not had the good fortune to be at your service," making a slight curtsy she added, "What would you like?"

The ice broken, both guys laughed introduced themselves and ordered omelets and home fries.

So now she thinks my name is Toby, this isn't good, thought Gregg

"Do you live in this town?"

"I plead guilty to that charge or question or whichever," Rebecca threw up her hands.

Both guys laughed as Rebecca turned and walked away to place their order.

"You're right, that girl does have style," said Joe, "maybe we should invite her to our little shindig tonight."

"You can only get so many people into that little camp, I've heard you invite half a dozen myself," answered Gregg.

"The more the merrier, besides half of the people won't show up anyway."

When Rebecca returned with the food, small talk took place and before the meal was finished Joe had added her name to the ever growing list of personal invitations. When Rebecca wouldn't commit, Joe told her they would be around the animal barns all day so stop over and just get to know them better before deciding. He handed her a day pass that would allow Rebecca free admission.

Gregg was left wondering why he didn't remember this girl from when he lived here.

❊

Behind the scenes a well-orchestrated effort to make everything run smoothly over the nine days fell to one man. It was the job of William R. Neilson to spend his time and energy for the fifty weeks prior to the fair planning all phases of the event. There was a history to The Skowhegan State Fair and the town took great pride in being labeled as the longest continuously running fair in the country. This year would mark the 145th year.

Just the planned agenda for today's activities showed what the challenge had been. Posters hung in all the towns within a fifty mile radius. Each day's events were listed in the newspaper and fliers were placed in all public places.

Horse Pulling and Harness Racing for the older crowd promised a busy afternoon. For the kids, in addition to the famous *King Reid Midway* complete with games and thrilling rides there were the animal barns to visit. On the track this evening *Joey Chitwood* and his dare devil drivers, *the Danger Angels*, would send their automobiles through walls of fire and into makeshift walls. The mid-way would stay open till midnight. These attractions were the visible signs of the General Managers job.

In addition— from hiring the parking attendants to coordinating with law enforcement and the fire department— it all fell to the general manager to be sure things ran smoothly. At least the weather looked like it would not pull any funny business.

William Neilson sat having breakfast at Whittemore's with Police Chief George Henry, County Sheriff Arthur McManus, and Fire Chief Russell Clement. They had met every morning for the past three weeks moving from restaurant to restaurant.

"I think this place has the best breakfast— though they're all good," said Sheriff Arthur McManus. Sheriff McManus who had to run for reelection every four years had learned a long time ago not to express an opinion that might lose a vote—unless it compromised his integrity.

If size were converted into job effectiveness, Sheriff McManus was the most effective sheriff inch for inch and pound for pound that this county, or any county in Maine for that matter, had ever elected.

Skowhegan Police Chief George Henry watched the sheriff make a stack of pancakes disappear. He didn't care much for the sheriff. This was his town and if Skowhegan didn't carry the dubious distinction of being the county seat, Sheriff McManus would be eating breakfast somewhere else.

Police Chief George Henry liked to be in charge. He had been an officer with the Maine State Police for a total of twenty years. He had taken a leave of absence to serve as a lieutenant in the Korean War. George was a relatively small man in stature and his mind tended to mirror his size. He stayed in shape physically though and had no tolerance for people who didn't share his 32 inch waistline. Wound too tight was a description of the chief held by the man on the street.

Always on duty he looked around the restaurant. The current conversation at the table didn't pertain to him. George seemed to be always mentally winding his watch, checking the time according to most who knew him, but was considered a good law man who didn't miss much. He didn't have much to say this morning, his men were handling everything outside the fair-grounds, while the sheriff's men patrolled the midway.

With the table talk focused on the day inside the fairgrounds George mentally removed himself from the table. He noticed Rebecca serving two young men at a back table who appeared to be enjoying themselves. Rebecca was a neat kid. One of the few kids in town who didn't seem to fit George's general opinion of today's teenagers. She seemed older than her years. *Might have something to do with having to be the parent in her house,* mused George, as he thought he picked up the word **party** from the conversation. Maybe he didn't hear it but rather read that young man's lips. Either way George knew the word party never seemed to bring joy. His experience as a law man noted the word transforming to the adverb **partying**, and he and his men nearly always had to crash the gathering; picking up the remains and many times depositing them on their parents doorstep. He hoped Rebecca was as smart as she seemed. Recent events in Canaan a town eight miles east seemed to reinforce the Police chief's belief that in fact the noun, **party**, needed a makeover.

❀

Away from the fairgrounds the roads leading to Skowhegan had been filling up for several hours. Families, friends, and it seemed entire communities were on the road. Busses loaded with children filled up in empty school yards, chaperones leading the singing of all the traditional camp songs— passing the time. Summer camps from the surrounding lakes would also sample all the fair had to offer, depositing kids from different states and cultures.

❀

Joe Gambino Jr. had hired Gregg Croteau to work the racing stables and the animal barns when necessary. His general description of what the job would entail omitted what could only be described as one very large detail— that detail stood over 6'4", weighed 255 pounds with a mean streak he wore twenty-four seven.

Marvin Higgins had no use for people—never had— he'd bullied and blustered his way through life and at age 47 he was at the peak of his game. He was effective with animals though— he was good at getting them to do what he wanted them to. For the last fifteen of his forty-seven years in this world he had been the man who was really in charge of the animal barns at this fair and fairs around the state.

Gregg was feeling good about the way he had the barns looking and was ready for all the kids to descend like the moose flies that kept tails flapping, racing forms slapping, and people from napping. He was in a light mood already looking forward to the party this evening whistling a happy little made-up tune when his boss filled the doorway. "Good morning boss," said Gregg, as Marvin lumbered into view. Marvin mumbled something unintelligible as his eyes swept the barn looking for a stray animal.

"This barn ready," growled Marvin.

"I believe so sir," giving a light hearted salute Gregg thought of the curtsy the waitress had made earlier and chuckled aloud.

"You an Army man?

"No sir."

"I can see that or this place would be a lot more spit and polished," said Marvin with a shit eating grin on his face.

Gregg's good feelings disappeared as the faces of several other assholes he'd run into over the past two years all merged in Gregg's mind. Gregg didn't hear the additional comments that Marvin was mumbling.

Marvin was in his element. He had no say on who got hired for these short time jobs but he damn well had a say on how the work would be done. Marvin got results from the animals by showing them right off who was boss figuring this valuable self-taught skillset ought to work with these short timers as well.

Gregg swallowed hard figuring he'd take the high road for now.

"Would you show me the areas that need work?"

Marvin immediately saw this as a sign of weakness. A real man would have challenged him, not get pushed around. Marvin was just about to test how much shit this guy would take when Joe strolled into view.

"Hi guys," he scanned the area, "the barn looks great don't you think Marvin?"

Marvin—in truth a coward and a bully— knew this was not the time to challenge Joe— after all the kid's uncle was his meal ticket. He'd just put this little conversation on hold for now.

"It'll do . for now I guess," Marvin dragged out the ending sending a clear message to Gregg that this wasn't over— not by a damn sight.

When Marvin left mumbling to himself, Joe motioned Gregg to follow him. They wandered to the wooden fence that circled the track and leaned on the rail. "Don't let that prick get to you, the last time he had a smile on his face was when his mother died in child birth."

Gregg nodded his head in agreement and the two young men watched the horses circle the track as they worked out.

"My uncle is Marvin's boss, if I say the word old Marvin will be drawing unemployment, so let me know if he gives you shit. I don't like how nosy he is anyway. The two men were silent for a time watching the horses inside the rail warm up— then Joe spoke, "Hey see that horse? His driver is wearing the red silks, red number 4 on the saddle, he's running in the sixth race today." The horse and driver passed, clumps of mud flying from the watering the track had received earlier to keep the dust down. With the clop-clop of hooves diminishing Joe finished his thought, "My father has spent like $40,000 on that nag, he's never been better than third—if he doesn't get it done today he's glue."

Gregg listened not commenting— Joe seemed to be mouthing the frustration of the father, not that anyone wouldn't be upset if they were on the losing end of that investment.

❀

It was 9:00 am. Though the gates would open at 10:00 the midway would not officially open for three more hours. No matter, the grounds were buzzing with people. The rides were spinning and twirling, diving and swooping— while voices and music blared through loud speakers. Lights flashed and winked trying to compete with the still rising and stretching sun for a little attention. The next three hours was final dress rehearsal for the first day.

Each morning of the fair would begin in the same way, garbage being removed vendors re-stocking food and drink. Workers who traveled with the fair lived in the tents and trailers parked behind the glitz and glitter. They stumbled about, coffee in hand, groggy from lack of sleep or the after effects of their own form of partying. The hard work had been done, the tents raised, rides assembled, wires placed and prizes hung to their best advantage. By noon they would all be in costume adding their own special invitation to step right up and win a prize or come right in and see one oddity or another. Come watch the dancing girls behind the green door.

The sheriff's deputies were hanging outside the church diner drinking coffee, munching donuts and kidding with one another.

Their work would not really begin until someone lost their kid, felt they had been cheated in some way, or darkness arrived. Things always got busier at night.

On the track, horses hooked up to the two wheeled sulkies were getting their exercise. Racing had been going on for a week prior to the fair but the purses got bigger with the influx of fair goers. Harness racing allowed the common man to stand a little taller. Going back to work after winning fifty or a hundred dollars brought you a little attention and don't we all crave a little of that. Just standing there in the warm sun or sitting in the grandstand studying the race program marking your next bet allowed a person to escape if only for a moment. Everybody had a hunch, or maybe a horses name held some significance, or a driver was due to win. For the two minutes or so the race lasted there was hope. For two minutes your yells just might make a difference. For two minutes time stops and you become part of something bigger than yourself. Horse racing is as much a thrill to the racing enthusiast as the scrambler or the cyclone on the midway is to a kid.

Already strung along the wooden rails lining the track, pockets of men armed with racing forms and their own significant knowledge watched horses that would be racing later in the day or days to follow get their morning exercise. The men were drinking coffee and trading information. Some were already nursing their first beer of the day. For many guys this is how they would spend every morning and afternoon during fair time. A fishing or hunting trip could not provide any more satisfaction than being part of racing at the state fair.

• LOOKING BACK

Sheila asked for a couple of hours off this morning.

She packed the stroller with diapers and a bottle for little Jeffery. Leaving the fairgrounds she walked down Madison Avenue into town. Large trucks climbing the long hill gasped for breath— the gray cloud of particulate streaming from their stacks offering a visual to their effort. She began pointing out landmarks to her son. She passed Whittemore's Restaurant on the left. The heads bobbing while raising coffee cups indicated a busy breakfast crowd. Sheriff's department cruisers and Skowhegan Police department vehicles present assured it would be a peaceful breakfast. Sheila spoke to her infant son, "As far as I know no one has been arrested for running down and killing your grandmother Jeffery, but let's hope they enjoy their breakfast."

She passed Blunt Hardware owned by the father of one of her classmates then watched her reflection in the windows of Knowles and Dressle the furniture store. She could see the reflection of the stroller— Jeffery appeared to be listening to every word.

Further along across the street was Hight Chevrolet, Buick. A gleaming 1963 Red and white Chevrolet rotating like a trophy in the window. Sheila couldn't dream big enough to show an interest. She crossed Elm Street where to her right stood the library, an imposing brick building housing the wisdom of the ages. Sheila spoke aloud to her son, "Charles Dickens is in there Jeffery, and I'll have you meet him if we stay." Further along the sidewalk was The Miles Carpenter Insurance Agency. Still talking to her son, at the window of Barry's Pizza which was closed this time of day she paused, and put her head against the glass. Memories of her friends from Jr. High Soccer, especially Ethel who she had stayed with briefly after her mother's death— meeting here to play pinball and eat pizza— flitted through her mind. *What would Ethel think of you little guy?* She chuckled as she boasted to her son about being second high scorer on one of the machines— *though nobody could beat the sheriff's deputy, Delbert.* They even posted my name and score on the wall. The owner, Mr. Barry was always nice to the kids on those afternoons. Sometimes he even offered the pizza free. She closed her eyes, she could smell it. Her mother was also a fan of Barry's pizza–she had worked nearby at Stern's Department store. The employees ordered out on Fridays and many times her Mom picked up the order. Everybody loved Barry's Pizza. She thought briefly of her mother as she passed Stern's windows, the mannequins her mother had dressed seemed to be missing her too.

Crossing the bridge over the mighty Kennebec she looked down into the lazily flowing water. Pulpwood dotted the surface, bobbing up and down on the way to Scott paper in Winslow.

She thought of her Dad bobbing her up in the air and bringing her back to earth at Coburn Park. A plaid blanket spread out and a picnic basket with her favorite cookies to follow, *if you eat all your sandwich honey.* His smell was suddenly with her. Her dad had drowned on this body of water up in Solon when he was helping break a pulpwood jam. Sheila was three at the time and didn't really understand what had happened— she just knew she missed his smile and the smell of old spice aftershave when he showered and shaved— Sheila standing in a chair alongside him. Suddenly the old spice smell had her thinking of Addison as well. She got angry and the stroller picked up speed. *Jeffery's father had no right to be here today,* "let's move on," she said aloud. It seemed weird, but all she could remember was her fathers' smile and his smell. He was buried in Waterville, a city to the south. Sheila had visited once a year with her mom till her mother became a marker herself. Sheila passed the Junior high school she had attended and the dairy treat she had visited a hundred times or more over the years. "You haven't had ice cream yet Jeffery. When we come back by I'll show you what you've been missing."

She crossed another bridge over the same body of water then walked past Peanuts Pool Hall. She had never been in but had heard stories of money changing hands as kids learned to play nine-ball. Some even learned to play Straight Pool which was a game that demanded great skill they bragged. Some of the older men in town competed in tournaments with players from all around the state. Peanut himself was one of the best she'd been told— she suddenly remembered, *her father an avid player had told her that— hey I do have another memory from Dad.* She passed Sturch's food market on the right then crossed West Front Street and climbed the Main Street hill towards the bus and car entrance to the high School.

Just a short distance from the entrance to the high school, gravestones and memorial markers began appearing on her right. "Here we are Jeffery your grandmother is resting here." She located the gravestone—bare— no flowers present— birth date 1930, died 1961 and her name Leslie Thompson.

Sheila sat on a grassy mound and told Jeffery stories of her mother. The love they shared, the hopes and dreams she had offered. She wept openly, and Jeffery joined in quietly, not wailing for a bottle or to be changed— rather grieving with his mother. When they had both stopped crying they wandered the paths between stones and markers a story at every marker if you were listening. On the return trip Sheila did buy a baby cone for herself. Jeffery was just an infant but it seems even they recognize the taste of a cold ice cream on a warm August morning. She had to smile when the infant tasted the sweetness combined with a coolness he had not experienced before, his face offering up a new expression.

"So that was your Grandmother you just met back there. I don't really have any history of my father to share. And your great- grandparents, well don't get me started." Your grandmother and grandfather never married— another strike against having any family. "Just you and I baby Jeffery, but we'll make it work."

❧

By the time Norma got the girls to agree on their days' schedule and un-ruffling all their feathers; "Yes you two sisters will stay together," it was nearly noon. As they entered the access road to the infield parking, the girls were quiet, solemn, and obviously not pleased. Norma smiled, she Looked in the rear view mirror at the two girls who appeared to have been sentenced to prison for the day. She had refused the plea of her oldest and youngest to ride shot-gun and asked Shellee to ride in the front. When they reached the ticket booth the girls brightened slightly as voices announced the teenage boys just ahead ready to direct them to a parking spot. When Norma reached the infield those teenage boys swooped down on their vehicle, waving their flags and laughing— enjoying their work. Anna ducked her head as she spotted John. The flag wavers were making so much noise Norma told the girls to raise their windows so she could give final instructions. Finally parked, Norma took a deep breath and began, "Look girls, if what I just witnessed is any indication of how this day is going to go then I will gladly be on my own." The girls smiled. "However," she repeated one last time, "Anna you and Ethel are to stay together at all times." The girls opened their mouths in unison.

"I don't care to hear it, I already set the ground rules before we left the house and that's that! And Anna don't forget we haven't settled the latest hot stove topic." She let that sink in. "Now we will meet for lunch at the Church Diner at 1:30pm. I have a surprise I want you to see. After that you're on your own until ten tonight. Anna, one last reminder, now don't roll those eyes— how you handle today will surely influence the next opportunity you'll have to see ten o' clock dark time. So let's check watches shall we?" The girls wanted to argue and it was clear Ethel didn't like the arrangement any better than her sister, they both were choking back comments. Norma was clearly in charge and any further protest might just find them heading back home. The last words spoken were Norma's, "I will meet you right here at the car at ten— don't make me come looking for you." The girls just rolled their eyes.

The three girls, feet heavy with the burden of having to endure one another wandered among the already parked cars and crossed the track to the midway. They brightened at the smells of Stan's French Fries, Anna, succumbing ordered a large fry and a coke. Ethel reminded her sister that in just over an hour they had to meet their mom for lunch, why not wait.

Shellee defending her friend, was more than a little tired of this brat, she finally spoke up. "Ethel, minding your own business might bring you as much satisfaction as these French fries," Shellee reaching into the plate of Anna's fries, waggled a ketchup tipped fry in Ethel's face. "Why don't you practice chewing on these today?"

Not to be out-done Ethel had a comeback. "Shellee I am surprised you would confuse me with someone who might give a rats butt for your opinion." The two stared at one another.

Anna could see where this was going to lead stuffed a French fry in both girls' mouths, smiled sweetly and began what was a second— soon to be a third— trip around the dusty ribbon of dirt. The sun not to be ignored, added heat to go with the brightness, the midway heating up faster than the girls cat fight. The two girl's continued the glare and stare contest. Anna too busy trying to keep the peace to enjoy her treat was stuck with a carton of cold Fries. She offered them to the two girls then dumped them with a big sigh when her offer was ignored. Boys with heads on a swivel were beginning to take notice of the three girls— speed walking by— turning their heads— making comments. This diverted the girl's attention and gave them a common enemy.

"They are so juvenile, I can't believe their parents let them out alone," said Shellee loud enough to draw a snide remark from one of the boys. Ethel said aloud, "I should have brought my soccer ball," then she smiled. Shellee and Ethel shook hands, calling a truce. Not ready yet to start riding the emotions of Tilt-a-Whirl and the Scorpion the girls decided to check things out from the top of the tranquil Ferris- Wheel, it would be cooler up there too.

❋

Norma walked past a knot of men leaning on the race track railing, several shouted out to her. Norma dressed in fitted jeans was proud of how she filled them. She waved and answered back using her wit when it was called for— but kept walking. Norma forced herself to slow down. She took a deep breath, there was plenty of time and secretly she savored allowing the moment of anticipation to last. As she entered the midway the first sense assaulted was her nose. The aroma of fried onions and French Fries hit her, followed immediately by grilled hot dogs, sausages and popcorn. Stimulated now, her nose began to separate smells within smells. Coffee and fried dough joined in and something else her nose couldn't place but Norma knew— more a feeling than a smell— it entered your head through your nose never-the-less— the fair— there was nothing like it. Norma worked hard and being a single parent was another full time job. Still a piece of Norma needed more—for a long time that need had not been dusted, waxed, polished or given any attention at all. Norma couldn't even identify it but she just knew something was missing. For a long time she thought it was the awkwardness of being a single parent. How do you discuss that with your kids? Then it happened. She smiled at the memory.

A year ago her friend Marla from work sat down during their half hour lunch on the bleaches at the little league field and suggested Norma come to a meeting with her. What kind of a meeting Norma had asked, she was tired at the end of a day and going to some meeting was the last thing on her mind. When Marla told her it was a garden club meeting Norma was sure she didn't want to go. Norma raised a few flowers on her window sills and that little effort made her feel good but a garden club— let's be serious.

She stood there in the middle of the midway knowing it was time. It was a short walk to the grand stand where so many performances had captured the imagination of hundreds of thousands of fair goers over the past century and a half. Norma didn't climb those steps though, she walked beneath the stands and joined a world that to her had come to make perfect sense. Norma had been rehearsing her lines all her life but only in the last year had she allowed herself to believe she belonged on this stage. Passing from a sunlit world with the smells of man, Norma was greeted by the earthy sweetness of flowers that comingled— gossiping among themselves. A babbling brook complete with stones and a water fall provided the flowers a path to follow. Live butterflies were fluttering through the air savoring the moment. This quiet little sanctuary beneath the grandstands offered a different form of visual stimulation. Soon the doors would be opened and the oohs and aahs of an appreciative audience would gaze longingly at– what for many of the older crowd would be the highlight of their day. After dropping a penny or a dime into the magic wishing well they would move on to look at the flower arrangements that lined the walls, each competing for that elusive blue ribbon.

Norma had created the center piece for this year's flower show. She smiled as she remembered that first meeting. At age thirty-four Norma was a beautiful woman who had two teenage daughters and no husband. She had been sure the group of ladies she hadn't met yet would not accept her. She was wrong. What she found was similar to the variety of flowers that now surrounded her— arranged to show their best qualities— there was a place for all. The common bond these women shared of working the earth creating beauty and life allowed them to move beyond wealth and age and education. Norma found after several meetings that she indeed had a talent for arranging and growing flowers. By the time spring arrived it became clear to the dozen ladies that Norma should design and arrange the entire Flower Show at this years' Skowhegan State Fair. Norma had told no one and today her daughters would get to see the small stone placed discreetly in the bottom of the reflecting pool. The stone carried a simple message: *Norma Gray, You have become our rock.* The girls would be proud of their mom. The real news she had to share would be even more exciting. Norma was going to be promoted at work. Norma found from her work with flowers that she possessed a remarkable talent for creating the big picture. Calling on all her courage she had submitted several designs at work for fabric patterns created from her flower arranging. As of today she had one more interview but she had been assured it was a formality. Norma had told no one this news either.

❀

Thursday, the first day of the fair is kid's day and by noon the noise level had been raised to just below screech as all the rides that spin, twirl, rotate, or slither are loaded with riders all trying to out-scream one another. Huge teddy bears hang just below the canvas ceiling of a dozen tents. Softballs thrown at weighted metal milk bottles, basketball hoops that defy entry, darts thrown at balloons, rifle shooting at small red stars, wooden balls rolled toward strategically placed holes— all the above compete for attention and your precious dollars. Tents containing glass enclosed electric arms allow you to guide a quarter to a place that will release a horde of its brothers—you are a lucky winner. Something for everybody. In the barns baby animals to ooh and ahh over. Farm animals raised and shown by young people from various 4-H programs. Horse pulling competitions for competing farms and woodsmen. A visit to the agricultural building to check on the vegetable displays. Keep moving along here where pie, cookie, and bread making competitions have been judged and ribboned. All the while appetizing smells darting along on sudden breezes compete for the dollars every kid is carrying— money they saved up all summer to spend today.

• EDDIE AND JOE

• THURSDAY, AUGUST 14, 1963

Late afternoon. Five miles north of the fairgrounds on the shore of Lake Wesserunsett Eddie Gambino was stretched out on a divan on the screened-in porch of a two room cabin he rented with his brother Joe. He had just finished a shift at Lakewood Theatre, performing numerous maintenance jobs. Eddie was a very talented young man. He understood wiring, plumbing, painting, and when not working— drinking and drugging, lying and cheating, violence and revenge. He also knew how to kick back and relax. Right now he was reading a good western paperback that was supplying new ways to tantalize and stimulate his desire to be a gun fighter. Eddie didn't identify with a story's hero, he liked the black hats. He could see the pitfalls the evil doer always seemed to fall into and would exclaim aloud at their stupidity. "I can't believe they would fall for that," he'd announce to nobody while vowing to himself to never let personal business ever cloud his judgment. "You don't talk it to death— you just shoot— you idiot!"

In reality though he had been really stupid assaulting that artist guy at the lake earlier in the summer. *Felt good though*, he mused. Older brother Joe was a role model for staying cool and he'd warned Eddie to keep a low profile. Eddie had also stolen money from the Theater, but he'd handled that better and a young local guy had been blamed and fired. The thing was he didn't really need the money so it was an unnecessary risk. Joe had been mad about that too. Joe had confiscated the money and promptly bought liquor with the money and hosted a party. Eddie got wasted and didn't remember how it all ended but he'd been the life of the party for a while.

Joe opened the screen door and shook his head when he saw Eddie sound asleep through the porch window. He sighed, not much bothered Eddie that was for sure. He entered the small kitchen, the late afternoon sun streaming through the kitchen window landed right between his eyes as he placed the bag of groceries on the counter. He turned away, allowing his eyes to adjust. Out the window that served as part of a wall between the porch and kitchen Eddie stirred in his sleep. Joe smiled, *probably rustling some herd of cattle or robbing a bank,* he smiled and shook his head. Joe emptied the bag grabbed a knife and began slicing a pepper to be followed by an onion. Good old Italian American Spaghetti for dinner. *The smell of onions and peppers and a little garlic frying up will wake the boy,* thought Joe. A half hour later, Joe and Eddie were seated across from one another on the only two chairs not broken. Joe poured a little Chianti and had placed a wild flower in a Crown royal bottle in the center of the table. Eddie looked the worse for wear. "No more parties for you Eddie you are out of control, and you let your mouth run when you drink."

"I'm sorry Joe it was that damn hard stuff, I'll stick to beer."

Joe pointed to the bottle. "That is more than a flower arrangement sitting there little brother, that's your new conscience at work. What you'll stick to is work, home, and your idiot westerns. Dad called me after the race. That nag finished sixth, Dad is pissed. He said the horse wouldn't bring a dime at a fire sale, then he just laughed out loud. It wasn't a ha-ha funny laugh, Eddie. Said he'll call me when he figures out what's next. Everything will work out but he doesn't need to be worrying about us. He's going to need us to help take care of this mess, his bosses are demanding it. That horse has go.

"These hick town coppers can't figure how to raise a roof ladder much less solve a crime, Dad needs to relax."

Joe Gambino Jr. chewed his own food slowly while studying his younger brother. *He doesn't even shut his mouth when he eats,* he mused. "Eddie we have less than a month left of work so dad simply wants us to relax— fly under the table— his words." Joe laughed at some of his father's analogies. Then he got serious again. "If we have to leave suddenly because you do something else stupid, even these hicks— as you call them— might put two and two together. We can't have our names associated with whatever happens to that damn horse."

"This spaghetti is really good Joe did you do something different?"

"Yeah I added a little dash of wisdom Eddie, so eat up and wise up."

Eddie raised his glass and offered a toast, "Here's to the guy who'd spit right in the eye of a blind-man."

Joe had to smile, "by the way we are hosting a gathering tonight, you will be designated bartender—this is a test Eddie". Eddie started to protest, Joe simply held up his hand and then turned it into a fist. That ended it. Joe chuckled knowing Eddie was right. Eddie did stupid things and saw himself as a throwback to the old west but it was he who could do evil and not raise a pulse while engaged in the act. Eddie would cooperate now that he had spelled it out for him. Eddie had seen what Joe could do when necessary; he'd felt the consequences of not listening to his older brother in the past.

❀

Sheila was working this first day of the fair in the little trailer behind the giant Ferris-Wheel. A small electric fan rotating left then right raising the edges of the papers on the desk that took up an entire wall. Sheila's baby Jeffery began crying when his mother sneezed loudly. Sheila picked up the tissue and blew her nose. Where in the world a summer cold had come from she had no idea but the stuffiness in her nose and the soreness in her throat left no doubt. She picked three month old Jeffery up and held him tight. She spoke directly to his eyes, "you are such a good little guy, you don't complain being stuck in that little carrier for hours at a time so mommy can work." She rocked him in her arms, "and you sleep through the night don't you little man. Your god mother will be watching you tonight so I can catch up with some of my old friends, that alright little man?" Jeffery quieted and closed his eyes. The thought of Jeffery's god mother, Madame Toussant who played the role of fortune teller for thirty five weeks a year brought a smile to Sheila's face. They met when Sheila was six months pregnant and immediately was taken under her wing. Madame was fifty years old and childless. A tragic fair accident killed her son when he was nineteen. Madame Toussant saw Sheila's plight as a way to be a Mother once again. She watched her closely throughout the pregnancy and a Mid-wife who traveled with the fair delivered the beautiful little boy she now cradled in her arms. Sheila lived in Madame Toussant's travel trailer these days.

Secretly Sheila had a crush on Gregg but after hearing Madame Toussant read her future shortly after her son was born she made the break from his living quarters. *I see a tragedy in your future, you and your son will survive but someone close to you will be injured in a storm.* Madame Toussant had reached across the little dimly lit table and squeezed her hand. Sheila trying to make light of this revelation had offered, "Seems like more of the same weather I have come to expect."

Madame Toussant put her finger to her lips and once more closed her eyes, continuing to hold Sheila's hand in hers. *This is a type of storm I've never seen before, you and your son will be taken away from me,* her hand squeezing Sheila's as if holding on for dear life. Madame Toussant had suddenly deflated like a balloon struck by a dart. Sheila never mentioned the prediction to Gregg but moved out, leaving Gregg thinking he had done something wrong.

Well here they were in Skowhegan, Maine. Her old hometown still looked the same. Two nights ago she and Gregg had hitched a ride to Ma Beane's and sampled some of her famous fried clams. Gregg had reconnected with an old teammate, Myron, and Sheila had been introduced. He was cute, Sheila decided. It was August and the weather promised to be hot and clear for the duration of the fair—which was unusual. Growing up it seemed at least two days during fair time attracted severe thunder storms complete with bolts of lightning and wash-out rain— the mid-way closed and races canceled. Sheila blew her nose, she really wasn't feeling that well. *I think I might just cancel that party plan Gregg invited me to.* She squeezed Jeffery to her once more and using the rhyming of Dr. Seuss she read to little Jeffery nightly, offered another good reason to stay home tonight.

"I don't like those Gambino's

No, not one little bit

They spit and they swear

Think they're both it."

She smiled and chucked Jeffery's chin, then finished her verse.

"Gregg says they lie

And thinks they both steal

They throw around money

It's their only appeal."

Sheila reached for another tissue, "Well we don't need their old money do we little fella," she sneezed," "we have each other."

• AUGUST 15, 1963

• EVENING OF FAIR DAY ONE

• GAMBINO CAMP IN LAKEWOOD

The little camp was lit like a candle, a record player competing with raucous laughter for attention. A galvanized tub loaded with ice and beer had replaced the Crown Royal bottle as centerpiece on the kitchen table. The screen door squeaked and squawked, keeping count of the beers being grabbed, opened, raised in salute, emptied— then deposited in a plastic barrel just off the porch.

11:00 pm on this Thursday evening found Eddie very much the bartender and sober host. Tonight he would try to fill a different yearning and there were several candidates for his attention. The camp couldn't house all twenty- something guests so the lawn, bathed in light from the windows, and a nearly full moon had guests strewed in little knots of conversation. The entry light just outside the screen door was hosting its own party as moths danced and flitted in and out of shadow.

Eddie approached his brother Joe and slapped him on the shoulder. "So who are these beautiful girls you have hidden in the shadows," he kidded.

Joe was standing with Rebecca, Toby, Anna Gray, and Shellee Fischetto. Anna and Shellee were asking for a ride home already. "We were supposed to meet my

Mom at 10:00, at the fair and I I'm in the dog-house as it is."

Rebecca ever the realist looked at the situation as a half full bottle of beer which she held up to the light exiting the camp. "It would seem Anna that even if we left immediately, the damage is done—true?"

Anna looking sheepish had to nod her head in agreement as she took another pull on her Schlitz, she grimaced, "Oh, I am in deep doo-do no doubt about that."

Shellee spoke up, tipping her own bottle to the gods of the night. "And I'm thinking I won't be bunking with you again any time soon," she drained her bottle.

Rebecca in full control waved her bottle at Anna, "So, since I am your way home and I really don't want to leave yet, I say let's enjoy the damage you have wreaked upon yourself." She toasted the little group. "To Anna, may the light of morning offer your Mom a softer view of your betrayal?" The group laughed in unison, all clinking their bottles.

Listening to all this, Eddie chuckled to himself, *this chapter looked like it might bear fruit.* "Introduce me to these ladies brother." With an innocent smile he became a white hat briefly, "I offer my own sober transport home ladies when the clock strikes midnight, so drink up you're safe with me."

The chips and peanuts disappeared along with the tub of beer. Eddie was a good sober host moving among the little knots of partiers offering up snacks.

After having consumed a six pack Joe motioned Toby (Gregg) away from the light and into the shadows of the trees just off the lawn. He began by emptying himself.

"I probably don't need to witness this Joe," kidded Toby.

Joe laughed, "Good one!" Zipping up he turned, "Can I trust you Toby?"

"Yeah sure, I mean of course, what's up?"

Joe was looking directly into the light coming from the camp, Toby was looking directly into Joe's eyes.

"I am going to ask you to do something for me. You won't be involved except to follow my instructions. Don't look or think or question beyond what I ask you to do. You will probably be fired for what I'm asking, but I will fix that later. You will also be paid for your trouble. Can I trust you to do me a simple favor?"

"Wow, this sounds heavy, can you be a little more specific?"

"If you promise me that if you don't agree, this conversation never took place."

"I can agree to that."

"Ok here's what I'm asking you to do."

❈

Eddie drove Shellee and Anna back to town with Rebecca and Toby closely following in Rebecca's father's car. Eddie dropped Shellee off first.

"I don't need to hear your Mom at this time of night, I will catch up on your sentence tomorrow." Shellee hugged her friend, said good night to Eddie and walked up her drive.

Rebecca dropped Toby off at the fair grounds and said she'd maybe see him at breakfast. He had seemed quiet most of the evening he obviously had a lot on his mind. He absently waved a little wave and wandered into the fairgrounds.

Eddie the opportunist wasn't ready for this chapter to end just yet. Anna the senior with impulse issues— enhanced by alcohol— saw consequences no matter the time she walked into her house. "Let's just go somewhere and talk," offered Eddie, I'd like to get to know you better, maybe we can come up with a legit excuse for tonight."

Anna, with her defenses down suggested a little used path that entered the back of the Drive-In Theatre. The two sat near the woods the car facing the darkened Screen. Eddie lit a joint of Marijuana and offered Anna a toke. New ground for Anna who had only heard of the product. She coughed at first but within a few minutes a buzzing added to her buzzing. All her worries seemed to dim as they pretended to watch a movie on the screen. Eddie described a romantic scene, then leaned in and kissed Anna. She responded. Eddie tried to move this to a bedroom scene and started moving his hands to places Anna didn't want to go. Anna tried to rejoin the present. She tried reasoning— though it was muddled— and kidding— and half-hearted. Everything seemed to be happening in slow motion.

Eddie didn't seem to be listening. He had his black hat on visiting a room above the saloon. Anna clearly said no— at least in her mind— the next half hour seemed as unreal as the first— but in a very bad way. When Anna stumbled into her house at 2:45am, her eyes were red from crying and her wrists rubbed raw— her body bruised beneath her sweater. Her mother was waiting up. Norma expecting her daughter to be defiant was taken aback by the passive nearly robotic responses to her accusations and anger.

"I am so sorry Mom," she managed," tears streaming down her face she blubbered, "You're right about me. I'm a horrible person I don't deserve your forgiveness." A new look had entered her eyes— fear. "There are bad people out there, just like you said." She grabbed the stair railing, "Punish me any way you want, I never want to leave this house again." Anna slowly climbed the stairs leaving her mother open mouthed, shaking her head.

Ethel was awake and listened to her sister crying in the shower. When Anna finally entered her bedroom room wrapped in a towel

Ethel had found her way to her sisters bed and was waiting beneath the covers. She saw the redness on Anna's arms. Anna made eye contact and began crying softly. Ethel held the covers open and Anna fell into her arms. Within moments Anna got back up and stumbled back to the bathroom. Ethel could hear the residue of a very bad ending enter the flush. A long time later when a shivering and whimpering Anna laid back down, Ethel hugged her back and shoulders, soothing her sobbing sister until a single sigh left Anna's lips and she slept. All the while Ethel thinking, *wonder how many times and locations a foot and soccer ball could make contact with a creep.* Then she too slept.

❁

Gregg, (Toby) entered his little travel trailer, got a bottle of Orange juice from the miniature fridge and slowly slugged down half a quart. He studied the moon as he held the bottle to his lips. He liked the look of Rebecca, *How do I tell her my name isn't Toby, this is all messed up.* The refraction of moon light through this particular lens suggested things are not always as they appear. The earlier conversation with Joe was playing in his head. *I just have a feeling saying no to Joe is not really going to be an option. He said I had a choice but do I?*

Gregg's next thought had him trying to figure out what was going on with Sheila. *I thought there was a real possibility there, I love her little boy and we were taking things slow. Just friends taking care of one another. I'm going to have to have her spell things out for me, I'm used to disappointment. Not sure she was even sick tonight.* Gregg stretched, took a leak and fell onto his bed fully clothed. He turned his head one more time toward the man in the moon but got no answers.

❁

• FRIDAY AUGUST 16,1963

• 6:00 AM

• SKOWHEGAN FAIR DAY TWO

Norma sat nursing her second cup of coffee replaying what the past twenty four hours had brought into her home. She had ushered her daughters into the cool and quiet serenity of the flower exhibit. The girls both expressed through word and hugs how proud they were of their mom. They were even more excited to hear of the job offer their mother shared. It had been the high point of the day. For the next few hours Norma had busied herself with quiet conversations with the ladies who had helped bring this exhibit about. The judging and placement of flower displays were critiqued as fair goers wandered through the building. She had entered the Methodist Diner and had coffee and Chocolate Cream Pie around seven. She wandered the mid-way not really looking for her daughters and not surprised she didn't find them. She was ready to leave by eight pm, tired and ready for a good night's sleep. She had spent the last two hours back in the flower exhibit sitting to the side sketching possible patterns she might develop in her new job. She was studying them even now as they sat in front of her, though her mind wandered and her coffee absently reached her lips. When ten o' clock had appeared on her watch face she stood in the vast parking area inside the race track. Lighting was dim but given the directions she had given the girls she should not be leaning on the fender of her car staring back into the lighted fairgrounds looking for three silhouettes to appear. At 10:02 one looming shadow appeared. A voice offered recognition as youngest daughter Ethel announced her arrival.

"I would have been here ten minutes earlier but I did one more walk-around trying to find those two bitches. They ditched me an hour ago at the women's bathroom." Ethel raised her fist to the sky.

Norma continued to lean on the fender but she seemed to slump a little, *and I thought this day was going to end on a good note for a change.* "Well we aren't going back in there for another look I can tell you that. Your sister may be only seventeen years old now but she is going to have to learn the hard way it seems." She hugged Ethel, sighed deeply and the two drove home in silence.

Norma had tried to get some sleep but each passing hour had her eyes opening wider. When a car pulled into the drive she had been staring out the window for a half hour solid, her neck stiff her back sore. The porch light burning bright had offered up a party for a hundred moths that had lasted a lot longer than usual. She watched her daughter slam the door of a car she didn't recognize then stagger onto the porch. A full minute went by before Anna had entered the house. Her clothing was rumpled her face like melted wax. *Something beyond the ordinary had taken place last night but Norma knew she just might be the last to know.* Her role was Judge, Jury and Executioner, no evidence offered. These kids covered for one another to their own detriment. *So be it.* Norma rinsed her cup took one look around her kitchen, snapped out the light and went to work.

❀

• 10:00 AM

I met with my buddies at the main gate. Still two hours till the midway opened but while a few cars entered only one of the new boys, was needed to assist us. Larry, John and my new running mate Paul walked the fence line with me looking for any new holes created overnight. "That was quite the shindig last night don't you think?"

I knew that simple little lead-in would take this conversation all the way around the perimeter— a full mile at least. "Gregg said it would be quite the party," offered Larry. "Say Myron, why do those two brothers call him Toby anyway?"

"Beats me," I answered, "not my business."

"What Gregg didn't tell me was who was hosting," announced Larry. "I told you when we got to that camp and I saw that guy through the window I'd had problems with him at Lakewood. I know he stole money and I got blamed. That's why I stayed in the damn car, out of sight."

"Well it was only for an hour Larry, so don't bitch to me, we didn't get there til after eleven and any way how was I supposed to know?"

"Myron's right Larry, and I'm glad we went," offered John. "I was considering forgiving Anna for her little camping trip but now after her ignoring me at the camp, forget it." He became animated, "Then tailing her back to town and seeing Shellee get dropped off then her and that guy— what's his name— Eddie, sneaking into the Drive In— that's total bull-shit."

Paul who had not been invited to the party remained silent but was thinking, *these guys seem to be part of a lot more action than I've witnessed I think I'm going to like Skowhegan.*

• 10:00AM AT THE HORSE BARN.

Gregg hung around the stable even after finishing his duties. He hadn't wandered into town for breakfast this morning, didn't want to see Joe until he had a chance to talk to Sheila. *I'm going to have to talk to Sheila about the conversation I had with Joe. And I need to find out what she's thinking about us, if there even is an, us?*

• 10:00 AM IN THE HOME OF NORMA GRAY

Anna rolled over and the wide awake eyes of her younger sister demanded an explanation. Anna sighed, "Let me go brush my teeth, I think I swallowed a dog turd, I'll be right back." When she returned Ethel had plumped up their pillows and was sitting against the head-board. "First of all there are a million reasons you can't tell anyone what I'm going to tell you. You have to promise me." Ethel nodded her head.

"Say the words Ethel."

"Okay, I promise I won't reveal what you tell me," she said somberly—then followed up hopefully, "did Shellee hook up with a Fair follower," she giggled.

"This is serious Ethel!! This is out of this world serious—someone hurt me last night." Anna told her younger sister the whole story and they cried together and they hugged together and they promised each other.

- ## FIRE AND RAIN

- ## SKOWHEGAN FAIRGROUNDS

- ## SUNDAY NIGHT DAY FOUR, ELEVEN PM.

The Grandstands emptied, a full house had witnessed the thrills provided by Joey Chitwood's Dare-Devil driving show. This was their last performance. Tomorrow night a country music duo would take over the stage. The vast parking area now resembled a long red necklace of taillights exiting the grounds. An occasional flashlight beckoned a car to hold up or move into line. The acrid smell of burning rubber and exhaust from the show was slowly dissipating. Comfort food smells of French fries, fried onions and hot dogs re-emerged, enticing the remaining mid-way crowd to eat up before the gates closed an hour from now. The car parking crew gathered at the main exit and divided their last duties of the night. The oldest and most experienced would walk the fence line. The youngest were dispatched with garbage bags and flashlights to clean the grassy parking area.

John, Larry, newbie Paul and I began our nightly trip. It was 11:20 pm. By midnight we had finished the walk and said goodnight to one another.

Paul waved good-bye to his new friends and turned on his transistor radio, moving to a bench to wait for his mom to pick him up. The hit song, *One Fine day* was playing and Paul hummed along. Seven songs and at least as many commercials later Paul realized his Mother must have fallen asleep on the couch again. His Dad had left early this morning to drive back to Massachusetts for three days of meetings with the Insurance Company he still worked at parttime in his retirement. Paul's Mother was excited about how well her plan for her son's senior year was working out. "I'll just pick you up at midnight, every night of the fair," she promised. "I might even pop into the activities some evening, who knows." Well she had managed to be late every night so far. Paul checked his watch, *wow I've been waiting over an hour.* He had observed the lights going out along the midway. Lights from food and fun booths soon followed. He sighed, *I guess I better call.* He wandered the now darkened area toward the one phone booth just outside the building that during the day and early evening housed the Sheriff's deputies. The building was dark but the light was on in the phone booth. As he got closer he realized someone was hunched down using the phone. Paul hung back, the collapsible door was partially open with the occupant back on his heels in a squatting position. Paul heard the words, *'Its a Go!'* A silence for what must have been twenty seconds followed. Then he heard, *'No sweat, all bases have been covered we got this. Talk to you soon.'* The caller stood up stretched and looked out into the darkness. Paul didn't know him, didn't recognize him as a fair worker, he was dressed too nattily to be one of them. He had an eerie feeling he had just witnessed what was intended as a private conversation.

Joe Gambino Jr. shuffled along the shadows heading away from the fairs main exit which was just a short walk away exiting to Madison Avenue.

Paul having spent the last few days in every conceivable nook and cranny of the grounds knew there was no exit available in the direction the man took. All exits except the main gate were padlocked by now. He waited a full five minutes before he entered the light of the phone booth and called home.

PART THREE

A BURNING RING OF FIRE

The first siren screamed at 3:28 am. A trucker entering Skowhegan from the south on Route 201 passed the Drive In and saw what looked to be an early sunrise, the sky aglow but in the wrong part of the sky. When his rig reached Madison Avenue and he was climbing the hill he could see flames chewing up the night. He got on his CB and announced, *THE FAIRGROUNDS ARE ON FIRE–ALL OF IT!*

By the time the person in charge of opening the gates was notified and on the scene, finger pointing had already begun. The fire Chief swore he had pointed out the main gate key hanging in the little wall box of important keys to his lieutenant.

Unfortunately the lieutenant had not completed the pointing out to his underlings. Twenty minutes of Fire trucks idling at the main gate allowed the fire to laugh in their face. A torrent of flame licked its chops and gnashed its teeth and chewed with its mouth open. The snaps and pops and explosions swallowed seasoned wood and fabric in big gulps.

Along with the acrid smoke, food smells mingled— hot dogs, sausage, onions and peppers whose smell enticed fairgoers— signaled surrender as they moved from done and ready to serve— to burned to a crisp in charred paper and melted plastic— exiting the fairgrounds as black smoke and smell.

Further down the midway screams emerged as animal barns exploded with igniting hay bales. New smells of wool and fur and hide, mingling with the screams. The horse barns were alive with anguish as well. Silhouettes of men darted to and fro, braving the blaze opening stalls sending horses running mindlessly up and down the midway. Several had found their way onto the track circling the darkened oval in a frenzy. The grandstands and everything under them were crushed as structural beams in the roof collapsed, straining spikes and nails squeaking their way to submission. Hissing sounds like a snake under attack emerged briefly as burning wood hit the water in the little babbling brook below. All the work Norma and her garden club had created covered in destruction.

❀

The light of day, as well as traffic, was muted for a square mile. The town police blocked off Madison Avenue just below what was called Cold Brook. South flowing traffic was diverted to North Avenue. A dark curtain of smoke blending with the inevitable fog that marked August mornings hung as a funeral shroud. Traffic coming North on route 201 was sent to North Avenue as well. The main entrance and exit for the town, Madison Avenue, for the next few hours posed as a persona non grata, with only official vehicles allowed. The Madison, Anson, Fairfield, Solon and Canaan fire departments had dispatched trucks to the scene.

Gawkers had found their way to the Russell road and parked within sight of the back entrance to the fairgrounds— sipping coffee, smoking cigarettes already armed with an opinion on how this had happened.

Both County Sheriff Arthur McManus, and Skowhegan police chief George Henry had their men laying out yellow tape well beyond the perimeters of the still smoldering buildings. Though not particularly fond of one another they were both professionals and stood comparing what they saw, smelled, heard and surmised.

"The State Fire Marshal is on his way, but it's pretty apparent to me these fires were set," offered police Chief George Henry.

"No doubt. This wasn't a forest fire jumping tree to tree and I smell gasoline in the smoke," said Sheriff McManus with his nose pointed skyward. "We have to shut this place down it's a crime scene, going to take the rest of the week just totaling losses."

Police Chief Henry nodded his head, "I'll have dispatch call the radio stations and try to get the word out in as many ways as possible. **Fair week is over.**"

Bill Neilson the fair organizer walking up heard those last words and opened his mouth to object. Sheriff McManus laid a hand on his shoulder. I know what this means to you Bill but what we have here is a real mess."

Fire Chief Russell Clement came running up, still listening to his walkie-talkie. "We've got a victim near the baby animal barn." His hand held squawked again. "What? A body just located in what's left of the horse barn. Repeat that." He held the device close to his ear. "The one near the animal barn is still alive but burned, a male."

Law enforcement looked at one another. "We now have arson and murder, I better call State Police Homicide," said Chief Henry.

Sheriff McManus made one more observation as he walked with the others toward what was now a murder scene, planned or accidental— no matter— someone died. "This didn't all happen because a guy spent ten bucks trying to win his sweetheart a teddy bear and not getting it done. Somebody had something to gain by all this."

Chief Henry found himself again agreeing with the County Sheriff. "Let's pool our resources Sheriff, two heads are better than one. The two men shook hands.

❀

Sheila had been awakened at the first smell of smoke entering the open window in the little camp trailer she shared with her son Jeffery and Madame Toussant. The trailers of most of the traveling fair workers were Located on the southern side of the midway behind a long row of mid-way tents but thankfully no wooden structures. As a group they had huddled and borne witness to the monster that devoured the western end of the fairgrounds as well as the buildings just to the right of the main walking gate. She had not located Gregg yet. The buildings across the race tracks spouted flames so high they towered over the grandstand— that would be the horse barns. She thought Greg might be sleeping there.

Bulbs popped in their sockets up and down the midway. Wrapped in watered down blankets the fair workers dodged embers and stood with garden hoses they used for their drinking water trained on the roofs of their little homes. Trapped, coughing, and helpless they stood talking, protecting their little town of tin just inside fencing that was designed to keep the bad guys out. Animal screams filled the night.

Sheila shivered, hugging both Jeffery and Madame Toussant. *Where is Gregg?* She recalled their conversation yesterday at lunch. He was not going to agree to what he'd been asked to do. They had also talked out where their relationship might be headed and had ended the conversation agreeing to just be friends for now.

Madame Toussant looked at the artificial light and the madness that was just across the way and realized she had in fact predicted the storm in Sheila's future. She too wondered where Gregg could be. Both buildings he was bunking down in this week were up in flame and smoke.

• TUESDAY AUGUST 20

• 9:00 AM

• SKOWHEGAN FAIR GROUNDS DAY SIX

The parking crew continued to work though the fair isn't running. The fairgrounds smell like a garbage fire, and our job is picking through the wet blackened mess for anything salvageable, or suspicious— filling strategically placed garbage cans with waste. Rumors are running as rampant as the fire that flattened the buildings. Since we're all employees we are going to be interviewed in the next several days. Larry and John seem nervous about the interview.

"Look I've already had to explain myself to the sheriff's dept. about that Lakewood thing. Not excited about going under a hot light about this," said Larry with his hands wringing.

"How about me having to prove I had nothing to do with Anna's fake kidnapping, I swear they didn't believe me till she showed up and the truth came out," offered John, holding out a blackened rag that smelled like kerosene.

"That might be something they will want to see so put it in this bucket" I said.

Paul the newcomer, listened to the chatter but in his mind he was back in the dark of that night listening to the conversation that emerged from the phone booth. He would be questioned and he wondered if he in fact held an important key to the investigation.

I listened to my two companions piss and moan, nodding in all the right places but my mind was elsewhere. *Where is Gregg?* I hadn't seen him since the fire. Sheila had not emerged either. The little trailer she and her son lived in was there but no one answered my knock.

• LAW OF THE LAND

• WEDNESDAY, AUGUST 23, 1963

• SEVENTH DAY OF THE FAIR

Sheriff McManus was still trying to piece this thing together. Bizarre was the word on the street and the sheriff would have to agree with that assessment. He obviously had more details than the community at large, but bizarre seemed the appropriate term for sure. He'd come to this job in an unusual way but now that he filled the office, both with his determination and his six foot-five two hundred and fifty pound body, he ran a tight ship. Sheriff Mac as he was called had been a woodsman for fifteen years. He had cut wood, bought and sold wood-lots and plowed driveways in the winter. He was known for his honesty, fair dealings, and common sense.

His decision to run for county sheriff came after an altercation at the State Fair in Skowhegan ten years earlier when he tried to break up a fight and was charged with assault. He was eventually exonerated but the lies that some of the deputy sheriffs had fabricated didn't sit well with Mac.

Today the peacefulness of those days in the woods— running a skidder and watching the deer play in the new cuttings, seemed mighty inviting. State Police detectives, The State Fire Marshal, newspaper reporters, and every elected official in the county were still clamoring for information while the smell of smoke was still in the air.

Some facts were clear. One person was dead while another was burned and in a coma. A fire, already determined to be arson, had leveled six buildings and numerous tents at the fairgrounds.

Sheriff Mac had not had the usual luxury of watching the rising sun find the eyes of each member of the group of men pictured on his bedroom wall for the past several mornings. When things were calm, these were the first people he saw upon waking. For the past three days Sheriff Mac drank his first cup of coffee well before the sun would hit their faces.

He loved to start his day with his wife Laura, a good cup of coffee and the paper. He loved to open his eyes just as the sun rose into his bedroom window and smile at that group picture on the wall. He had fought with these men. Not a single member of this group was from the area. In fact they didn't stay in touch—yet they had shared a trauma that was indelible as the photograph that had been enlarged, spoke to him silently every morning.

He felt out of sorts— his routine wrecked, more attention than he wanted— not a happy camper. This pre-dawn time at the kitchen table filled with artificial light was his only guaranteed quiet time lately. The news both national and local was spread out on the kitchen table. Sheriff McManus didn't spend much time on national headlines this week. The death and fire had created bold black headlines locally, moving national concerns to the inside pages.

A supposed attempted kidnapping that originated just days before opening day of the fair— with his troops already stretched thin— ended only when the kids again supposedly escaped from a makeshift campsite in Canaan. At least that was the story being told by the girls. Lots of man hours had been wasted in the Sheriff's opinion— and this morning after an update last night, *hopefully I'll hear the truth of what really occurred.* It was a rare an unusual beginning to the dog days of summer.

This morning's paper tried to capsulize all that had transpired in the normally quiet town of Skowhegan, Maine. *An arson fire had destroyed several main buildings as well as the animal barns and part of the horse stables at the fairgrounds late Sunday night. The death of a fair worker and hospitalization of another, followed what had been an attempted kidnapping in nearby Canaan. Both cases were open investigations. The Sheriff's Department and Skowhegan Police Dept. were both working on the attempted kidnapping. They were also involved investigating the fire and murder along with the State Police. The State Fire Marshall had determined the fire was arson.*

Sheriff Mac drained his cup, rinsed and set it beside his wife's. He looked in on his wife Laura. He glanced up at the framed photo which seemed to kick start his day even when he could not linger over the images. Sighing, he quietly closed the French doors.

Laura would be up soon getting ready for her own work day. Thinking of his wife, Sheriff Mac smiled as he padded quietly to the mud room to slip on his leather shoes and light jacket. *I could walk blindfolded anywhere in the house and find everything in its proper place,* he mused. Laura had to be the most organized woman he knew. She had shown through married life she had the most courage too. When the outside world screamed chaos and confusion Sheriff Mac knew Laura would provide the stability and sanity he needed to unwind and remain centered. *Love that woman* he thought to himself as he quietly closed the door.

Sheriff McManus greeted the dispatcher and entered his office. It was more of a meeting room than your typical office. A long table took up the middle of the room with steel folding chairs lining the sides. Sheriff Mac when asked why he didn't put something a little nicer in their place replied, "Nobody should get too comfortable in the Sheriff's office." There was a double meaning to the statement. Elected every four years by the general population after a long primary just to get your party's nomination, the real campaign followed with lots of negative feelings emerging. Bad feelings many times remained in place and were as difficult to remove as a fallen tree across a logging road— both ends forming scar tissue just out of sight of a passerby. Sheriff Mac had survived two of these campaigns and wasn't sure he really wanted another.

On a small desk at the end of the room a much younger Laura McManus looked all visitors' right in the eye, just daring them to lie to the law. Another door led to a bathroom stall, a shower and sink. There were no windows in the office, each wall covered with maps of county towns. An American flag hung over the sheriff's desk. On his desk a green blotter framed with messages tucked into the edges— a day planner with positive thoughts and quotes— along with that framed picture of his wife.

When sitting across from the sheriff a visitor would be looking directly into Laura's eyes. Many times Sheriff Mac began a conversation by asking, "You wouldn't lie to me right in front of my wife would you?" He'd ask this question deadly serious. On a small table the same height as the desk, a miniature skidder with a twitch of logs seemed to echo a message written in Calligraphy framed and sitting adjacent. The message was clear and cut through all the lies and politics that might enter this room. *DON'T TRY TO HAUL MORE THAN YOU'RE EQUIPPED TO!*

This morning Sheriff McManus asked the dispatcher to round up the night officer when he came in so he could get up to speed on any developments in the on-going investigations. He poured a cup of coffee, his second of the morning and would hold off on any more till he could catch breakfast at Whittemores. Trying to coordinate and cooperate with other enforcement agencies was as delicate an operation as removing a tree that got hung up when it fell the wrong way. Breaking bread with the Police Chief and Fire Chief and lately the State Police detective in charge of the murder investigation at different breakfast places in town at least provided an opportunity to start the day on the same page. *But breakfast would have to wait,* Sergeant Gene Sylvain was waiting in the corridor.

A half hour later two morning sergeants and Sheriff's detective Patrick Fitzmaurice joined Sheriff McManus and the night officer.

"Case is solved. I think it was a good idea to let their parents have a go at them first, Sheriff. One of the parents called just before this meeting. Not sure if they had to beat it out of them or what but it seems the kids spent a night partying and a day sobering up and another night trying to come up with an excuse for not getting home the first night— Kids!"

The men all nodded their heads in agreement and smiled as their own experiences both personal and professional flashed through their minds.

"Never really thought you could have a group kidnapping anyway, especially a group of teenagers." The men laughed at that. "That young girl who triggered all this she's got some explaining to do," said the Sheriff. "I'll call her Mother later this morning."

With one case seemingly solved it seemed a little levity was in order. "I've got to tell you a funny story before we get back into the serious stuff," said Sergeant Leblanc, an army veteran. "You know how awkward officer Delbert can be. You have to hear this. Maybe I should get him in to tell it."

"Just do your best, we can all picture Delbert delivering his lines," said the sheriff chuckling to himself.

"Once we heard those kids were missing old Delbert he had it in his head he was gonna solve this mystery all by himself. He was sure one of these fair followers was involved. *Some of them get here a week early you know,* he told me. Anyway, this is just the way Delbert explained it to me. He had been up the night before watching a John Wayne war movie where he placed himself in a tank, riding tall and in battle mode beside old Duke"

This group had all heard and seen Delbert imitate John Wayne which brought a collective smile before the story even unfolded. *Imagining Delbert with sounds leaving his mouth like rapid machine-gun fire— while a little insensitive— it was still funny dammit.* "This story took some time in telling as you can well imagine but I'll just deliver the reader's digest version."

'I was making the circuit around the tents and trailers.' Sergeant Leblanc paused to convey the seriousness of Delbert's mission. *'I viewed the young boy peeling potatoes for French fries as an Asian orphan in a smoky village in the Pacific.'* Smiles all around. *'I hailed the boy, he looked at me oddly then a raised middle finger snapped me back to reality and I felt foolish.'* Laughter this time.

'I heard sounds, they were setting up and testing equipment. Normal midway ride noises along with flashing lights, but in my mind they became bombs landing and planes taking off.' Sergeant Leblanc paused.

"Here comes the best part." *'I heard what sounded like a scream and began a zig- zagging movement toward the sound. I saw a tent flap move about fifty yards ahead. Nobody else would have picked up on that.'* Belly laughs beginning around the table.

'I began a side to side movement, one I've watched dozens of times in those war movies, I became stealth-like. I heard the noise again, something between a scream and a plea. Just eight yards from the tent now I was already planning to hit the culprit with my leather sap just not sure where.'

The Sheriff had tears streaming down his cheeks.

'The flap opened, I steeled myself. Practically falling out of the tent was not a prisoner of war but our very own Roxanne, sputtering as she struggled to close the gap of her blouse. Then the Fair fella he come out. He was trying not to let this occasion end, so he offered up, "I thought we meant something to one another."

Roxanne struggled to say what she meant. "We did— we do— not right now though—we might later on," *'Roxanne was fumbling her words as she continued to struggle with her blouse. She just started running, the further she got down the midway the more she was checking her options. 'She looked over her shoulder and hollered,* "I'll probably be back Stanley, probably after dark, maybe probably I'll be missing you by then."

'I managed, morning Miss Roxanne.' "Delbert said he tipped his hat as Roxanne brushed past him." Gales of laughter.

Roxanne sputtered, "This ain't what it appears Delbert so you just go on and solve a stolen bike mystery," *finishing,* "and it's not a very good morning I can tell you that!"

Sergeant Leblanc was bent over double as retelling the story rekindled the original laughing fit he had experienced.

Everyone in the room continued laughing having all heard a Delbert original as only he could tell them. After continued chuckles and side bars the men all got themselves another cup of coffee.

Sheriff Mac raised his hand and yielded the floor to Sergeant Gene Sylvain. "On another matter tell these guys what might just be an important clue that has come to light." Said the sheriff.

The night man on duty, Sergeant Gene Sylvain, a World War Two veteran, not one to dramatize, embellish, or exaggerate was not about to raise any hopes either. "Probably doesn't mean anything, but patrolman Ware caught a teenager breaking into Lakewood Theater last week." Silence followed.

Night officer Sergeant Sylvain didn't expound on his statement.

Sheriff Mac waited, he finally had to prime the pump.

"What did the kid offer up as a reason for breaking in?"

"He didn't offer up anything," Gene let the silence thicken. Finally he added, "I had to do a little bartering first."

The other officers were looking at one another expectantly, waiting for the shoe to fall.

Sheriff Mac had all the patience in the world and knew Sergeant Sylvain was having a little fun with the boys.

"Okay Gene cut to the chase, I've watched wood grow faster than you getting to the point."

Gene smiled then, "Well officer Ware wrote up a summons and let the kid go. He's local and Officer Ware knew him from the football team. The kid has been fretting about it and didn't want his family to find out. He came in and asked if he could just pay a fine. I interviewed the kid last evening, here at the station. Seems this teenager worked at Lakewood Theater over the summer and was let go when some ticket money disappeared. The boy swears he didn't take the money but he knows who did." The room began to get restless. "Anyway he said he went back there last week after the first night of the fair to get some clothes he'd left." Another long pause, Gene winked at the Sheriff.

"He said the manager told him the sheriff's office had been informed of the stealing incident and if he came back for any reason he would be charged with trespass. His mother has been asking about his clothes so he needed to get them back," said Sergeant Sylvain.

Sheriff Mac added the next line. "Seems Lakewood never notified anyone about the alleged theft, Sergeant Sylvain checked." The sheriff stood up, "But out of this seemingly harmless little drama we might just have a lead to the arson fire." He had everyone's full attention now.

Sergeant Sylvain puffed his chest ever so slightly, "The boy— who now works at the fair parking cars— said two guys, older than him have been staying in one of the cottages near the theater. Seems one works at the theater painting scenery and doing electrical stuff. He thought they were college age, maybe twenty or so. Anyway they have been throwing small parties all summer— by invitation only. The kid says he knows Eddie, the one who works at the theater stole the money."

The other officers continued to squirm.

Gene held up his hand, quieting the restlessness. "He can't prove it but he said the beverage of choice greatly improved after the theft. They went from

Dawson ale to Crown Royal Liquor the night after the theft," the boy told me. "He said, Eddie kidded to everyone at the party, then again at work that he'd played a leading role in the best mystery offered up at the theater this summer."

Detective Fitzmaurice yawned and stretched. "Can you give me a little more yarn here I'm not sure if we're darning a sock or knitting a sweater?"

Sheriff Mac smiled, these were good men he worked with and they knew how to play one another. Good police work came about by noticing and questioning and being easy with one another.

Patrick Fitzmaurice a navy veteran had worked in intelligence in the service and was a steady as she goes investigator. Sheriff Mac was glad to have these navy men aboard.

Sergeant Sylvain continued, "Playing good cop I asked him what else he could give us that I could take to the sheriff— the only one with the power to maybe make this break-in disappear. He said he didn't know anything else. I went fishing anyway and asked him one last question. Does Eddie have a last name, and do you know where he's from?"

Silence was the only sound in the room. The Sergeant continued without being prompted. "The boy said he was always bragging about being from Boston and in fact he did know the last name because part of his job had been handing out checks all summer.

Gambino, Eddie and he assumed his older brother, had the same last name, Gambino." That's all he knew and he said he hoped that was enough because if his mother got wind of any of this he didn't think there were branches big enough. I don't know what he meant by that but it sounded like he might rather face you sheriff— than his mother."

Detective Patrick Fitzmaurice was suddenly at attention mentally fashioning that garment he'd mentioned. It was beginning to resemble a sweater. He cleared his throat and supplied his own yarn.

He cleared his throat, "I've just heard that last name for the third time this summer. First time was in June regarding a beating of a student from The Skowhegan Art school in East Madison. I was involved because some items were taken. The art student is not a kid he's a thirty-five year old aspiring artist who was wandering the area doing facial sketches of rural Mainers. Seems he chose a young man he saw near the water in Lakewood. He didn't ask the young man for permission. At some point as the art student was filling in back ground of the lake the young man wandered by and recognized himself in the picture. He immediately pummeled the artist, ripped up the sketch and took the artists paints and brushes with him. A local witnessed the assault and called it in anonymously. Gave the name Gambino but that was it. The artist refused to cooperate and we had no idea who this Gambino was or where to find him." Detective Fitzmaurice had everyone's attention now.

Sheriff Mac smiled, I thought that you had mentioned that name to me at least once in the past several months."

"That Gentlemen is the way good police work is conducted, gentle persuasion I call it," boasted Sergeant Sylvain rising to pour a second cup of coffee.

Detective Fitzmaurice continued. "The second time I heard that last name was just yesterday." Detective Fitzmaurice rose and stretched, then moved to the head of the table like a teacher about to begin a lesson plan.

"The State Fire Marshal determined the fire was deliberate. They believe separate fires were set to muddy the waters. This is all still speculation but the state police believe and we would agree— the horse stables were the main target. Four horses burned up. One person died in that fire. We believe the fire under the grandstand was started to create a diversion to confuse any investigation. The fire at the

Methodist diner and the exhibit hall were diversions as well. The baby animal barns we believe caught fire when embers from one of the other fires hit hay bales stored there. It seems whoever set these fires figured with that much area up in flames most any evidence would be wiped out by water, scrambling fire teams, as well as the general public trying to help. And it was."

"How did the Gambino name come up regarding the fires?" asked Sergeant Sylvain.

"Well it wasn't directly related to the fire. That's why you haven't been aware of the name. We checked on who owned the horses that died in the fire. Guess who owned two of the horses that burned up. Joseph Gambino Stables out of Malden Massachusetts." The other two horses were owned by locals. We have not spoken to Mr. Gambino, we were told to direct any questions to his counsel." Detective Fitzmaurice returned to his seat.

"Sounds like we might have a reason to talk to the Gambino brothers," offered Sergeant Leblanc who spoke up for the first time since telling the funny story.

"On the surface I'd say you're right," said sheriff Mac. "But let's consider this a little bit. The only things we know for sure is two members of what we believe might be part of Boston's crime family are living in our county and one of them possibly beat someone up. Further, Brother Eddie might have stolen some money from Lakewood Theater, a crime that didn't get reported. What we will do by interviewing them is alert them that we know they are here." The sheriff stood up and stretched— this time he faced the table— he had a story to tell. "When I worked in the woods somebody was always trying to steal fuel, equipment, wood, or all of the above. I could have set in those woods every night and probably never caught em; they skipped around from logging site to logging site. So a bunch of us woodsmen laid a trap.

During a poker night a group of us fashioned a story then quietly let word out about a big logging operation that was about to start with lots of equipment being used. We gave a remote location but made sure it was near a main road. The Paper mill worked with us and let us use a piece of their land as the site. We put some old equipment in there and a bunch of fuel. We took turns staking it out— the Sheriff's dept. cooperated. Hell they were glad to, they had been sending deputies to one theft after another and coming up dry. Anyway as I said the six outfits took turns and on the fifth night— pay dirt. Four men snuck in with little pen lights looking for fuel, skidder chains, chainsaws, and anything else worth selling. They exchanged high fives and were congratulating themselves when the bigger lights came on. We held rifles on them till the deputies arrived. They didn't have to sneak out with flashlights when they left, the whole area was lit up as they slunk out— wearing cuffs. The Sheriff's dept. traced these guys to a whole string of night time activities. The point I'm making men is we need to develop a plan before we speak to these two individuals, in doing so we just might get a whole lot more than we even know about."

Over the next hour plans were made to do some digging, discreetly. Detective Fitzmaurice would head up a new investigation of all the incidents that might now be related to the Gambino family. No patrol officers, State Police, public officials, not anyone— including wives or girlfriends were to be given any information. The detectives would report directly to the sheriff after they compared information daily. They would be removed from their daily routines. "You will be conducting interviews in conjunction with the police department and when necessary the State Police." When we have enough information to share regarding the Gambino boys we'll share— not before, no sense muddying the waters."

As the men filed out Sheriff Mac realized he had put together a crack investigative team that were local, seasoned, not prone to flying off the handle and loyal. *Maybe I will run again,* he mused, *though Laura wouldn't be pleased.*

❁

Sheriff McManus had met with his men earlier and now sat across the table from Police Chief Henry. "I would like you to schedule the interviews, you and your men know some of these kids better than we do."

"I'd be glad to, I would like one of your detectives to work with my lead investigator as well, if that works for you."

The two men shared all the information they had received regarding the fire. Then Sheriff McManus asked Chief Henry if he knew an Anna Gray, Norma Gray's daughter.

"Actually I do a little. Why do you ask?"

"She was involved in that foolishness out in Canaan and I am going to have her in for a chat. Wondered how easy I should go with her, those kids had us chasing our tails for a couple days. Media got involved too. City papers suggesting we are all country bumpkins out here in the foothills."

The Skowhegan Police Chief cleared his throat, "She's not a bad kid, a little impulsive maybe. She started a protest at the high school last year regarding the length of skirts allowed. We got called when about twenty girls refused to leave a Civics classroom and go to their next class. It got loud and there was some pushing and shoving. Truth is the girl wasn't involved in the confrontation but she had started the petition and made some posters. She got inschool suspension as the ring leader. One of my deputies was called to clear the classroom. I've known her mother for a long time. They are good hard working people."

"That's what I heard from one of my deputies. I have to decide whether to counsel her, scold her or charge her- for I don't even know what- maybe wasting tax payer dollars?" he chuckled. "Well any way if you want to send your investigator in I'll have him sit with my detective Pat Fitzmaurice and they can frame their questions in light of what we know and surmise."

• WHO KNOWS WHAT

I was the first of the boys to be interviewed. Detective Fitzmaurice had a list of questions written down. He and police dept. Detective, Vincent Noonan had spent an hour framing a dozen questions that if answered honestly and without hesitation might prove useful in solving this thing. "We'll tag team them, you ask their name and what their function with the fair is. I'll write down their answers," suggested Detective Fitzmaurice. "Then I'll ask the second question with you recording their response. By the end of question seven we'll know whether they know anything or anyone who might be connected to all this." The two men nodded to one another. Detective Fitzmaurice stood and moved to the door, he looked down at his list, "Send in Myron Therrian."

Detective Noonan asked me the first question. Just as Detective Fitzmaurice had predicted by question seven one more name to be interviewed emerged from a question I had asked.

"I have a friend, Gregg Croteau, he was working at the fair in the animal barns, I haven't seen him since the fire. And a girl, Sheila, I can't find her either— do you know if they are okay?"

Detective Fitzmaurice looked Myron up and down, nodded to himself and decided I was one of the good ones. "Myron, we don't have a name for the young man burned, he has a skull fracture. He is presently in a coma in the hospital, you say his name is, Gregg Croteau?" Detective Noonan was writing this down and smiling at Detective Fitzmaurice, they were hitting pay dirt.

I began shaking like a leaf. Detective Noonan asked me to tell them what I knew of this Sheila, where was she staying? When I left the interview the two investigators high fived one another, one interview, two new possible leads. Larry and John followed but they had no information, they were nervous through-out the interview but clearly had no knowledge of the fire or anyone who might know something.

Paul Leland answered all their questions honestly and they were about to dismiss him when he suddenly took a deep breath and described what he had witnessed on the night of the fire. No, he had never seen him before.

"Beyond what you heard that night what made this incident stick in your mind?

Paul closed his eyes briefly as if to recall that night. "It was really dark. The only light coming from the phone booth but when that guy left the light he wasn't having any problem finding his way, he definitely knew exactly where he was headed."

Detective Fitzmaurice followed up, "and you heard the words, *we got this?*"

Paul nodded his head.

Detective Noonan looked down at his notes, "Dark hair, maybe just under six feet, twenty or so. That's what you remember?"

Paul shook his head yes. "I hope it helps."

The rest of the day's interviews offered nothing new and when the men wrapped up the day they agreed to meet with the Sheriff and Police Chief at six this evening. They had several valuable leads to follow up on.

❖

The patient stirred, uncomfortable and stiff, arms covered with bandages. He gingerly felt the gauze and a terrific pain replaced the ache that was constant in his arms. Senses began to kick in. The room brightened his eyelids, though he wasn't able to see— something covered his eyes. The smell of coffee reached his nose. He could sense someone in the room and tried to focus. A voice was reaching out, bouncing off the canyon walls of his mind echoing words he couldn't quite string together. He focused with all his might and every third word or so found its way through. McManus— days— alive— fire— a string of adjectives and adverbs— descriptors with no meaning— not yet. He slowly closed his eyes as the words faded to footsteps receding, even those out of sequence.

• WEDNESDAY, FAIR DAY SEVEN

• 6:00 PM

• SHERIFF'S OFFICE.

The Police Chief and Sheriff McManus sat across from one another, the chief commented on the log truck and the calligraphy. "That about sums up the very reason we have jobs sheriff," he raised the mug of coffee to his lips and made a decision. "Say when we get this whole mess cleaned up, would you like to go fly fishing?"

Sheriff McManus raised his own coffee, "I would indeed and maybe later in the fall I can offer a couple days at my hunting camp. We drink, we play poker and— occasionally someone gets a deer— although that's secondary if you get my meaning." A knock on the door produced the two investigators both laughing and kidding one another.

Seems like some good might just come out of this mess, mused Sheriff McManus.

An hour and a half later the Sheriff and the Police chief sat alone once again. "Tomorrow morning first thing we'll have William Neilson in and see if he has information about any young men working for the fair who might fit this description. In the meantime let's get two investigators to visit the camper this girl, what's her name again?" He checked his notes,

"Sheila Thompson, lives in."

Chief George Henry, spoke up. "You know with the fair shut down most of these fair people have moved on. I believe they go to Windsor next. Good bet we find her at the next stop."

Sheriff McManus rose, stretched and reached out to shake hands. "I believe I'll get moving George, that picture of my wife there on my desk is a constant reminder of what a lucky man I am. I can smell a casserole from here," he chuckled.

"You are a lucky man Sheriff, I will be dining at Whittemore's this evening and though the food is good, the companionship is usually pretty sparse."

"I'll see you at eight in the morning then." Two official looking hats were raised and lowered at the same time, the light switched off and the door closed.

❀

Detectives Fitzmaurice and Noonan strolled down the midway. Black brackish water and smoke scum framed ever receding puddles. Residue of smoke clung to the remaining buildings a layer seemingly becoming airborne each time a breeze arose.

King Reid shows had moved on. One burned out camper remained, the tires flattened showing signs of a scorching heat that had its way with it. The men studied the whole mess in front of them. "What a waste. What's the world coming to?"

"You got me there Pat. Nobody here to talk to, looks like a little road trip to Windsor might be in order," offered Detective Noonan."

"What a friggin mess, a lot of people hurt by this, not counting the dead and injured. People wait all year to show off their hard work and effort. Others raise a little hell, a lot of laughing during fair week. My wife is yakking at me already to solve this," said Detective Fitzmaurice as he continued to look at the destruction.

❀

• THURSDAY AUGUST 26

Sheila, holding her little boy, Jeffery— named after the bright little nephew in Florida she had so come to love— sat in the waiting room of the Redington- Fairview Hospital. She had been trying to get in to see Gregg since she found out he was in the hospital badly burned and in a coma. Gregg's mother entered the room and the two made eye contact. The two had not been introduced. Gregg's mother shook her head slowly, "He's still not fully awake, looks like he's going to make it though."

Sheila breathed in deeply, hugged her baby. *I sure wish he was awake, I'd know what to do with what he told me.*

"I can call you if things change, is there some place you're staying?"

Sheila introduced herself. She answered the question before it could be asked. No, Gregg is not the father. "I'm staying at a friend's house at least temporarily, give me your number, that might be easier," thinking, *who knows how long I can stay there.* Sheila rose, calmed her baby who had begun fussing and took the elevator to the cafeteria in the basement of the hospital.

Sitting quietly with paper and pencil sketching designs that might perk up the sterile walls of this place Norma Gray looked up and smiled as little Jeffery announced his entrance from the corridor. Just as Sheila reached the table her friend from middle school, Ethel Gray joined her mother with a tray of food.

"Any change from yesterday, Sheila?"

"No he is still in a coma, coming around slowly they think. I met his mother in the waiting room this morning, though."

Norma Gray opened a packet of sugar. As she slowly added it to her coffee then stirred it in she appeared distracted, seeming to wrestle with the proper way to respond. "I worked with that lady for ten years, she never offered that she even had a son. I have bragged about my girls, brought in pictures of their successes but she has never even acknowledged that she had a boy."

Ethel added, "Anna said he was the best runner on the Cross-Country team when he was a freshman, she was in most of his classes too.

No one ever knew where he went or why. The kids all thought the family must have moved." Ethel slid a wrapped sandwich across the table to Sheila, "Tuna on a roll Sheila, eat up. Let me hold the baby for you."

Sheila handed little Jeffery to Ethel. "I can't thank you guys enough for taking me in this way," her eyes watered, "I just couldn't leave Gregg and just go on to the next town. I have to talk with him and find out what happened. He was worried that something was going to happen and now it has."

"You can stay with us for as long as you need to Sheila, we'll figure out some way for you to get back in school this fall. The tough part will be finding someone to watch little Jeffery while you are in classes," offered Norma. She checked her watch. "Well girls I'll get you home, I need to get at least half a shift in."

❀

Bill Neilson entered the Sheriff's office. Sheriff McManus and Chief Harvey both rose to greet him. "Can I offer a cup of coffee or a soft drink, Bill?"

"I'm good. What you can offer is some good news. The damn insurance company is already reading the fine print. It's going to be a struggle."

"Sorry about that, but we're struggling too. Maybe you can help us out." The metal folding chairs complained and scraped as the men seated themselves around the table.

"Do you know any men around the age of twenty, dark hair, well dressed, who would know their way around the fairgrounds in the dark, who maybe work for you or someone else during fair week?"

Bill Neilson cupped his chin, tilted his head backward and studied the light fixture. "I don't really get that involved in the hiring, why do you ask?"

"I can't really comment on that, but who would be able to answer that question?"

"Well let's see Sheriff, I suppose if you are talking about working for the fair itself, my assistant Tom Quinn would be the man to talk with." Bill squirmed around in his chair and looked at Chief Henry, so you two have a suspect?"

"As the Sheriff said, no comment. The less you know the better right now." Chief Henry followed up, "Who else does any hiring for this week?"

"Well Marvin was part of hiring for the horse barns and the whole agricultural part of the fair for that matter, but he had a boss too. No idea who. Marvin's dead, so I'd start with my assistant, let him piece-meal this together.

There's the racing part, the betting, the parking, the food vendors. Advertising. A lot of moving parts so yeah I'd talk with Tom." Bill rubbed his hands through his hair looking distracted and about ten years older than when the fair began.

"Can you call Tom? I've met him— seems like a capable guy," offered the Sheriff, "see if he can come down. He sells land and homes for most of the year. He still live in Embden?" Bill Neilson nodded. Sheriff McManus looked toward Chief Henry, "I bought a wood lot from him years ago. He don't miss much. He just might lead us in the right direction."

❁

Joe Gambino Jr. turned in his sleep, the sudden brightness from the window reached into his dream— the dark night in his dream quickly morphing into a flash from the recent fire. He'd watched as each of the fires he and his brother set joined forces and become an inferno— from just outside the fence. He woke to the morning sun and an already warming breeze finding its way through the screen. He lay there content, nearly everything had gone as planned. He stretched his six foot frame—his leg touched the girl—she twitched and sighed in her sleep. He moved his body to fit her pattern and nestled. He became aroused and began rubbing her shoulders. *Yep everything was moving along nicely, too bad about Toby but it couldn't be helped.*

Rebecca was having her own dream and Joe's heated body moved things along nicely as well. She wriggled her body allowing her panties to slide off her hips. One hand deftly removed the obstacle while the other guided Joe into her wetness.

An hour later the two were sitting at the kitchen table, mugs of coffee serving as chess pieces to their next move. "I'm heading back to School at the end of the month but I would really like to see you again."

Rebecca liked this young man. He was more mature than her peers and seemed to have a plan. She was intent on joining the Peace Corp but she still had college to get through after her senior year of High School. She intended on going to The University of Maine herself. Joe would be a senior and she would be just starting, but a year together, well who knows?

Thinking back to that first morning she had met him in Whittemores she just had to ask, "Why did you play it so cool when we first met and even at that party you didn't really talk to me?" "I am a very careful guy I like to watch for a while before I warm up to people. I watched the way you handled yourself— and by the way— I watched that little movement your butt makes— that is a definite turn on." Then holding up his hands in surrender he finished, "though I could see it was totally unconscious on your part."

Rebecca smiled, "Anyway I'm glad we met and I wouldn't mind being courted by a college man." She reached across the table and touched his hand. Another thought, "what's going to happen to Toby, I haven't heard anything?"

Good question, I'm sure there must be some insurance coverage but I haven't been able to talk with him—still in critical care as of yesterday."

"The rumors are running rampant, some are saying he started the fires. I don't believe that, do you?"

Joe put the mug to his lips— his next words became muddied in the amber liquid, heating and hiding his treachery. "I know he and Marvin were having problems and Marvin spoke to me— his words," *'I want his ass fired!'* "He never said why. Guess he can't now. Toby himself said he was tired of ass-hole bosses and he intended to stick up for himself if it came to it." Joe sighed, "Personally I don't think he did it but who really knows anyone."

"Well I don't believe it either. Anna grew up with him, she said he was always a really nice kid. He moved away. She was shocked when he was at the party the other night. She also was confused when you kept calling him Toby. She hadn't seen him in two years but his name was Gregg back then. If she hadn't been quite so shit faced the other night I think she would have held a conversation with him. Gregg or Toby seemed to have a lot on his mind as well. He seemed to be in a daze when I dropped him off at the fairgrounds.

Joe was about to respond when Eddie entered the kitchen, gargled a glass of water in the sink then filled a cup from the pot, lightened it and scraped out a chair to join them. "Morning all, Miss Rebecca you're looking like the new school Marm who just arrived on a stage from Tucson."

Rebecca looked at him quizzically. Joe responded. "This brother of mine reads way too many westerns, and he only understands the short words, so pay him no mind."

Joe rose, "well let me get you back to town we can finish our discussion in the car. Eddie don't forget to carry out that little assignment today I really need to have an answer."

"Yes sir I'll just mosey into town poke my head in a few places maybe find a varmint." He smiled at Rebecca. He seemed to be studying her.

Rebecca didn't like the look in his eyes, they were not filled with merriment, devilry possibly, or was that pure evil she was observing, she shivered.

Eddie noticed, "You might want to get a shawl wrapped around our little teacher here, she appears chilled."

❀

Norma was at work, Anna was in her room while the two younger girls dried the breakfast dishes. Baby Jeffery dozed in a towel lined laundry basket just outside the reach of a sunbeam.

"Your sister is not the carefree girl I remember— kicking the crap out of us with pillows when we talked too late in the night— then bunking down beside us on the floor wrapped in a blanket, is she ok?"

"Listen Sheila, I'm really glad to have you back in my life but things are a little sketchy here right now. I promised my sister I wouldn't tell anyone anything. But you are right she's changed."

"Fair enough, after what I went through last year I'm the last one to want to poke into people's lives." She paused, tilted her head then as if making a decision she nodded her head and began.

"I have a secret of my own though, think you could guard it as well as your sisters'?" I need to share it with someone, it's eating me up."

The two girls left the baby just inside the screen door and moved to the two chairs on the porch. A butterfly flitted above the many flower planters hung on the porch railing. Sheila looked out from this porch, fifteen hundred miles north of where she had fought for Jeffery's future. Remembering the vast manicured cultivated lawn, the flower gardens and fruit trees she had viewed on that morning, somehow this porch held more honesty and integrity. It was clear these well-worn chairs had been the seat of many discussions and burdens. Hopes and dreams had been revealed. Looking out over this small back yard. Sheila took a deep breath. She took Ethel's hand. "I'm scared Ethel, really scared, I think Gregg might have been hurt because he wouldn't help do harm to some race horses." She suddenly deflated as the air surrounding her words carried her worry. She sunk into the chair looking for all the world like a junior-high schooler. "I don't know if anyone else knows or if anyone knows I know." She continued to explain and when she was finished Ethel was left with overlapping secrets— the last name Gambino, was part of both.

❀

The investigators entered the Windsor Fair grounds and went immediately to the Waldo County Sheriffs building. They had called ahead and alerted the deputies that they would like to interview one of the fair workers. The two investigators walked towards the little silver trailer that Sheila had stayed in. Madame Toussant sat in a plastic chair just in front, nursing a cup of tea. The two investigators introduced themselves and Madame Toussant invited them to sit. There were no chairs so they shrugged and shared a portion of the narrow step leading into the trailer. After being told Sheila had not come to Windsor, Investigator Fitzmaurice asked if Madame Toussant had any idea where the girl might be. "All I know is she was originally from Skowhegan and she had touched base with some friends early in the week. I was with Sheila when the fire started so I can assure you she was not involved with that fire."

"Did she give any reason for not continuing with the fair?"

Madame Toussant decided to tell the men about reading Sheila's fortune. When she had finished, the two men looked to one another. "So you predicted all this and even predicted her friend getting hurt?"

"That is correct and I believe that is part of the reason she did not stay with me. She believes she carries misfortune with her. We talked after the fire and she believes I correctly saw all that was to happen and she does not want to see any more."

"So you think she stayed in Skowhegan to be there for her friend, the boy injured in the fire?"

"I believe that to be true, yes."

❀

It seemed as if dead ends were the order of the day. Two full weeks after the fire there had been no arrests. Scoop Plummer sat across from Sheriff McManus. He wet his pencil lead with his tongue and said, "Let me get this down correctly Sheriff, you have no concrete leads in this case."

"I didn't say that, Scoop, what I said was we have not made an arrest— big difference."

Scoop was a little man with bushy eyebrows and a constant gleam in his eyes that seemed to be burrowing straight into your conscience. He wore a Sherlock Holmes type cap that announced he was a seeker of truth.

"I noticed that load of wood there and the message Sheriff, do you need to call in the big guns?"

Sheriff McManus smiled across the desk, "should I have asked for the owner of your paper to conduct this interview or do you feel equipped to handle it?"

Scoop squirmed for a moment but caught the Sheriff's message, "I'll keep digging on my end and share as long as you keep me in the loop.

It's a terrible mess isn't it?"

"It's certainly something I never thought this town would have to weather, but we'll get through it as long as we don't start doubting one another."

"You're right, sorry about that." With that he rose, adjusted his hat, and turned to leave.

The sheriff spoke, "We still have people to interview, some we haven't located, and the damage is done. School's about to start and when that damn smell dampens down we'll have football to watch."

Just as Scoop was about to close the door the Sheriff followed up, "That's when people let down their guard you know, when normal sets in."

• SCHOOL DAYS

• SEPTEMBER 1963

We had been practicing for the up-coming cross-country season for the past two weeks. Paul is indeed a gifted runner and once he learns to pace himself he will definitely be a top five runner for our team. He is in my senior English class as well, so I am getting to know him on and off the field. This afternoon after practice we wandered onto the bleachers and watched the football team go through their drills. Larry and John gave us a head nod and went about their business of punishing the underclassmen who are being asked to stop the varsity's offense. "Glad I'm not a freshman" said Paul.

"Glad I don't play football. I have enough trouble dodging roots and rabbits," I laughed.

We small- talked about the team, our shared English class, the cafeteria food, a girl in English class Paul seems attracted to, and finally the devastation we both witnessed and can still smell when we're running.

"I thought it was cool the way Mrs. Merrill is going to use the fire as a way to research and write about our towns past, present and future," Paul offered.

"Yeah sounds like this first quarter will be interesting. Who are you going to invite in to speak?"

"I'm new so I don't really know anyone, though I did meet the police investigators. Maybe I'll invite the Sheriff or the Chief of Police."

"Well I'm thinking about inviting the head of the fair association. I've met him before—find out what the plans to rebuild looks like."

The afternoon sun had warmed the wooden bleachers and the boys semi-dozed with their eyes open.

I finally re-joined the present when an extra loud whistle on the football field sounded and the team began the first of three, one hundred yard sprints— the groans were nearly as loud as the whistle. Soon we were joined by John and Larry climbing the bleachers sweating and swearing softly. They stretched out and put in their two cents worth regarding the first day of the rest of their lives. When Anna's name came up in conversation John was quick to say he had no further designs on the girl and offered up, "good luck with her, she's a good kid but for me there is the trust issue, I could never trust her again."

He went on to tell Paul his sad summer story, while Larry and I heard the tale of woe for the umpteenth time.

"I just told Myron I thought she was cute, I didn't say I was going to marry the girl," Paul offered after John had finished.

"Hey, anyone going to Ma Beane's tonight? Heard she got a new load of records on the juke box," said Larry changing the topic.

❀

Anna's first day back in school was painful. Everyone was excited to be back for their final year, while she had to fake feeling any sense of well-being at all. The fire seemed to be the hot topic of the day. Kids she hadn't seen over the summer, all had to give their opinion, on the who— the what—the why—and the how. Anna had decided— though she hadn't shared it with anyone— to invite her mom in to speak about what the fire had destroyed beyond the loss of buildings. The personal loss would offer a different perspective. She walked home and went directly to her room. Her friends Shellee and Rebecca were the only two who picked up on her quietness. Anna had no intention of sharing what had happened with anyone beyond her sister and would just have to be better at disguising her anguish.

According to Shellee, Rebecca was very excited about a boy she had met and thought she would be seeing him every other weekend. The girls didn't have a chance to really talk since they were not in the same classes and Anna left before Shellee could give her any details.

❀

Sheila started her sophomore year of high school sharing all the same classes with her friend Ethel. She got re-acquainted with some of her friends from Jr. High School and enjoyed her first day at Skowhegan High School. She hurried to the home of the elderly lady who was watching her four month old son Jeffery. All day, friends had welcomed her back and encouraged her to join the soccer team. Sheila didn't shrug from telling them she had an infant son who needed her more than the team did. Some raised their eyes in astonishment but most realized there but for the grace of God, good contraception or strict and nosy parents— go I.

"Jeffery is an angel," reported Mrs. Bolduc as Sheila joined her on the screened in porch. Jeffery was napping with his pacifier securely inserted, little sucking sounds indicating his contentment. Sheila was content and grateful as well to have found this former workmate of Mrs. Gray living on the same street and newly retired. Sheila hated to ask but did anyway; "Could I leave Jeffery for an hour longer I really need to go to see Gregg?"

❀

Sheriff McManus again entered the hospital room of Gregg Croteau. The young man had been moved from critical care to a private room. The Sheriff had demanded a private room since he wasn't sure if he was dealing with an arsonist and potential murderer or a victim. Either way he was insisting on a level of security. The room was the last one on the floor and visitors had to sign in. The Sheriff and Police Chief had created a list of people allowed to visit. If your name was not on the list the Sheriff's office would be notified immediately.

The Sheriff approached the bed just as he had for the past three weeks. No longer hooked up to monitors— burns appeared healing— Gregg Croteau could have simply been taking a nap if one didn't know better. In the last hour he had awakened to a degree that prompted a call from the hospital. The Sheriff cleared his throat, "Gregg can you hear me?" The blankets stirred but nothing was verbalized. "Gregg I am Sheriff McManus and I have been coming in to check on you for nearly three weeks now, ever since the fire at the fairgrounds, do you remember the fire?"

A low groan and a raspy unintelligible sound left Gregg's throat.

"Can you hear me Gregg?"

No sound but a slight head movement in the affirmative brought a sigh of relief for the Sheriff; *he's coming around at least.*

"Gregg I'll be back tomorrow, we'll try to talk then."

The Sheriff left strict orders for no one except hospital staff, not even family be allowed to go into the room until he had a chance to interview this young man. "I'm sending over a deputy to sit outside his room. If you have to lie to his parent's— so be it— say he's had a slight relapse and you are taking special precautions. I'll be here by ten in the morning."

❀

Sheila walked from the top of Madison Avenue, retracing her every other day visits to try to see Gregg. She had snuck in when he was moved from critical care but he had been non-responsive. Today there was a deputy sitting just outside his room. She never made it that far. When she stopped at the nurses' station she was told there would be no visitors allowed today. No explanation was offered since she was not family.

❀

Paul arrived home from practice around 5:30, his dad's car was in the driveway. His father was home from three days in Massachusetts where he now worked part-time for the same Insurance company he had retired from. His father was sitting on the porch looking out over Lake Wesserrunsett from their cozy cottage. He was smoking his pipe but still had his suit and tie on. He only wore his suit when he was attending to business. Paul and his mother greeted him as they entered the kitchen, when he didn't leave the porch they opened the screen door and joined him.

"I didn't think you'd be home until Friday Dad, what did you bring me?"

This was a little joke between Father and son that had become a ritual over the years. Even when the family lived in Massachusetts, Paul's dad had traveled and every Friday he brought a little trinket for his son. From hotel gift shops mostly, and it didn't matter the item it was their thing and it had continued. His dad continued to draw on his pipe and didn't answer immediately.

Paul's mom filled the void. "Have you eaten? Since Paul started on that running team he eats like a horse so I made plenty if you're hungry?"

"I'm going to take a shower," offered Paul, "I'll see you at the table. I'm starving." Glad you're home dad."

Home-made Macaroni and cheese, sliced fresh tomatoes from the garden, ham steaks and Apple crisp for dessert. Paul soaked up the juice from the tomatoes with a biscuit and seemed content to eat and not talk. Nobody seemed to have any comments that weren't reinforcing how good the dinner was. Mrs. Leland who was a peculiar lady but genuinely loved her husband and son basked in the warmth of an early September evening. All at the same table, well fed, seemingly happy— her sigh was one of contentment.

Finally Paul's father still in his suit pushed himself away from the table and asked Paul to walk with him down to the lakes edge. Two Adirondack chairs stood as sentries perched on the very right hand side of the lawn looking out over the water. A thirty foot aluminum dock— with a small sailboat tied down at the end— was gleaming as a last gasp of sun began seeking evening's shelter behind a range of mountains on the horizon. Mr. Leland took a seat and lit his pipe. He motioned Paul to sit. Shaking the life out of the match he drew in a mouthful of smoke, watching the tobacco embers glow. He took several draws. When he was satisfied the bowl would sustain itself he removed his pipe and looked directly at his son.

"I've been given the duty of handling the insurance claim for the death of two race horses that were insured with our company. I don't really like this a bit. The owner of the policy is a company headed by a man who supposedly has ties to organized crime." Paul turned his head. "We're talking about those horses lost in the fire at the fairgrounds?"

"The very same. And the conversation we had about you seeing someone on the phone that night, if this is what I think it is, or could be anyway, I don't want you involved, no way no how."

"But dad I've already told the police what I saw."

"That's true but you haven't identified who you saw. This is a small town, they are going to figure out who was on that phone. Mr. Gambino has let it be known to my company that he expects no trouble in receiving the full value of his claim. Hell he had my boss quaking in his boots. Didn't come into the office alone, he had three oversized deli sandwiches with him if you get my meaning."

"So what are you telling me dad?"

"I'm saying that I have no doubt the person you saw has ties to the Gambino family and it's in all our best interests for you not to make an identification. We are going to pay the claim and not do further business with this man. Let someone else figure this out."

"But dad!"

His father changed the subject, "Look at the way the water is reflecting the leaves. Looks like autumn coming up from the bottom of the lake. Going to be a colorful fall. I plan to spend a good deal of time myself— reflecting on how fortunate this family is— sitting right down here at the water's edge. We don't need no big waves clouding up our lives son." Another tack, "Let's take the sailboat out tomorrow, maybe we can even get your mother aboard."

Mr. Leland looked down at his dead pipe that he had not attended since the one sided conversation began. With a shrug he reached for his tobacco pouch, rose and wandered back up towards the cottage. Paul sat there looking out over the water once again. It was certainly calm. He recalled how quickly that can change. He closed his eyes remembering their second summer on the lake when a tornado emerged from those mountains to the west followed the river then jumped to the head of the lake. Their roof was torn off, trees in the drive spun off their root system as if they had been placed in a pencil sharpener. The storm had sounded like a freight train dragging its brakes in a feeble attempt to miss a car on the tracks. The family had huddled in a hallway just outside the bathroom and hugged one another. In the thirty seconds it took to do the damage— it seemed like hours had passed. The storm continued south and tore big sections out of the hearts of trees in Skowhegan and then veered east toward Pittsfield. A rainstorm followed on the heels of the storm and pelted the now roofless cottage with an inch of wetness. Paul's dad had expressed frustration with their home's insurer and had to fight to get their claim settled.

Maine doesn't have tornados they had been told. The wind damage was just a natural occurrence of lightning and thunder storms. In the end, they paid but never did concede it had been a tornado, even with a dozen eye witnesses to the contrary. Plausible deniability, Paul's dad had called it. That very fall he put in for early retirement but agreed to service business on a part time basis. But not during snow season— he was not going to travel during the snowy winters— he was going to cross country ski on this very lake. *Dads a fighter, always has been but he's telling me to back off, this doesn't sound like dad.*

• IT IS STILL SEPTEMBER 1963

• THREE PM.

Sheriff McManus had put off talking to Anna Gray about the foolishness out at Lake George but he needed to complete the report his deputies had started. After talking with Chief Henry who knew the mother and respected her, he was going to finish this up in as painless a way as possible. In the end no one had been hurt and he had much bigger fish to fry.

"Send the girl in." He took a pull on a quickly cooling cup of afternoon coffee and rose from his desk. Anna entered, her eyes cast down, her shoulders slumped. Sheriff McManus gave her a wide smile. "It's not the end of the world young lady I just have a few questions to ask you."

"Yes sir."

"Please sit down, over there at the table. Let's keep this as informal as we can" When they were seated he offered the girl some water but she shook her head. "Tell me what happened that weekend and don't lie to me. We have spoken with about everyone who was there by now, I just need your version and we can all go on about our business. I think you would agree this town has bigger problems right now."

Anna told the truth and took full responsibility for arranging the party and agreed it was her idea to suggest the kidnapping.

She seemed almost eager to be punished. Her demeanor remained passively despondent.

"Well Anna I appreciate your honesty. I've actually heard some good things about you so I'm going to file this case for now. If your name doesn't surface in a bad way in the next year, we'll just close the case. How does that sound?"

Anna nodded her head but offered no comment. Sheriff McManus who had no experience with counseling teenagers felt stymied.

"I could just put you through the justice system Anna, is that something you'd like to experience?"

Anna's response surprised the Sheriff.

"I probably deserve it. I have disappointed everyone in my life by now. But thank you Sheriff, my life sucks right now and it's all my fault. I won't let you down that much I promise."

Sheriff McManus decided on the spur of the moment to throw this girl a lifeline. "Say, are you working after school or playing a sport?"

Anna shook her head. "No sir, actually I need to find something. I'm planning on going on to college. I worked the past two summers in the drapery factory with my mom. After my little escapade— which everyone knows about it seems— I don't think it's a good idea to apply there."

"How would you like to work in the sheriff's office?" Do you know what a dispatcher does? You're seventeen and a senior, this might just be a good opportunity to see what kind of havoc is caused by a simple case of poor judgement."

The Sheriff gave her a tour of the little office that housed the dispatcher. "We have a wonderful, compassionate, no nonsense guy who works the 3-11 shift five days a week. He's off today. If you're interested, come back in tomorrow at four o'clock and meet him. If you two get on, well maybe we can do a little paid internship. Maybe work till nine during the week and to the end of shift on weekends. How does that sound?"

Anna smiled for the first time since she'd entered the room. "Actually it sounds fantastic sir, I won't let you down." She caught herself repeating her promise but suddenly it seemed important to say it even once again as she rose to leave— "I won't let you down." Sheriff McManus felt good about the end of the conversation. He had no children of his own. He was whistling as he left his office and got in his cruiser. Instead of entering High street to exit left on Madison Avenue, He drove past the Milburn hotel and glanced left to see what was playing at the Strand Theatre. He chuckled to himself when he saw the billing. *Days of Wine and Roses.* He certainly wasn't feeling wined and dined. Demands from the public, town officials, the media and the rumor mill had him wanting to look straight ahead. But that was not the personality of Sheriff McManus, he was curious by nature.

❁

The autopsy of Marvin Higgins had been complicated by the degree of burning his body absorbed. He was alive when he died, smoke inhalation in his lungs indicated that. Head trauma was finally ruled as the cause of death. It took an entire month to simply reinforce what the Sheriff had known from day one. This was murder. The man had been buried in his original hometown of Smithfield. The Sheriff attended the simple graveside ceremony witnessed by four others, the Sheriff noted no tears were shed.

❁

He turned right, the giant A&P Grocery stood on the corner, abandoned shopping carts dotting the parking lot indicated people were out and about on this late September afternoon. He joined the one way traffic that circled the middle section of downtown businesses. A left had him looking at Barry's Pizza across the sidewalk. The place would be busy in an hour as increasingly pizza was being brought home for dinner. He hunted and fished with Jerome Barry and local crimes were discussed and even sometimes solved on those trips. Barry's was a magnet for young people and Jerome heard lots of bragging and boasts. Most was harmless. When he heard something that could cause real damage— a fishing or hunting trip might get planned with his buddy. Jerome had not heard anything regarding the death and fire at the fairgrounds. He would in time though, these teenagers were pretty good detectives themselves.

Sheriff McManus turned west onto water street and pulled into the parking lot at the town's municipal building. Police Chief George Harvey was waiting on the granite steps and walked out to the cruiser. On the way to the hospital they discussed them damn Yankees probably winning the Pennant and World

Series again this year, the Red Sox fading now like one of their beloved hats after being worn during haying season. He asked if the Chief had been informed of the autopsy results—he had—they walked into the hospital to hopefully gain some insight on how this all came to pass.

The smell of wood smoke hung in the air. Late afternoons already chilly enough to break the chimneys pledge to stop smoking.

They had to wait while the nurses performed the rituals that a hospital stay requires no matter the degree of injury or illness. After what felt like an hour to the two men who sat spinning their hats and drinking more damn hospital coffee, they entered room 336. The deputy at the door stood, nodded and sat back down.

The room was in shadow the mountains to the west about to call it a day. Still light enough to see a blaze of color from this height though. A painter's palette would not be able to create what the sheriff saw from the window even in the fading light. *Dare I look,* thought the sheriff as he turned to face Gregg Croteau— the boy was awake. Chief Henry let the sheriff take the lead. "Can you talk Gregg? I'm Sheriff McManus and this is Police Chief Henry." He pulled a chair up to the bed. The chief moved to the window for his own evening foliage tour.

"Let me tell you what we know Gregg. That might make it easier for you to fill in the blanks. I wouldn't normally give a possible suspect or accomplice any information I have but I believe you are an innocent in all this." The Sheriff went on to lay out all that was known of what took place on that Sunday night.

Gregg listened and heard for the first time of the death of Marvin Higgins his old boss. He was told the degree of destruction to the fairgrounds and loss of animals from the baby animal barn where he was found. He was told of the loss of four race horses, burned to death.

Gregg spoke for the first time in a husky halting voice. "I'm sorry for all that happened." He cleared his throat. "I'm not sure what I can add, something knocked me unconscious." He asked for water. Beginning again, "I apparently swallowed some smoke and I have some burns on my arms. And my head has been hurting like hell. That's all I remember."

The sheriff looked Gregg straight in the eyes. "I'm going to tell you something else, something no one knows but myself and the chief— someone pulled you out of that baby animal barn— someone saved your life!"

Gregg's eyes widened, thoughts bombarded his brain; *did Eddie have second thoughts after he brained me with that tent peg.* It hurt to think. Gregg closed his eyes. He opened them and offered all he felt he could to the sheriff. "All I remember is smelling smoke and going to investigate. I was bunking in the baby animal barn. I started to open a pen, the roof was on fire, something hit me and that's all I remember."

"Do you remember what time that was?"

He thought, then winced at the effort, "It was well after One am at least. The lights go out around midnight, I went to my trailer and had a beer." He began to sweat from the effort he was making to talk and think. He steeled himself— as if doing that last quarter mile of a race, what seemed like a hundred years ago— "I'm thinking it was closer to 1:30am when I got back to the barn and went to sleep. I'm not sure what time it was when I woke up smelling smoke. There were flames everywhere, I got up, started to look around. I got hit with something, maybe a falling timber, I don't know." This last effort clearly drained the boy and the sheriff nodded. "As I said someone pulled you from that burning barn. Any idea who it could have been?"

Gregg shook his head, physically drained, "if I did I'd certainly tell you, I'd want to thank them myself."

❧

• EDDIE AND JOE AWAY AT SCHOOL

The two brothers sat across from one another in the three room apt. they shared in Orono, Maine. Joe a junior in college and Eddie beginning his second year were both studying business. This morning they were discussing family business. Joe was nursing a Coke while younger Eddie had poured his Pepsi in a glass over ice. Joe began, picking up his coke and visually presenting it to his brother, "We don't agree on much do we younger brother, can't even agree on colas?" Eddie tipped his Pepsi glass in salute and bit into a piece of toast. "In the end though Joe, we got it done. And no one's the wiser. So once again I say, here's to you!"

Joe shook his head."Think about this for a minute Eddie we got a dead guy and a hurt guy. The hurt guy knows we intended to get rid of those horses. He didn't agree to help. Will he talk? Probably not. Can we take the chance? Knowing Dad, probably not." Eddie rubbed his toast across the butter dish, crumbs blackening the butter dish and the half stick remaining.

Joe just watched in amazement, shaking his head. "Right there is a perfect example of what I'm talking about. You leave messes Eddie, everywhere you go, everything you do."

Eddie looked down at the butter dish.

Joe rose and went to the Window. The street below was lined with trees in full celebration. The scene brought to mind the raging spectrum of colors he had witnessed as the stables, animal barns, and what appeared as the entire midway challenged the night sky. He took a deep breath. "I spoke with dad. You are to stay here in Orono, go to class, come back here, read your damn westerns and chill. No parties, no girls in— for the forseeable future. You will play the part of a monk little brother. Dad is dealing with the insurance company, putting pressure where he can. This whole mess is not simply going to go away. The money is the least of dad's worries. He turned around facing his brother.

"Even if Gregg— that's his name you know— keeps his mouth shut we may have a problem. Someone pulled him out of that animal barn, Eddie. That someone might have seen you or me and what we did."

"What you did you mean, I didn't club Marvin you did. I just chased a guy I thought was setting fires and when he attacked me I hit him first. Self-defense pure and simple." Eddie stretched, leaned back in his chair, pleased with himself and his response.

Shaking his head Joe sighed, "Like toast through butter Eddie you are so wrapped up in your stories you don't see the pictures that don't lie."

He rose, walked up to the back of the chair where

Eddie sat, looked down and once more gave Eddie the bottom line. "You stay put, Dad and I are going to figure this out. I have a girl— remember Rebecca? Well she's going to be visiting me every other week. She'll know what's going on. Those high school kids will be trying to figure this all out." Like talking to a small boy, Joe continued, "What we need to know is who pulled Gregg out of that barn. I'm sure the Sheriff is trying to figure that out as well. Dad is sending someone to follow the fair circuit, ears to the ground. Find out if it was a carney who saw something and saved Gregg. We need to have a little chat with Sheila too. Make sure if Gregg talked with her, she keeps her mouth shut. Everything is circumstantial unless someone puts us at the scene."

He put his hand on his brother's shoulder and squeezed. "Do we have a deal brother or do I call Dad, let him handle it?"

• BOARDING UP FOR WINTER

October winds had leaves leaving their seat of business. Airborne and out of control they struck and stuck in every nook and cranny. Some hit window panes begging for entry to escape what would soon follow. On Lake Wesserunsett Paul's father was seated on a farm tractor that doubled as a mower and snow plow. He looked out over a sea of blue, small white clouds scudding overhead. The wind kept the water pulsing, no reflection offered for his troubled mind. He hooked a chain to the dock and was easing it out of the lake. He loved the feel of something he could control. The crisp air made him feel alive and vibrant. *Why don't I just quit this working foolishness, it's turning me into a damn fool. I'm making my son ashamed of me for God's sake.* The dock slowly slid up the embankment, a plywood sluice acting as a lubricant to ease friction. The screeching of the dock on plywood mimicked the sounds the geese had made as they flew overhead on their way to a winter vacation. Leaves had already taken up residence on the aluminum decking. He had just hauled the dock to where it would stay for the winter when his wife hollered from the porch. "Irwin you're wanted on the phone, it's the Sheriff."

"Tell him I'll call him right back."

Irwin completed his task and parked his tractor in the small shed. He looked to the mountains to the west where a peak had aged overnight, the white hair visible from here. "I'll be putting chains and the plow on this thing next," he muttered to himself. *Decisions, decisions, decisions, and it looks like I'm about to make one I'll have to live with,* he sighed. He took off his work gloves laid them on the bench and trudged to the cottage still muttering to himself.

❋

An hour later Irwin Leeland sat waiting in the Sheriff's office. Ten minutes after that he was sitting in the chair opposite the sheriff.

"Can I get you anything Mr. Leeland?"

Irwin shook his head no, "How can I help you Sheriff." "Well you can help me in two ways actually. First, your son. I feel like he's dodging me. I know he goes to school and is on a team but he hasn't made himself available since that first interview when he said he saw someone on the phone the night of the fire. I have some pictures he needs to see. Can you get him in here?"

Irwin nodded his head, I'll see to it sheriff I'm sure being a kid, he doesn't realize how serious this is. I'll call your office after I talk with him. What else you got on your mind?"

"I understand you are handling the investigation for the insurance company for several of the horses destroyed?"

Irwin breathed deeply, "yes and it looks like we're about to make a settlement on that."

The Sheriff fidgeted, not comfortable with what he was about to ask. "Can you stall that for a bit, I'm sure your company wouldn't want to be wrong on this? I'm going to tell you something and I want it kept in this office. We think your client had reason to want those horses killed. We also have an idea who did it and we certainly know how." The sheriff waited for this to sink in then continued, "What we don't know is what, if anything Marvin Higgins— he's the man who was killed— had to do with it." The sheriff took a sip of his coffee, "We do know he was hired to oversee all livestock and horses and had been doing it for some years. We don't know why a young man lies in the hospital with a fractured skull and some burns. We don't know what he might have to do with all this." The Sheriff sat up straight, his size suddenly filling the room, stealing the oxygen from the air. "Off the record what does your investigation conclude? Wait don't answer that yet. Here's something else we know. We know your company's client is associated with organized crime, gambling in particular."

Irwin made a decision from his mulled over list of decisions he had pondered earlier. He got up from his chair and walked around the room looking at the little reminders the Sheriff had strategically placed, each designed to make lying a tougher choice. "I particularly like that log hauling scene displayed there Sheriff, kinda says it all. Well here is what I know and what you're up against." Irwin sat back down. He folded his hands looking for all the world like a man in confession. "My company has insured a Mr. Joseph Gambino Sr. for the thirty years I've worked for them. He has sent a lot of good honest business our way. The payback is when he makes a claim it is handled discreetly and always in his favor. He is demanding this situation be handled in the same manner." Irwin cleared his throat, "so in fact there is no investigation from my end, the company intends to pay the claim. I am simply window dressing."

"I appreciate your honesty Mr. Leeland. I do need to talk with your son however; he may be a material witness."

"I will talk with him tonight, you have my word." He rose to leave and then turned toward Sheriff McManus, "He's a dangerous man Sheriff, please keep my son's information— if he has any— out of the press. I would be lying if I said I'm not worried where this is all going to lead."

• THE INVISIBLE PEOPLE EMERGE

Roxanne, feeling a little blue on this late October afternoon walked into the Milburn Hotel. She entered the bar, allowed her eyes to adjust, then found her usual stool unoccupied. She ordered a Schlitz. *Stranger on the shore,* was playing on the juke box. Roxanne loved instrumentals. Music didn't lie like words that leaves people's mouths. Roxanne had heard every lie known to man and spewed by man by the time she reached the ripe old age of twenty-seven. Those lies had started when Roxanne was just thirteen when a friend of her father's offered to take her fishing. She pulled a knife used to cut bait and offered to put a bit of his worm on a hook. That ended that, but in that moment she knew you just couldn't believe the words that leaves a man's' lips. Time had proven her right. She just loved this song though and she closed her eyes imagining a shore line that didn't have a pile of rocks that could trip you up leaving you hurt. When the song ended she wandered across the lounge and looked at the long list of songs she could choose from. The juke box offered no opinion on which heartache best suited your mood. Just pay up. Roxanne put in a coin and replayed the song she had just heard. *I might just play that song all night long,* she thought, then spotted a Frank

Sinatra tune. She chuckled and put in another quarter thinking, *I've had a fair share of Strangers in the night.* Her last stranger in the night was long gone. Out of state with the fair circuit by now. "Just as well," she said into her beer, "just as well."

"What's that Roxanne?" Favor the bartender had big bunny ears and missed nothing.

"I said, all is well if you must know you nosy Nellie, and I repeated it so's you wouldn't miss a beat, you must be slipping Favor. Favor just grunted.

Roxanne went back to studying her glass, *I probably should get the hell out of Dodge myself.* The thoughts of that night still bothering her as much as anything bothered Roxanne. *They should be pinning a medal on me, my little short stranger in the night too for that matter.* She toasted herself. *Course I had to threaten the little bastard to get him to move his ass. We did it though, we saved that young man's life.* "I need another beer down here Favor and how about giving up a bowl of them peanuts you're hoarding, I'm a paying customer for hell's sake."

Two beers later the just got out of work— stop in for a quick one crowd began arriving. Delbert the deputy was among them. "E-e-vning Miss Raw-raw-xanne, aw-aw-lways nice to see you." Delbert tipped his hat.

"Hmmph, at least you lie real polite-like Delbert, you always did even back in grammar school."

"Mi-mi-ss Roxanne y-y-ou have me a-a-ll wrong. L-let me buy you a beer." *Stranger on the shore* was playing in the background for at least the sixth time.

"I love th-that song don't you Mi-mi-ss Roxanne? N- no words, l-let's your mind wander, I-I like that." H- hey F-f-favor how about a li-li-ttle respect for law en- enforcement down here, d-d-don't make me r-run you in," he kidded.

The two sat one stool apart, Roxanne her guard slowly slipping as her third beer receded said, "Can I tell you something in confidence Delbert?"

"I-If it don't con-con-cern a life or d-ddeath situation I-I'll take it to my g-g-grave Miss Roxanne," he said solemnly.

"What if it did Delbert, what if it did?"

"W-why I'd be duty bound t-t-to try to save you Roxanne, J-J-John Wayne never let his per-personal feelings mu-mu-ddy the waters, h-h-he was duty bound, and s-so am I."

She studied Delbert for a moment, *harmless, happy and hopeless,* then she sighed. "Well John Wayne couldn't fix what I'm carrying Delbert, so never mind, just never mind— move along."

"A-aw-lways nice t-t-talking with you Roxanne."

Delbert left the stool scratched his head, finished his beer and left the bar. He walked like a man dodging invisible bullets—one foot landing lightly as the next seemed to study the terrain before making a decision.

Roxanne picked up a handful of peanuts watching Delbert make his exit. *He's alright in his own way. I could do worse,* she smiled chewed on a peanut, *hell I already have, a dozen times.*

Delbert stopped into Barry's Pizza ordered up an Italian sandwich and chips. While he waited he played a game of pinball. He loved sending a wrecking ball up the chute and into the midst of a towering inferno. With his hands on the flippers, using a slight shoulder movement—one he believed he had created when this place first opened—he could keep that ball circling and for a few moments in time Delbert Dominski was in full control of his world. "Your order is ready Delbert," Jerome Barry announced. He watched Delbert give the pinball machine one last look, shake his head as if he was leaving a best friend, knowing he could have kept the game alive for another five minutes. He paid up then tipped his hat to a customer at the door and entered the real world.

Barry shook his head. Delbert was definitely a lost soul. He had never fit in to this world. Barry had watched him try to fit in. During his high school years Delbert spent nearly every afternoon and evening playing pinball. There was nothing mentally wrong with Delbert. His problem stemmed from stuttering and its collateral damage. It affected his body language as well. Simply put Delbert was awkward. During his high school years, a group of his class mates had kind of adopted him. They took him places with them. They took him to football and basketball games. They spent hours eating pizza and playing pin-ball. They taught Delbert how to play poker. Those four years of high school seemed to be his happiest time. Then they moved on to college and jobs. Suddenly Delbert had no one. Jerome felt sorry for him and hired him to help clean the place and stock shelves twice a week. He couldn't put him behind the counter— people could be cruel. Delbert didn't drive so he never left town. Barry recommended him and he started with the Sheriff's office as a custodian. Four years ago Sheriff McManus decided to make Delbert a special deputy. He didn't drive so his job was to walk the streets of the seat of county government—Skowhegan, tipping his hat and keeping his eyes open. Everybody in town loved Delbert— from a distance.

Delbert walked to his little two room apartment on lower East Front Street. As he sat watching the evening news the war in Vietnam was beginning to take up a good hunk of the news. "Wh- wh-ere in h- hell is V-v-ietnam anyway?" he asked the TV.

Television was his best friend.

When he turned out his light at exactly nine pm. The last thought that entered his mind was, *I wonder what's got Miss Roxanne so stirred up, I kinda like her. Maybe I'll see if she'd like to go see a John Wayne movie with me.* Delbert didn't stutter in his mind.

❁

The next afternoon after Cross-Country practice Paul jogged from the high school to the Sheriff's office. He stopped running when he reached the railroad bridge that spanned the Kennebec River. Water seemed to ease his mind nearly as well as the sound of his own heartbeat when he ran. His dad had walked with him down to the lake's edge just as the sun was setting last night. The wind had stilled and the lake reflected the last surge of color to appear before November's chill shook the remaining leaves from their moorings.

"I was wrong Paul." That simple statement followed by his dad's explanation of the conversation with the sheriff assured him he should help in any way he could. "He's going to try to keep your name out of it, you're still just seventeen anyway, still a minor." The river was moving, white water from the power turbines churning offering up an occasional piece of pulp wood that had gotten hung up earlier in the summer. His earlier effort now dry on his skin, cooled him and he shivered. He began the last quarter mile jog to the Sheriff's office.

Sheriff McManus had been busy. He met with Tom Quinn and had a list of young men who had been hired for this year's Fair in Skowhegan. All the boys who had parked cars were listed. Men and boys and girls who cleaned and maintained the restrooms, swept the grandstands and handled the garbage at the end of each day were listed along with their photo identification. All of this was a long shot but Sheriff McManus was hoping for the best. From the description offered by the young man about to be interviewed, maybe one or two of the identification photos he had in the file was at least possible. He had two more photos in a separate folder, they had arrived in the mail in the last several days. Sheriff McManus had Chief Henry sitting at the table when Paul entered. "Thanks for coming in, you've met Chief Henry before."

Paul nodded his head. "Sit down at the table there, would you like a soft drink, water maybe?"

"Water would be good I just finished running three miles before jogging down here."

"How's the team doing, have you competed yet?"

"We won our first three meets. We have some good runners."

"From the scores I've seen in the paper the football team could use some good runners as well."

Paul chuckled, "We probably wouldn't be much use to them we're all pretty light. Nobody trying to tackle us either."

Sheriff McManus poured a glass of water then sat down opposite Paul. "I guess you know why I asked you to come back in Paul, I have some photos for you to look at."

Paul nodded. "I'll do my best, but it was pretty dark."

"The phone booth was lit up though, right?"

Paul cleared his throat, clearly nervous, he managed, "Yes sir it was."

Six photos of young men were laid out one at a time on the table by Chief Henry. Nothing was said until all six were staring Paul straight in the eye. Four of the pictures showed young men in casual attire. Two had young men in suit and tie.

Paul studied each one in turn, saying nothing, but one immediately had caught his attention. He began to smell his body as new heated perspiration combined with his earlier effort. He cleared his throat, his father's reminder to just tell the truth steeled his nerves. "It's that one, he's the person I saw that night." Paul was pointing at the smartly dressed high school graduation picture of Joseph Gambino Jr.

Sheriff McManus let Chief Henry respond.

"Are you absolutely sure this is the man you saw in that phone booth on the night the fairgrounds were set on fire and a man was killed?"

"Yes sir, that's him, who is he anyway?" The two men looked at one another. "I'm not at liberty to say, son but he won't know it's you who identified him. We'll try to keep that in this room. Don't tell anyone."

"What you saw could very well be the break we need, so thank you for stepping up, thank your dad too. He's a good man," finished the Sheriff.

When Paul left the office his father was in the car waiting to drive him home. "You've got your license Paul why don't you drive. Let's stop in at Hight Chevrolet, your Mother and I talked, we think it's time you had a car of your own. You are a grown man son."

Chief Henry sat studying the photo then looked to the Sheriff. "You had any run-ins with this Gambino kid?" Sheriff Mc Manus shared all his department knew of the boy and his brother. He also told Chief Henry of the possible mob ties of his father and the ownership of two of the horses that perished in the fire.

"What are you planning to do with all this?"

"It's still all circumstantial, so we need to keep at it. But I can tell you as sure as I'm sitting here that young innocent looking boy in the picture there. He set those fires. I think his brother the other kid in a suit, I think he helped."The Chief rose, rubbed a twinge in his lower back and responded. "Let's get our two investigators back in here and lay it out for them and redirect their efforts."

• 1963 WORST NOVEMBER EVER

It seemed the weather was foreshadowing the gloom that would enter our lives during this month. Cloudy days kept the temperatures from freezing but the sky wore a funeral shroud eighty percent of the time.

Our cross country team that had done so well during the regular season must have peaked with the leaves in October. We lost at regionals, not qualifying as a team for states. Two of us, Paul and myself finished in the top ten and qualified for states as individuals. We were the only two still running and training for individual glory. Our coach let us pretty much decide on our training schedule and routine. To motivate ourselves this afternoon we ran the fields of the Dionne farm located a couple of miles from town. We ran various tractor paths that dotted the property, dodging cow flappers and scaring up partridge. At least we knew no one would be hunting in this area since it was all fenced off. As we drove back toward the school we talked about girls and dating. Paul was driving his newly acquired car, a 1959 Chevrolet coupe. WSKW the local station was playing at a low volume but when a song from a British group who had not yet made it to our shores came on, I cranked it up. *She loves me*, was a catchy tune and we both sang along. When the song ended Paul turned the radio down and continued, "We should double date, maybe go to a movie." He was sweet on Anna and they had actually just started seeing one another outside school. I had my designs on Sheila the sophomore who was staying at Anna's house. How convenient. "You know she has a baby, right?"

"Of course I know she has a baby, a little boy. I'm finally going to meet him this weekend."

"That's cool. So see if Sheila would like to hit Ma Beane's for a burger then go see a movie, *The Birds*, is playing, supposed to be scary as hell. I already ran it by Anna, she said double dating was a good idea." Paul frowned then added, "I'm new at this dating business but I thought the idea was to be alone together."

"Anna said she wanted to take this slow, actually brought up the idea of you asking Sheila."

"I'm a rookie in all this myself Paul, it's just this year girls have started seeing see me as more than a sounding board for their boy problems, so don't ask me anything about what dating is supposed to look like."

> *Just to give a little perspective on what was taking place in Skowhegan in November of 1963 I am taking the liberty to summarize what individuals knew or were feeling. No walls are thicker or more difficult to navigate than what goes on in our head. Much of what finally emerged from that year took years to uncover and discover. The following is what individuals knew before the darkest days of that horrible month stole all our attention for a time. And had an impact for all time.*

- Gregg knew the Gambino brothers set fire to the fairgrounds, tried to kill him and caused the death of Marvin Higgins.

- Sheila was quite certain the Gambino brothers were involved in the fire based on the request Gregg had wrestled with. She needed to speak with Gregg to confirm it. She had shared her thoughts with Anna's sister Ethel.

- Sheriff McManus and Police Chief George Henry knew but could not yet prove the Gambino brothers set the fire and were at least accomplices in the death of Marvin Higgins and injury of Gregg Croteau.

- Paul Leeland knew he was the only known witness to the fire but he had no idea the identity of that person.

- Anna was the victim of a rape by Eddie Gambino but because of the uproar her earlier actions had caused, shared that information with no one but her younger sister Ethel.

- Ethel the real innocent in all this, now had a connection to her sister's rape and the fire at the fairgrounds. She was not one to divulge secrets easily.

❀

The town itself had slowly returned to whatever normal looks like. The football team finished a so-so season with a loss to Madison our arch rivals. Going to be a long winter.

Paul and I finished in the top twenty in the states. Probably good enough to get a small scholarship at a really small college.

Norma Gray began her new job designing patterns for a fabric company and though still upset about the fire was more concerned with her older daughter's personality change. *Maybe her new job in the Sheriff's office would help. Going to be a long winter if she doesn't come out of her funk.*

• NOVEMBER 22, 1963

Through-out history monumental events have been captured by the technology of the time. For centuries the spoken word handed down around campfires painted in caves or shouted in the streets gave us the news. Later the written word, paintings, illustrations, verse or song inspired and aroused. The camera unleashed to the world the phrase, *a picture is worth a thousand words.* Camera stills morphed into film and our emotions could be manipulated in theatres around the world.

On November 22, 1963, the newest medium, television, allowed the American people to watch their president murdered in their living rooms. I for one, a high school senior who had taken about everything in life for granted, grew up that day. We were actually in our American government class talking about the impact of the fairly recent Cuban Missile Crisis. The war in Vietnam was too far away for us to really wrap our heads around— though our knowledgeable teacher Mr. Blood tried. Anyway the intercom came on and with a simple announcement our graduating class went in to shock. "The Russians did it, was the first blurted response."

There was a half hour left of class but there was no lesson offered. We simply milled around exchanging thoughts hugs and real tears. Rebecca who had her sight set on joining the Peace Corp was especially distraught. She had poster pictures of the handsome president and his family plastered on her bedroom wall.

Where were you when defined our generation after that day. It decided career paths, and created doubt in our government. For me conspiracy theory became a noun. I would later read the Warren Commission Report that concluded there was a lone gunman and read it as a cover-up. The grassy knoll, the underpass, the book depository, the Zapruder film, Oswald, Jack Ruby, the Mafia, it was all just too much to absorb. To this day it is debated and written about.

In the end it was simply that the first hero of my generation was stolen from us. Many songs were written about that terrible day. I couldn't listen for the longest time. It was only when I heard a song that let my imagination run wild with the possible implications that I was wrestling with that I embraced the words of Simon and Garfunkel. *The Sound of Silence* became my inner anthem. It spoke to me in my pain. It erased all doubt. It defined my politics.

That first night the evening of the 22nd, of November my friends and I gathered at Barry's Pizza. Angry silence was the first emotion conveyed. We didn't have enough information to put words to our anger. The pinball machine got jostled as our body language betrayed us. The big winner that night was the machine. The message **TILT** along with the accompanying shut down of lights and sound made us even angrier. Jerome was behind the counter. He was angry too. He let us take a lot of anger out on his machines before he finally spoke. "Boy's go beat on some trees, time to call it a night." We all filed out and truthfully I don't recall spending any time with my friends over the next four days. We were all glued to our TV's watching first the drama of Oswald being arrested, then shot right in front of our eyes. All those images occupy space in my mind. Our anger turned back to grief as the funeral procession for John Fitzgerald Kennedy was broadcast around the world and we were given a seat in the house.

Skowhegan, Maine was like thousands of other little towns throughout America and around the world. It grieved. Lyrics that would later put words to our actions and inactions during that time flood my mind.

Darkness did seem deeper. Silence was more solemn.

I don't recall long conversations with my friends about the unspeakable act that had taken place. We walled ourselves off and dealt with the pain in our own ways. I never ran harder or longer. The bleakness that defined the month of November in Maine that year seemed to now make sense. I ran alone, I ran for me. I cried for me. I believe that it was the same for people around the world. We all shared a grief that would take root in our hearts and it would always be personal.

In another part of town, Gregg Croteau ran as well.

Gregg Croteau had been discharged from the hospital supposedly into the care of his mother back in early October. No fanfare, no announcement in the press. Spirited out in the dead of night by the Sheriff himself.

In reality the county was presently paying for the lodging of Mrs. Croteau and her son in an unused portion of the Skowhegan Women's Reformatory located a mile from town on the back road to Norridgewock.

Only recently the reformatory had begun a new approach to rehabilitation for the many women from all walks of life who found themselves incarcerated. After careful screening, young women of high school age would move into a family setting in a farmhouse adjacent to the prison. They would be going to the local high school, taking classes and hopefully receive their high school diploma. Other girls and older inmates after passing the screening would join the work force, save some money and build a new life. The new term for what was a changing attitude towards rehabilitation became known as, Halfway House.

Gregg was not happy with this new arrangement and had voiced it in no uncertain terms to the two leaders of law enforcement who sprung it on him in his hospital room. "Your life is in danger whether you choose to believe it or not, Gregg. We know you worked for these two brothers. We also believe you know more than you are saying. When you decide to cooperate we can arrest them and put them where they belong."

"So basically you are putting me under arrest unless I accuse Joe and Eddie of starting that fire."

Sheriff McManus not one to beat around the bush, nodded, "Yup, you are a material witness, one of at least two. We haven't located the person who pulled you from that fire, but we will. Until then you are the only game in town. We know there's been some asking around about your condition and when you might be released," the Sheriff looked as stern and serious as the situation warranted, "it hasn't been the local paper asking."

Gregg took a deep breath, he knew the Sheriff was right, *Joe and Eddie would be wanting to compare stories.* He spent the latter part of October picking late blooming apples on the farm that made up part of the reformatory property. The sheriff had arranged for a friend of his from the local shoe shop— a man he trusted— to set up a work bench and teach Gregg to hand-sew shoes. A good hand-sewer made top money in the shoe industry. Gregg was glad to have something to keep him busy in the evenings. His mother had taken a leave of absence from her job. She spent her days smoking, reading magazines and making herself miserable as she went through withdrawal from alcohol abuse. There was counseling and basic medical assistance available at the reformatory so the choice of where to house Gregg and his mother had a positive side to it.

Gregg was feeling stronger and a desire to run was re-ignited. The reformatory had originally been a farm of over two-hundred acres. Created through an act of the state legislature the farm buildings multiplied to four and in 1918 a two story brick building was added. Another story and a hospital wing followed. The reformatory raised their own food including dairy. A church was started, fire protection initiated and a wing for children including an adoption agency. This little community within a community was quickly changing in 1963 but the buildings were all still there.

Gregg ran the fields and paths created by farm equipment, all the while angry at the situation he found himself in. The winds moving dark clouds overhead mirrored the storm of emotions he wrestled with. November had always been his favorite month to run. The season he had been a member of the Cross Country team had been fun but when the seasons ended he began the runs that allowed him to free float, both physically and mentally.

This morning, cold air stimulated him as steam poured from his lungs. He fueled his run with the anger and confused feelings for both his mother and Sheila during those runs. He had yet to speak to Sheila. He did know she was still in the area, his mother had told him a girl seemed to always be in the waiting room with a baby. Today's run did nothing to clear up his confusion. Sweating and spent he walked a quarter mile to cool down then entered the little apt. he shared with his mother. It was less than a week before thanksgiving and he was feeling sorry for himself. He was sitting on the couch with the television on, providing company but not companionship. He suddenly thought of his father. He had no idea where he was. He heard from his mother relentlessly how neither father nor son had returned from that southern trip. She was out right now so he could think in peace. Draped with a towel over his shoulders, he was steaming warm. He loved his father and if he could find him maybe he could join up with him and get away from all this. He was about to rise and take a shower when his attention was suddenly drawn to the screen. A special bulletin ribbon crossed the screen accompanied by a sound Gregg had never heard. **Special Bulletin** the noise announced. Walter Cronkite, the anchor of the evening news was seated and solemn. The President of The United States had just been shot. Gregg jumped up and turned up the volume. He spent the next week doing what millions of Americans were doing, hanging on every word.

In the course of that week he came to realize the Sheriff was right in secluding him. If the President could be assassinated in broad daylight Joe and Eddie could certainly find him and silence him if they wanted to.

• WE ALL NEED TO GET BACK TO WORK

• DECEMBER 1963

Time may seem to stop when tragedy enters our lives. Pens may pause, phones may silence, quiet may seem a bit louder, but the world moves on.

In Skowhegan for a large number of citizens getting back to work– meant getting the kids up—dressed and fed— gulping a second cup of coffee then driving to work at one of four remaining factories in town.

Not a lot of opportunity for gossip or conspiracy theories, the two shoe factories the drapery factory and the spinning mill were all about production in industries that were hanging on for dear life.

In schools, especially high schools, whispers and gossip rode the wind. In Skowhegan, in our American Government class the assassination of our president dominated discussion. The quiet anger we had been feeling was given voice, our teacher helped us move on by asking us to write about what the event had meant to us. Having to put the written word to our feelings forced us to think through some of our earlier outbursts. *Just let the words seep out of your bones,* we were instructed.

The fire at the fairgrounds was quickly becoming a distant memory for most of us. Paul still had the fire on his mind however and needed to talk with someone about it. He was dating Anna now. She was working at the Sheriff's office in the afternoons. She heard things, some of the things she heard added to her painful memories of the summer. On her first day the Sheriff had sworn her to secrecy on anything heard within these walls or over the scanner or anywhere else for that matter. "You are representing law enforcement Anna, give me your oath."

❀

Paul sat in his car holding Anna's hand. They both had a lot on their minds but Paul spoke first He was not on a fishing expedition he simply wanted someone he trusted to understand how helpless he was feeling. He began simply enough, "You know that fire at the fairgrounds was set, right?"

Anna having dealt with how hurt her mom felt when her hard work went up in flames and was still angry wanting answers, said, "Oh indeed I do."

Paul cleared his throat, "Well I might have seen the person who set that fire. I had to look at pictures of possible suspects, and I picked one out. I don't know who he is, and they won't tell me. They said he won't know I identified him, but this is a small town, I'm scared as hell."

"Wow that is scary!" her eyes opened wide. "How old did he appear to be?"

"About our age, course I don't know if that is a recent picture or not. But I would say he's young."

"Could he be in our school, you think?"

"I haven't spotted him if he is. I would say he's out of school, the picture looked like maybe a graduation photo."

Anna liking this police work she was engaged in decided it might be fun to play detective. She threw out the idea of them going to the school library and looking over pictures of graduating seniors from the last several years. "Let's find the sucker, shall we." Anna decided this was not the time to tell Paul this relationship was not going to work out. And she certainly was not going to tell him why.

Rebecca waited on the sidewalk in front of Gene's restaurant for the bus that would take her to Bangor. She hadn't been up to see Joe for nearly three weeks. The death of President Kennedy had hit her especially hard. The posters of her hero hanging on her bedroom wall were still hard to view. She had been saturated with images of the man and the aftermath, all the while crying for her loss. The Peace Corp seemed to take on an even greater urgency for her future. She would honor him in the only way she knew how. The diesel pusher pulled up and whisked Rebecca to the land of make believe— that's what Joe called it at any rate. He refused to live in a dorm. He shared an apartment with his brother Eddie in downtown Bangor now having moved from Orono. He drove to his three day a week classes in a brand new Oldsmobile Cutlass. He was waiting at the station when she pulled in.

She brought her writing assignment from her Government class with her, eager to hear Joe's response to the tragedy. Joe wasn't a phone person, so beyond making plans to get together they did not hold long conversations. "You never know who's listening" he would kid her, "nobody needs to know my business but me."

The ride and the numbing sound of tires on tar had given her time to try to best frame something she needed to talk to Joe about.

She and Anna had been friends all through school. Not the stay at my house overnight pajama party kind of friends but two girls who both loved school and were in most of the same classes and study halls. It was in a study hall held in the library due to overcrowding that the subject of Rebecca's new boyfriend came up. When Rebecca revealed that Joe

Gambino was the young man she was seeing, the color drained from Anna's face.

"Oh my god Rebecca, are you sure about this guy?"

Rebecca gave her friend a strange look. "What does that even mean?"

Anna recovered, then whispered, "I'm sorry it's none of my business. I'm sure he's not like his brother, that's all I can say."

"What makes you say that? You only met Eddie once that I know of— at that party. I agree he's a little strange, ok weird even, but he seems harmless, he wasn't even drinking that night."

"He did drive me back to town though as you remember." She took Rebecca's hand, "He hurt me Rebecca." Anna's eyes told the rest of the story. "Just be careful. His brother completely fooled me."

Rebecca thought that was all that was going to be said on the subject. She studied the back of Anna's head and mulled over what had been shared. The girls went back to their studies. When the bell rang to switch classes the girls rose to join the herd in the hall. Anna took a deep breath and ushered Rebecca to an alcove.

"Rebecca I'm pregnant with that little turds baby. I've missed my last two cycles. You are the only person other than my sister, Ethel that I've told. Please don't tell Joe or Eddie. You just need to know who these people are, that's all. I may have to leave school once I start showing. I'm going to have to tell my mom too." She shook her head from side to side, "I'm not telling her who the father is though, cause she would go crazy!" Anna took Rebecca's arm. "Promise me you won't say anything!"

"I promise."

Rebecca came out of this reverie of remembering armed with a plan—watchful waiting she decided. Eddie lived with his brother and was around like a lap dog most of the time, so she was going to study him, be nice to him. As for Joe, she liked him a lot but they both knew it was not a lifetime commitment they had going. *So just keep your mouth shut Rebecca and watch.* She gave Joe a big smile. The new Cutlass smelled like a new Cutlass should smell.

The afternoon sun poured through the window warming her face. Joe didn't talk much when he drove so Rebecca was left with her thoughts, interrupted only by the song on the radio playing— *She's a fool*—by Lesley Gore.

Rebecca had to chuckle, *hopefully Lesley Gore is not trying to warn me too.*

Joe glanced over, "What are you so happy about Miss Rebecca, that glad to see me?"

"Oh yeah there's that."

❁

Sheriff McManus sat across the kitchen table from his wife Laura. The baked potatoes were still steaming in the unwrapped foil. He reached for the plate of deer steaks, which told of another successful season of hunting, he was smiling to himself.

Laura spoke up. She was always reading his mind. "I hope your other hunt goes as well, people in the shop are anxious. When I'm walking floor to floor handing out their checks they want more from me than just their pay." She waited a heart-beat before continuing. Laura knew better than to pry into her husband's business— and she wouldn't— but she was curious as well. "Any news at all?"

Sheriff McManus shoveled some peas onto his plate then ripped open a hot biscuit. "Laura you are by far the best cook in the County."

They ate is silence for a time then Arthur spoke. "If I told you who caused all this, I'd have to lock you up for your own safety," he didn't smile, he was deadly serious. "I can tell you this much, I'm not the only one who knows what happened. There are a lot of moving parts to this puzzle. We have witnesses who don't even realize what they know." He searched his mind for an analogy

Laura could relate to. "You remember all those mud seasons I paced this house waiting to jump back on that skidder? All the pacing didn't do a damn bit of good. Things just had to dry up naturally. That's what's happening here."

Laura listened. Then she smiled. "Got it."

• I'LL HAVE A BUE CHRISTMAS WITH OUT YOU

Anna broke up with me just before Christmas. School closed on Friday the 20th. We had half a day of classes, which was mostly class parties, the Chorus put on a concert at 11:30 which closed out the day.

We were walking down the steep path in front of the school, everyone in high spirits. No snow or ice on the ground to send us skidding to the side. When we reached the sidewalk on West Front Street Anna took my hand. "Paul, we have to talk."

My mom had driven me to school this morning. She was going to help me pick out a gift for Anna this afternoon.

"What's up, this sounds serious," I kidded.

"Can we go somewhere and get a cup of chocolate." She still looked serious.

"Sure, let's go to the Three G's. I'm meeting my Mom there at 1:30," I checked my watch, "so we have an hour."

The hot chocolate was good, the message not so good. Not even Christmas music providing a cheerful background nor twinkling lights and a waitress wearing a Santa hat could soften the blow.

"I can't be your girlfriend Paul, I'm very sorry, you are a great guy."

Maybe the hot chocolate wasn't so good after all. "Did I do something wrong?"

"It's not you. I can't explain but I'm sure you'll hear all about it in time." Anna began to tear up. "I am really sorry Paul." With that she rose and left me sitting there staring after her, listening to the strains of *Silver Bells.*

When my mom arrived an hour later I was still sitting there with two cups of now cold, hot chocolate and a dazed expression. "We won't be needing the shopping trip Mom, Anna broke up with me."

❀

Sheila spent Christmas with Norma Gray and her two daughters. Ethel the same age as Sheila, had really bonded with baby Jeffery who was making repeated attempts to crawl. Six months old now, he was an alert and happy little boy. The two girls were in the living room sitting on the floor with Jeffery rolling over and slipping and sliding his way to one then the other. Anna entered and went directly upstairs. She didn't say a word to her sister or Sheila.

Sheila didn't miss much and had noticed more than a personality change in Anna. "Would you be upset if I told you what I think is bothering your sister? Or maybe you already know?"

Ethel picked up baby Jeffery and hugged him to her chest. "I do know, and you're right. And it's even worse than that. Can I trust you to keep this to yourself?"

"Of course you can. You guys have been wonderful to me and my son."

Ethel whispered, "Anna's going to have a baby, you guessed that." Ethel whispered even lower, "She was raped this summer."

Sheila took a deep breath, "That's horrible! Does your mom know?"

"No, but when she figures it out which won't be long from now— if you can tell— she's going to go nuts."

Was it the boy she used to go with?"

"No, it was some out-of-stater, here for the summer renting a camp, she said Greg knew him." Anna went to a party at that camp.

Sheila nearly swallowed her tongue, His last name wasn't Gambino was it?"

Ethel's eyes widened, "you know him?"

"Oh my god Ethel, Greg worked for them at the fair. Those are the two brothers I told you about. Joe and Eddie. Joe's the oldest."

"Anna said it was Eddie, he gave her a ride home from that party. She had been drinking way too much. He gave her pot then he raped her behind the Drive-In theatre." Little Jeffery began to get restless and started fussing. Sheila picked him up and began to sing to him. She shook her head, "Bad, bad guys."

❁

I called Sheila to ask if she could come to my family's Christmas party. "Bring little Jeffery with you, mom says she's missed having a baby in the house." I started laughing, "When dad heard that he about crapped himself, he closed his bible, started sputtering and left the room."

Ethel had to add— just so Sheila would know what she was getting into, "By the way this Christmas party will actually just be the five of us, Jeffery included in that number."

Sheila listened without comment.

"Anyway it's going to be early on Christmas Eve. We only have to stay an hour or so—that's all they can take in the being sociable department anyway. I thought maybe we could go out for a while." I explained I was to interrogate her. "Paul wants me to find out if you know why Anna's so upset with him. He really likes her." I continued to babble. "Mom said she would love to watch Jeffery for an hour or two. I get to drive the family tank. Between you and me, I think I'm getting the beast as a Christmas present.

Secrets have holes in them in this house."

Sheila spoke. "You covered a lot of ground there Myron but it sounds like fun. Your family sounds umm, interesting, can I make anything, a dip or something?"

"No, but if you know any Christmas hymn's you'll be a hit with my father."

Sheila was left thinking, *how much can I tell him about Anna? This house— with me included— is just full of secrets and not a hole in sight.*

❁

Rebecca spent three days with Joe in Bangor. He was as nice as he could be, very attentive. They strolled the down town. He bought her a charm bracelet. Joe picked out the first charm that would hang from the sterling oval. "Italy, my grandfather's birth place. He came here with nothing and started the family business. This charm will bring you good fortune."

Rebecca had to admit to herself, *Joe could be charming.*

They had dinner at Mama Baldacci's with Joe giving the waiter a hard time by ordering in Italian. Mama herself came out of the kitchen and they conversed in their native language. They hugged and when the meal arrived, you could tell it had been put together by mama herself.

Rebecca didn't see Eddie until the third morning when he came dragging in, looking like he had spent the night fighting over an overcoat and he'd lost.

Rebecca's hair was still wet, she was in Joe's bathrobe, sipping a cup of coffee when Eddie entered the kitchen. He noisily dragged a chair away from the table and sat down. Immediately his head was in his hands. He didn't speak.

Joe was in the shower.

Rebecca thought, *vulnerable moment perhaps.*

"Good morning Eddie, I was hoping to see you before I go. How have you been?"

Eddie raised his head only slightly, "Been better." "Could I get you some coffee?" Rebecca started to rise.

"Nah, I already tried that, this cowboy just needs to sleep."

"Anna says hello."

Eddie allowed his head to rise a little more. He shook his head, "Yeah? She is quite a little cayuse that one, not surprised she remembers me." He puffed up slightly, remembering his ten seconds in the saddle.

The remark and the body language that followed told Rebecca all she need to know.

Joe came into the kitchen and looked at his brother. "Jesus Eddie, you just don't learn do you? Well I have news, Dad wants you back home ASAP."

Eddie looked up then, completely oblivious. He squinted, the kitchen light attacking another sense. "What did I do now? Man, dad needs to get a grip. He's getting to be an old woman."

Joe smiled, "I think he's going to get a grip alright little brother and it's going to be on your neck. In fact I think he might just step on it."

He noticed Rebecca then, "I'm sorry Rebecca you don't need to hear this." He looked at Eddie, "get some sleep you have a bus ticket at three this afternoon." He put up his hand as Eddie began to respond. "That's it, it's a done deal. Don't talk just walk."

For a brief moment Eddie looked like he might challenge his brother.

Joe read his thoughts, "That would be interesting Eddie, but it wouldn't end well—just go to bed. I'll wake you when I get back from seeing Rebecca off." Eddie stumbled into his room grumbling.

Rebecca returned to Skowhegan on a bright sunny day. As the wheels on the bus droned on, Rebecca went over what Anna had told her and what she now believed to be true. Eddie Gambino is a very bad guy. *Joe's a peach though,* she thought as she studied the charm. *Very old world.*

❃

It was three days after Christmas that Anna summoned her younger sister into her room. "Ethel I'm leaving. I'm not going to tell you where I'm going so Mom won't be able to shame you into telling."

Ethel looked shocked. "But, but, why….?"

"I've drained my savings so I've got money. Look I've let Mom down way to many times this past summer and she doesn't need to be saddled with another kid in this house." She took her sisters hands—their ritual of intimacy— it's been good having Jeffery and Sheila here it's helped me grow up. Sheila is not allowing herself to be a victim, I'm not going to be one either." Letting her younger sister digest this she rose to take a shower.

Ethel sat on Anna's bed looking at the posters. Elvis, Paul Anker, The Beach Boys, they all watched from the walls— their background music to this drama sat in a rack of LP albums. She held the little cloth Raggedy Ann her sister placed on her pillow every morning when she made her bed. She took the little dolls hands in her own wondering and worrying if she should tell her sister what Sheila had shared with her in secrecy?

Anna toweled her hair dry. Sitting at her mirror combing out her tangles she watched Ethel's body language— still handling Raggedy Ann— she seemed to be wrestling with herself.

Anna spoke to the glass while eyeing her sister. "I'm going to talk with the Sheriff before I leave town. I like him. He has given me a chance. I'm going to tell him about what happened. He can't do anything but he needs to know why I'm leaving."

Ethel squeezed Raggedy Ann willing her to speak. *Guess not huh Raggedy, it's going to be up to me to let Anna know just who messed with her.* "There's something you need to know before you talk with the Sheriff, Anna."

Anna turned from the mirror with a quizzical look on her face. "And what would that be oh wise one?"

"I'm not kidding. I can't tell you who told me, but Eddie and his brother Joe set the fire at the fairgrounds."

"What?!"

"All I can tell you is Gregg knows the truth but he's not talking. And no one knows where he is."

Anna tried to process all this even as she packed a small suitcase of clothing. "Look when Mom gets home just tell her I've gone to spend a few days with a friend." She took her sisters hands, "You won't be lying. School doesn't start till Monday so she won't over analyze. Just say I need some time by myself."

Ethel hugged her sister and went to the room she was sharing with Sheila and little Jeffery. Her bed was made and all her clothes had been picked up— Sheila was amazing. She laid down on her bed to try to sort through all this. The world Ethel knew was falling apart and she felt helpless to fix any of it.

❀

Gregg had spent Christmas in his little— lock-away— as he called it. His mom had moved back home since getting sober. She had come for Christmas dinner, a dinner she had purchased at the one restaurant that opened at one pm. Christmas day. They ate sliced ham, baked potatoes and peas. An apple pie sat waiting for dessert. "How long are they going to keep you here Gregg, have they said?"

"Not a clue but really right now I don't have a choice. They could be making it a lot tougher on me so I'm not complaining. They could have me locked up in the county jail. I don't really have anywhere I could go anyway."

His mother didn't seem impressed.

"Look I'm supposed to see the Sheriff next week, hopefully he'll have some news. I'm fine mom, a little bored but I am learning to hand sew. And I'm being tutored. I can get my diploma by the end of next summer or maybe I'll join you in the shoe shop business." He smiled.

"That's not funny Gregg. You need to go to college. I know I drove you out of the house and I'm sorry for that but it's not too late. I'd like to be a better mother. The last two years have made me realize both you and your dad had plenty of reason to strike off on your own. If you'll let me back into your life I'll try to make it up to you." She began to cry silently.

He didn't interrupt. He would be gentle but closeness was out the window.

❀

Anna walked to the Sheriff's office. It was Thursday January 2, 1964. The skies were clear, a pale winter blue, like Paul's eyes. The light poles along lower water street were still wearing shiny green garland with the message, *Season's Greetings* in red and white letters. Anna checked her image reflected in the window of *Gagnon Jewelers. Alan's Cut Above* barber shop was to her right. The *Strand Theatre* marquee announced the movie *Bye Bye Birdie,* was playing for two full weeks. *How prophetic is that,* mused Anna as she tugged her stocking cap a little lower— Bye Bye Anna.

The secretary who at times doubled as a dispatcher greeted Anna warmly. Mrs. Noonan brought a sense of motherly concern to what was otherwise a Man's world kind of operation. "Anna you look like a little lost soul this morning, come here give me a hug. After the embrace, which lingered— Anna drawing strength from this kind lady— Marion Noonan announced the Sheriff said he would see her as soon as she arrived, so go right in. Anna entered the Sheriff's office and stood in front of his desk. Sheriff McManus was intently reading. Anna had called to ask for this meeting so she cleared her throat and began. "I am sorry to bother you Sheriff but things have changed for the worse in my life."

Sheriff McManus raised his head, his reading glasses perched on his broad face giving him a Santa Claus persona. He smiled, "Good morning and Happy New Year young lady, what's up?" The Sheriff pointed to a chair, "Sit down, you look like you're carrying an armload of firewood and don't know where to place it."

Anna had to smile, she had come to hear all the woes of the world explained in terms that involved the woods business in one fashion or another. Most of them made perfect sense actually. Suddenly she knew how to frame her dilemma. She pointed to the sign that held the message, *Don't Try To Haul More Than You're Equipped To.* "That sign is me right now, Sheriff Mac." She had come to like this man and he had insisted she call him by his nickname— only in private though.

He studied her through furrowed brows.

Anna was squirming, she cleared her throat and gushed out a long run on sentence, "I'm going to have a baby, Sheriff Mac, and I'm leaving the area. I have a ride arranged to Waterville then either by bus or train I'm going to California." She looked like a little kid who had just lost their breath blowing out way too many candles in hopes of getting their wish immediately.

Sheriff Mac sat back astounded but remained calm, "That seems like a long way to transport your load Anna. Does your mother know about this?"

Anna composed herself, "I'm eighteen now Sheriff Mac. I'm a legal adult, and no my mom doesn't know yet. It's complicated, the father doesn't know either and I'd rather not run into him again, he's not a nice person."

"So what can I do for you Anna, seems like you have your mind made up?"

"You have been very nice to me Sheriff, I won't forget it." She cleared her throat. "I'm going to give you a name— Eddie Gambino." Anna started crying softly but continued, "He raped me." She took a deep breath and continued. "Nothing I can do about that now. I should have done something when it happened but I was already in trouble for that stupid party," she seemed to be as angry with herself as she was Eddie Gambino. "I just found out he might have had something to do with the fire at the fairgrounds too."

Sheriff McManus sat up a little straighter. "I am really sorry Anna, seems like this kid has caused trouble for the whole town and then some." The Sheriff got up and began pacing his office. He massaged his chin, pondering, then he asked the question he already had an answer to. "You had a birthday recently didn't you?"

"How did you know that Sheriff Mac?"

"Honestly, when you caused that ruckus this summer I had to decide whether to charge you with a crime. I saw you were only seventeen at the time and as a juvenile the whole effort wouldn't be worth the time. Judge Eames would have given you a slap on the wrist. He's much harder on adults."

Anna sat absorbing all this but it didn't change her circumstances any, she was leaving town.

Sheriff Mac nodded to himself like he had just made a decision he had yet to share. "What if we could help each other out Anna— together I think we can make this Eddie Gambino pay for all his crimes, would that work for you?"

This time it was Anna who looked quizzical.

"You do realize you were a juvenile when Eddie assaulted you, he's an adult, nineteen I believe. If I can get someone to place him at that fire, I could use a rape charge to get him to talk, will you help me out?"

"How can I help?"

"First you write out a statement of what happened, all the details. Include anyone else who might know of what happened or at least knew you were with him that night. Then I have a safe place for you to stay for the next couple of months while we put the squeeze on this guy. You can get tutored and graduate on time. How does all that sound? Your Mom can even visit you."

Anna looked relieved. Her body unfolded and she sat up straight. "Really, you can do all that?" She smiled, "Thank you Sheriff Mac." She stood came around the desk and shook the Sheriff's hand vigorously.

"I'll talk to your Mom before you have that conversation you've been dreading." He smiled then, looking at the same load of wood Anna had studied earlier, "I'll just lighten that load you're hauling Anna." He rose and gave her a hug. "You go on home

I'll be in touch in the next day or two. I'll have your mom in tomorrow. Things will work out, trust me." Sheriff McManus called in his lead detective, Patrick Fitzmaurice. "Fill me in on anything new you've come up with. I have a new twist to add." Detective Fitzmaurice noted the Sheriff seemed buoyant, almost happy. He sat, he waited.

"I think we just got dealt an ace in the hole, Detective and I want to strategize when to play it." The two men slogged their way through two cups of coffee, the files, what they knew to be true, then adding Anna's revelation to the mix. "We have to convince Gregg Croteau to speak with us."

❀

Skowhegan is a small town and paths cross and re-cross many times with a nod of a head the only communication or acknowledgement. The woman sitting in the waiting room at *Med Wed Footwear* looked familiar but Laura McManus couldn't place where or when she might have met the woman. Laura was the bookkeeper and oversaw the two secretaries that handled phone calls, appointments, and the pesky salesmen that were always trying to get in to see the owner. Laura was first in the office this morning and after making the coffee decided to be gracious. "Could I get you a cup of coffee? No answer. Are you here for a job?" When the lady merely blinked up into the fluorescent lights Laura decided to take a different tack. She held out her hand, "I'm Laura McManus the office manager, what's your name?" The woman studied the hand briefly then put her hand into the sturdy grip offered.

"My name is Roxanne." She didn't provide a last name. "I would like that cup of coffee," she managed, "and yes, I would like a job as well."

Roxanne got a job in the stitching room in the adjacent Drapery factory also owned by Med Wed Footwear. She would work under the watchful eyes of newly promoted Norma Gray.

Roxanne lived in the basement of her grandmother's house on Turner Avenue. She had the place fixed up with wood paneling and carpeted floors. She had her own entrance. One wall had daylight windows.

Roxanne planted window boxes of flowers to the side of each of the three windows. When she was introduced to her new boss Norma Gray she recognized the name from the beautiful flower display she had seen on the first day of the fair.

Roxanne might be invisible to the town but she didn't miss much. She didn't mention the flower show but based on what she had seen beneath the grandstand she was already feeling she had found a boss with a heart.

Roxanne had been a stitcher before at Norrwock shoe in Norridgewock. Her boss there had been a married man she got involved with. She was stupid enough to believe he wanted more than a roll in the hay. One more lie had left a man's lips. It did not end well and Roxanne had begun a downward spiral of bad choices that always ended in a bottle with no good way out— unless a Genie should appear suddenly—that hadn't happened yet.

Norma wheeled a rack of cloth pieces in front of Roxanne's work station. Speed and accuracy were fundamental to a good days pay. An inspector would check the pieces Roxanne stitched together for any mistakes which would then be returned to Roxanne for repair. You don't make money making repairs. Roxanne had done this type of work for four years— though it had been leather pieces and shoes the product— the skills and speed needed to make a living were the same.

Norma spoke. "Prove me right Roxanne. Several people saw you sitting out there. They saw fit to approach me and offer their unsolicited opinions.

They said I shouldn't hire you. They don't know you or your work but offered their opinions anyway. This is a small town and people can be small as well." She nodded and went about her business.

Roxanne went about her own business as well and when the day ended she had made forty dollars. A good beginning, she would get faster as she learned the machine better.

She left the shop and noted the sun was already staying in the sky a little longer on this cold clear afternoon. She walked behind East Front Street to French Street heading for her apartment entering Mill Street where the sidewalks had not been plowed. Gingerly climbing the slight incline, Route 201 with the main flow of traffic stopped her progress. The bridge spanning the Kennebec with open water near Central Maine Power's dam drew her attention. The water flowing was on a journey that mirrored Roxanne's own. Roxanne sensed this as little sticks and branches rode the surface, buoyant and glad to be free of the prison of ice that had interrupted their search for the sea. Roxanne crossed the road and turned left at the Dairy Treat, the Junior High to her right. The swinging bridge which hung from cables creaked and moaned like a rheumatic knee when you stepped on it, stood at the end of what served as the parking lot of the school. You bounced and tread awkwardly for the entire crossing. When she emerged from this year round fair ride she entered Alder Street. After a deep breath of relief a quick left on Bridge Street a fairly steep pitch, had Roxanne breathing deeply once more. A light sweat emerged cooling her neck. Turning right onto Turner Avenue her house came into view. A large tree on each side of the driveway remained stark, their naked limbs shuddering in the late afternoon. She entered her basement apartment down its own set of steps and entry door. Inside she removed her coat and hat looking around all the while at the neat little world she had created underground. She looked out her basement window and smiled to herself, at this level all she could see was two feet of tree trunk but maybe she would plant some flowers around those trunks this spring. She felt inspired for the first time in ages, this job just might work out. She turned on the radio just as Hank Williams reminded Roxanne that a job was only part of what was missing in her life. *I'm So Lonesome I Could Cry,* sung with such feeling that it seeped into your bones had Roxanne weeping silently on her couch. *'Dammit Hank don't remind me, one problem at a time if you don't mind.'* Roxanne fell asleep on the couch and for the first time in a month she didn't make it to the bar. The next morning she began walking the same route coming— and in reverse— going to work every day. This pattern would not draw attention in the first months of Roxanne's employment—but later this route would draw scrutiny from several parties.

❋

Joe Jr. got a call from a guy who knew a guy who knew another guy. Finding Gregg had proven fruitless— Gregg seemed to be the name he was going by these days. Sheila on the other hand was living in town and going to school. Joe was given the address and sat pondering his response to the news. *On the one hand she might know nothing about the fire. It was nearly six months removed from the media's attention and Joe hadn't heard a peep. Gregg obviously had not spoken to anyone and probably wouldn't. If it was up to Joe he'd let sleeping dogs lie. His father though saw it as a loose end and Joe always did what his father said. Maybe I should take a trip to Skowhegan. Take Sheila out to lunch ask about Gregg in a concerned way. Maybe Rebecca can arrange it. There you go, I have a plan.* He stood, did several deep knee bends, stretched and walked to a window overlooking the street. Dusk was falling, steam starting to rise from the street. Street lights offered a little light to the shadows that were slowly eating the houses one by one. He put on a jacket and took the stairs in pairs. He locked the outside door. His car sat along the curbing, he shrugged did a little dance step and decided to walk the half mile to Mama Baldacci's.

Wednesday was called Prince Spaghetti day in his family when he was a kid. He remembered his mother calling him and his brother home using the line from the commercial he had grown to hate but couldn't forget. *'Anthony'* she'd yell. Truth was she was a lousy cook. Now Mama Baldacci, that lady can cook. Joe's mouth was watering as the smell of Italian cooking reached him before he could even see the place. Tonight— Chicken Marsala to celebrate his plan.

❀

Norma Gray and her daughter sat on the edge of the bed holding one another.

Sheriff Mac true to his word had called Norma Gray and they held a sit down. Norma thought they were meeting to discuss Anna's new job and a possible violation of the conditions the Sheriff had set for her daughter. The Sheriff sitting down behind his desk looked very serious. "Thanks for coming in Mrs.

Gray." He paused as if looking for a way around a felled tree in the path, "what I am about to tell you needs to stay in this room. For your family's sake and in particular your daughter Anna."

Norma Gray found herself shaking with nervous anticipation of what Anna could have done that could be this serious. "You suffered the effects of that fire in a personal way. I saw your display of creativity first hand," he nodded. The rest of this conversation was going to be difficult. "The young man who we believe was part of causing a death and a serious injury as well as the fire is a very dangerous man. He is also a criminal who has harmed your daughter Anna in the most personal way possible."

Norma Gray waited for a shoe to drop.

"I promised I would speak with you about this in a general way and offer a way for Anna to be safe from this animal." The Sheriff was having trouble guiding this twitch of wood to the yard. Finally he just came out with it. "Eddie Gambino a nineteen year old from Massachusetts took advantage of your daughter after a party at his camp. He sexually assaulted her." Norma armed with the truth of that night began connecting dots. Her held breath released, "I knew something was troubling her, she hasn't been the same since the summer, she sighed." Norma was suddenly cold and had to hug herself. "Is there another shoe to drop Sheriff?"

"I'll let Anna tell you the rest of the story. What I'd like to offer you is part of a solution and the safety we can provide."

When Norma left the Sheriff's office she was so angry she could feel her pulse in her teeth.

❀

Anna moved into a room in what was called the Half Way House at the Skowhegan Women's Reformatory. This was the first publicly funded facility of its type in the United States. Ward Murphy arrived as Superintendent for the reformatory with a different approach towards rehabilitation. With the cooperation of local businesses and the school system girls were reintroduced to the community after showing their willingness to change their ways. Several older women were among the ten housed in a dormitory type setting comprised of four bedrooms, a gang shower and a small kitchen where the girls could make sandwiches and coffee or cocoa. Their meals were served in the prison cafeteria at a different time than the general population. Girls of school age went to the local high school while the older women filled jobs in the local factories. Anna would be bunking with two other teenagers. Anna would not be attending classes she would receive her assignments via these girls and once a week a teacher from Skowhegan High School would tutor her and administer tests. Anna did not know Gregg Croteau was just a stone's throw away from her building. One of the older girls, twenty two year old Celia Stanley got a job in the stitching room at the drapery factory. Her boss Norma Gray, her co-worker Roxanne.

• FEBRUARY 1964

• A MONTH WITHOUT SNOW

Gregg Croteau sat at his little bench deftly pushing the awl through the leather upper that was positioned on a wooden foot shaped piece of wood called a last. He was becoming quite proficient as a hand sewer. The waxed thread ends and oversized needles lay ready to turn the leather pieces he had softened— by soaking them in hot water— into a hand-sewn moccasin. This was a skill where you gained speed by repeating the steps over and over and over. His hands were beginning to toughen to the task. He tapped the edges of the leather pieces that would be sewn together with a special hammer-plier tool. He gazed out the window at an overcast but balmy morning. Overnight the temperature had actually risen as cloud cover offered a warm blanket to stifle the February cold. He sighed, *February 14, Valentine's Day,* he desperately wanted to talk with Sheila. He finished the case of twenty-four pairs he was working on and rolled the rack to the wall. He worked his fingers, easing their stiffness. *People make a living like this?* He asked himself. By 9:00 am the sun was making marginal progress at putting in an appearance. Gregg turned on the radio.

It might not be summer but it seemed insects had taken over the world any way. He had watched the

Ed Sullivan show when the Beatles made their appearance and heard the screaming that nearly drowned out their music. *Can't buy me love,* was blasting the airways this morning. Gregg was restless, time for a run. He rose, stretched his long frame and dressed in a thermal long sleeve shirt with a tee shirt over that. His legs never got cold unless the wind was blowing so he pulled on a pair of shorts, socks and added a stocking cap. He tied his running shoes in a double knot, ran in place for a minute his feet ushering him out the door.

The winter had not offered up much accumulation of snow so far— an open winter was what they were calling it. Gregg stretched each muscle group, absently studying the terrain then entered the plowed paths and driveways of the reformatory. He did several laps around the plowed area before exiting onto the back road to Norridgewock, heading west. His internal engine warming and smoothing out he covered two miles then turned back just as the sun was finally breaking through. He picked up his pace feeling his heart settle into the rhythm he sought. He changed gears after a half mile and ran full bore back to the drive heading into the reformatory. Breathing deeply and sweating profusely he slowed then— stopped briefly putting his head to waist level to recover. As his heart slowed he looked around once more breathing with satisfaction at his effort. His cool down jog repeated the circuit of driveways and parking lot. Feeling both mentally and physically invigorated he took a deep breath, *yeah he could handle whatever comes,* he decided. He looked to his left when a door to what was called the half-way house closed and a girl appeared. He looked twice. He shook the cobwebs away, could that be? He squinted his eyes. He looked more closely, then he spoke, "Anna is that you?" Anna looked his way. "Holy crap, Gregg??"

They moved toward one another both dazed.

Anna spoke first. "Everyone wondered what happened to you, especially Sheila, wow this is unreal. So the Sheriff has us all rounded up it seems." "You know Sheila?? Gregg gasped, "Is she okay? My Mom said she came to see me in the hospital but they wouldn't let her in. Where is she living?"

Anna took a deep breath, "Boy do we need to talk, are you staying somewhere in this place?"

❋

Paul found out in January when classes resumed that Anna was no longer living at home or going to school. When classes began he was actually glad he didn't run into her in the hall. She had hurt him, but weirdly he thought he must have done something wrong. Avoidance seemed the right recipe for the moment. He had English class with me and when the bell rang he pigeon holed me at my locker. "Myron, where is Anna? What do you know? Has Sheila told you anything?"

I put up my hands in defense. "Whoa there Paul, Sheila has been sworn to secrecy. All she would tell me was Anna has left the house and that's all she knows."

"Why did she leave the house, did her Mom kick her out or something?"

"I forget you don't live in town Paul, take a deep breath. The word bouncing around like a pin ball at Barry's Pizza is she's going to have a baby."

"WHAT?!" Heads turned and several teacher poked their heads into the corridor thinking a fight might be brewing.

I nodded. "I asked Sheila? She would neither confirm nor deny."

Paul was visibly shaken. I tried to calm him but he wouldn't listen.

The bell to the next class rang but Paul ignored it. He walked out the back exit to the parking lot sat in his car and stared at the brick building, his mind racing. He fumbled with the keys his hands shaking nervously starting the car. He turned up the heater and looked into his rear-view mirror at himself. He saw a frightened young man looking back at him though he knew he played no role in any of this. The radio was on but he paid it no mind until the Beetles announced that, *We Can Work It Out*. His eyes opened wide and he said to himself, *not so sure about that!*

❀

Police Chief Henry, Sheriff McManus, Detective Fitzmaurice and Detective Noonan each claiming a corner of the folding table Sheriff McManus used as a command center studied and passed hand to hand the photos of Joe and Eddie Gambino. All eyes lifted to the Sheriff, "its February men, these two yahoos are still out there. I'm sure, feeling really good about themselves. One's out of state and the other is going to school like a normal kid." He threw up his hands, "Where are we with this? Do we need to charge this Gregg Croteau? I don't want to do this but if it will get him to talk maybe it's something we have to do."

Heads nodded.

Detective Fitzmaurice spoke. "We have interviewed dozens of people. No one saw anything except that boy who witnessed the phone call. I'd say tighten the screws Sheriff.

"I'll go see Gregg Croteau today."

By the way Sheriff where's that cute little dispatch intern gone?"

"She might just be the key to unraveling the truth.

She's in my safe keeping for now. So don't ask."

With that the Sheriff rose, signaling this meeting was over.

As the men filed out the Sheriff finished up, "We'll meet again when I have something new to add. Chief will you stay a minute I have some news you might want to follow up on.

❀

Gregg and Anna were meeting at the same time law enforcement was making plans.

Gregg brought two cups of steaming coffee to the kitchen table. "Didn't think I'd ever drink this stuff but there you go, lots of new things entering my life." He removed his cap and wiped the sweat from the recent run from his hair, walking back to the fridge he grabbed a bottle of milk. "Sugar is already in it, let me know if you need more." With cups placed like chess pieces on opposite ends of the table he began. "So tell me Anna what brings you to our little village at the top of the hill?"

"It's a long story." She wasn't sure where to place that pawn. "I don't really know where to begin. Maybe a little defense first. "Good to see you Gregg, you look good for all you've been through, just one little scar there on your right cheek."

Gregg smiled, "a couple more you can't see but yeah I'm ok." He cleared his throat, "What's happened to you Anna, obviously you're going to have a baby but there has to be more to it than that if you're bunking up here?"

Anna sipped her coffee added a little milk stirred the brew and took off her jacket. The sun was taking over now adding little vignettes of light to objects in the window over the sink. Anna took it all in, hesitating to begin. She sunk lower in her chair but settled her mind. A very deep breath ushered a rushed sentence. "I was raped Gregg, by Eddie Gambino." She seemed suddenly smaller, younger, child-like.

Gregg was speechless. He covered his shock by taking a long pull of coffee, burning his mouth.

Anna, continued, "The Sheriff knows he and his brother set that fire and killed that man and hurt you in the process. I'm in protective custody. I didn't know you were too."

Gregg continued to listen eyes wide, he couldn't wrap his head around all he was hearing.

"I don't think you know this either— Sheila is living with my family— She told my sister Ethel all that she knows and surmises."

Gregg cleared his throat, started to speak.

Anna held up her hand, "Let me finish, this gets weirder and weirder. I was dating a guy in the fall, a new kid in school who worked with Myron at the fair. He saw a young guy making a phone call at the fairgrounds the night of the fire. He has identified him but the Sheriff won't say who it is. I think it was either Eddie or his brother Joe." All that revelation came out in what seemed like one breath.

Gregg sat back all color had drained from the rosy cheeks of his earlier effort. "Wow, Wow, Wow! Anna, does Eddie know you are pregnant?"

"No and we don't want him to know till the baby is born and we can prove he's the father. The Sheriff hopes to get him to talk because I was seventeen when it happened and he can be charged with rape no matter what story he tries to dream up. He's dangerous Gregg, as you well know."

Gregg took a long sip of his coffee that had cooled considerably, "What you don't know is his older brother Joe is even more dangerous, he's the planner in all this."

"My god, Rebecca is dating him and thinks he's wonderful!"

"I don't really know Rebecca. I met her the night of the party and she drove me home. this summer but sounds like someone might want to warn her."

"That's the night I got raped Gregg, remember Eddie driving me home cause I had too much to drink? It was that night." She looked across at Gregg,

"What are we going to do?"

"I have to talk to Sheila."

❖

The main office was filling up with roses. Teen age boys publicly impressing their girlfriends. Valentine's Day was a pain in the ass for the secretaries. The Principal a no nonsense individual was never-the-less no fool. He had all he could handle trying to keep a dress code that allowed no long hair or facial hair or blue jeans from causing a rebellion. He decided to pick his battles and let this day unfold with him playing the good guy. "Deliver the damn flowers and be done with it."

Sheila received a single rose from me. We sat at the lunch table trays of Tuna P. Wiggle and crackers in front of us, looking into one another's eyes. "Glad I met you Sheila," I said, smelling the rose she put under my nose.

Sheila smiled, "I like you too Myron, thanks for the rose, I never got flowers before." We began to eat.

Paul came and sat down. He studied Sheila briefly, then said nervously, "The girls don't think I had anything to do with Anna's condition do they?"

Sheila wiggled her tuna wiggle around in her plate. "Paul rumors are flying, nobody knows what to think" then she raised her eyes to meet Paul's, "and I promised Anna not to answer any questions. You are the new boy on the block so a lot of people don't really know you." She took a bite then pushed the tray away. "Let's just say I don't think you are being given the benefit of the doubt. How do people eat this," shoving the tray away. "I know what happened and Myron knows some of what happened but for now you probably are not loved by lots of girls in this school. I'm really sorry."

Ethel pulled up a chair catching the end of the conversation, "Well I know the truth and this town better wake up pretty soon to more than just what happened to Anna." She looked directly at Sheila who was caught trying to wash away the taste of terrible and began coughing.

Ethel seemed to be waiting patiently for a response. When Sheila had control back she nodded her head. "I agree Ethel but who knows where to begin?"

• MARCH BLOWS IN AN ILL WIND

In the back of our minds suspicions were beginning to form on a lot of fronts. Jack Ruby was convicted of killing Lee Harvey Oswald. The brazen shooting of Oswald— with law enforcement surrounding President Kennedy's assassin— added fuel to our speculation that more than one person was involved in the assassination plot. Shortly after the president was killed President Lyndon Johnson formed an investigative commission headed by Supreme Court Justice, Earl Warren. Four months into the probe we the public remained angry. The investigation was conducted behind closed doors with no deadline spelled out. We read and heard the reports of police officers describing a gun shot from in front of the presidential motorcade. A silent film of the assassination was being kept from the public which furthered our suspicion that a cover-up was being fashioned. All our news came by way of the three networks nightly broadcasts. We trusted the news anchors completely. They entered our living rooms with the latest updates on topics ranging from the war in Vietnam to cultural happenings. They too however seemed to be kept in the dark regarding the most important event in our recent past.

On the local scene the curtain that covered the stage at the opera house where we would hold our senior play could just as easily have shrouded the entire town of Skowhegan. The mystery of a death and fire at the fairgrounds continued to effect the lives of ordinary citizens in dozens of ways.

❋

Rebecca was at her locker fuming about the discussion just held in history class. To her it seemed her peers were already forgetting about their slain leader and taking for granted that Lee Harvey Oswald alone committed the killing. She read every magazine article on the subject she could find. Every week it seemed another possible scenario emerged. The Mafia, Fidel Castro, the Russians, the CIA, even President Johnson was not above suspicion. Rebecca wanted answers. Nobody else in her class seemed to care. Paul and I stopped and patted her shoulder. "I think some of us care Rebecca, we just don't know what we can do so we're leaving it to the warren Commission to figure it out."

"Thanks guys, I realize I can go a little overboard but this man was my idol. You should see my bedroom I can't even take the posters down. I'm still so angry." The boys turned to leave.

"By the way Myron, congrats on getting the lead in the senior play, you will make a cool Japanese interpreter."

"Yeah thanks Becca, I actually think, *Tea House to the August Moon* might be fun. Mrs. Merrill gave us an overview in class today. I have a month to learn all my lines. She is going to show us the movie in English class next week. She said that should raise the interest level for all the other parts." I laughed, "The guys will like that they can pretend being drunk right in front of their parents."

The principal, seldom seen in the corridors was walking by at that moment and heard me use the word drunk and looked at me oddly. "That's how rumors start sir— it's all about the play."

The Principal who was known simply as— the Principal— seldom walked the hallways. His attempt to remain anonymous— an omniscient voice over the intercom— (the voice of god we called it), allowed us no one to debate the rules with.

The days were getting longer, the first day of spring arrived on a Saturday and it seemed everyone was ready for it. It had been a long winter. Not a terribly cold or snowy one but so much had happened in our town and the whole Country in the last eight months— It seemed winter had started in August. Well we seniors were about to enter our last quarter of education at Skowhegan High School and graduation couldn't come soon enough for us. Barry's Pizza was full of pin-ballers this early afternoon and there posted on the wall was the point leader for the new game, *BIG TOP*. And there pointing to his name on the leaderboard was Delbert. There must have been ten of us guys standing around the three machines. All were watching Delbert deftly guiding the ball up the shoot. Using body language that nudged the machine lightly— not allowing the deadly tilt message that killed a game in a heartbeat to appear. Delbert's fingers hovered. When a ball headed to an exit he pushed the button on each side of the machine that controlled sets of flippers sending the ball madly back toward the top with lights flashing, sounds pulsing. He set a new record right there in front of us gamers. We looked at Delbert with a new respect. Delbert nodded, walked to the counter in his odd gait, and retrieved an Italian sandwich with extra oil and pickles. He tipped his hat on the way out.

We were left shaking our heads, a silent testament to the phrase, *go figure.*

Delbert turned right and walked past Stern's department Store he gazed in the window at the mannequins dressed for spring in the latest fashions. In Barry's we had been discussing this years' prom, Delbert heard every word. Delbert never got to go to a Prom. Hell Delbert remembered going to a dance once and just sitting there. Girls on one side boys on the other. Seemed like a crossing into no man's land with the risk of being shot down— your heart wounded— then having to return to the teasing of your supposed friends— no fun at all. Delbert continued his walk looking down at the water that carried small chunks of ice from up-river. A security guard waved and hollered, 'Hey' from the doorway of the Spinning Mill. Delbert waved his bagged Italian sandwich at him and turned into the Fire Station on the Island. Two men were on duty, the Fire Chief Russell Clement was sitting in his personal vehicle chatting with the men. Delbert wasn't on duty but the men kidded him anyway.

"Hey Delbert, you keeping us safe on this glorious first day of spring."

"Ju-uh-st getting suh-um lunch, guys."

Delbert had come to adopt this place as a safe haven. Also he could watch the comings and goings of Roxanne without her seeing him. Right on cue she came into sight. The drapery shop was doing well apparently— this was the fourth Saturday in a row she had worked. Delbert half listened to the banter, his main focus was watching Roxanne turn left and navigate the swinging bridge on her way home. He smiled at the way the bridge seemed to take over your legs. *Welcome to my world,* he thought then smiled. He made a decision. He mumbled an awkward so long and crossed the street. Roxanne was three quarters across the two-hundred foot span when Delbert yelled. Roxanne nearly lost her balance as she turned to the sound. Delbert tried to run across which merely amplified his awkward gait. He reached Roxanne just as she reached dry land. He took a deep breath. Her smile relaxed him. Delbert imagined himself navigating a pin ball machine and spoke. "Roxanne, I br-ought lunch." He held up the sandwich.

Roxanne smiled again. She too looked beyond the moment and imagined herself with someone who might actually care about her.

"Why that's very nice of you Delbert, where were you thinking of having this lunch?" She smiled and winked, "I wondered when you'd make your way across that damn bridge."

Delbert feeling sheepish remained silent but knew he'd hit the jackpot, a new high score in his private life. He smiled.

Roxanne reached out and took his hand, "Of course I've been watching you watching me Delbert." Together they navigated Bridge Street.

❀

Back at Barry's the talk covered the gamut, from tonight's poker game to who was grounded, to who was responsible for their friend Anna's woes. I offered up nothing. John denied everything. Paul who had driven me this morning simply listened. It got a little heated when this last topic was raised and I found himself defending my friend Paul.

"John I can tell you with certainty Paul is not the one. I can't tell you who it is but it's not Paul, so let's move on shall we?"

"Good idea gentlemen!" Jerome Barry shouted, he allowed no nonsense. He gave the group *the look* from behind the counter.

For a while the pin ball machines made the only comments heard.

❁

Rebecca was at home with her Father on this first day of spring. Her dad was forty-five when Rebecca was born. He had worked at Med Wed Footwear for years. When the Woolen Mill shut down after World War Two, Durwood Tully found himself no longer a Foreman making good money. His skills no longer needed he entered the shop and worked in an assembly room grinding the excess leather from the bottom of shoes before the sole was glued and stitched on. This was a job for a much younger, quicker man. Her dad was a nervous wreck. His job was a piece work job. Speed was paramount. The grinding machine did not discriminate. Leather, skin, even bone sometimes found contact with the spinning wheel of misfortune. He was still out of work recovering from his latest mishap. Rebecca tried to reason with him, encouraging him to find something else. Too old she was told. Their conversations tended to be of about that length. Singular responses on any subject raised— too young— too fast— too slow— tonight— tomorrow— too bad.

She loved him though. Her Mom died five years ago which had shortened three word conversations down to two.

"I have a friend coming to visit me for the weekend Dad, is that ok? He's going to stay in my room."

Her dad merely looked at her, then uttered "Growing up."

He turned to the TV. turning up the sound— this too was a way to communicate.

Joseph Gambino signaled right on to Mechanic Street and turned right again into Rebecca's driveway. No other vehicles were in the yard and for a moment Joe thought maybe no one was home. Rebecca saw him out the living room window and entered the small porch facing the street. Joe smiled through the windshield and turned off the engine. He exited, raised his arms to the sky welcoming the warming sun. He removed and hung his sunglasses on his shirt opening. He closed his door and turned back to Rebecca. She had left the porch and was standing in front of him. She pulled him into an embrace— "Missed you" she murmured.

"Right back at you beautiful. Easy don't crush my sunglasses."

Mr. Tully had left the living room for his bedroom and the door was closed. The TV. offered a lighted screen but was tuned to a channel that didn't have a signal, showing a screen of white noise. *"That man can still find ways to communicate,"* thought Rebecca shaking her head.

"Anybody else here Rebecca, or do I have you all to myself?" He hugged her from behind.

Rebecca sighed, "Don't crush those glasses Joe," she kidded. "I think it's safe to say we will not be bothered." She took his hand and led him to the stair case.

❁

Joe arrived back in Bangor with no more information than he left with. Rebecca seemed to know nothing of what had happened to Gregg and said she had yet to meet Sheila. She seemed obsessed with a possible conspiracy in the killing of President Kennedy. Her bedroom walls were covered with posters of the Man. Lying there, recovering from their energetic love-making Joe had looked the man in the eye and thought, *I hope it was me she was with just then.* President Kennedy remained silent on the issue.

❁

Anna had her baby two months early. The doctor who delivered the child expected the worst but was dealt a little miracle. The child while small appeared fully developed. Certainly her lungs were operating at capacity. "We will do some tests but I believe you have a healthy little daughter."

Mom Norma and sister Ethel were in attendance. Waiting down the hall bouncing little Jeffery on her knee was Sheila.

The baby girl was in fact healthy. Anna had been brought to the hospital late Sunday evening. She endured a relatively easy birth and was holding Layla Ray Gray wrapped in a pink blanket dotted with blue elephants.

Norma watched her daughter bonding with the baby and began to cry softly. "Not the way I envisioned becoming a Grandmother, but how can I be angry when I see such a beautiful little bundle."

Anna responded in a whisper meant only for her mother's ears, "I'm angry enough for all of us and he's going to pay dearly for this."

Ethel got to hold the little girl for a moment before the nurse whisked the baby away.

Anna continued whispering, "The Sheriff will be in later today. We finally have a plan and little Layla will be at the center of it. Anna continued to whisper to her mom.

Ethel entered the waiting room and told Sheila the baby was going to be okay and Anna wanted to talk to Sheila. Jeffery reached for Ethel and she began a soccer shuffle with the little boy in her arms.

Sheila knocked. She took Anna's hand, eyes meeting, sharing an experience that most girls their age don't face. Then they got down to business. Norma left to join her daughter Ethel.

Anna began, "Gregg has been in town all along. The Sheriff has him in protective custody."

Sheila sat on the edge of the bed, eyes wide.

"Can I see him, I really need to talk with him?"

"Sheriff McManus is coming in later he has a plan— and it includes you— can you ask Mom and Ethel to take care of Jeffery for a few hours?"

"I'm sure they won't mind."

❀

Sheriff McManus was taking no chances. A blood test of baby Layla was ordered. Sheila and her child were going to be moving to the reformatory and by Thursday. Anna and her baby would be back there as well.

When the Sheriff headed home early Monday evening he was feeling pretty good about bringing this case to a conclusion. He and Police Chief Henry would be meeting with the county prosecutor in the morning.

He was whistling when he entered his kitchen. Laura had cooked up a pasta dish, the kitchen windows were steamed up and the Sheriff could smell garlic bread toasting. "Seems like I have struck gold twice today honey, that sure smells good on a cool windy night."

"You're in good spirits, anything you wish to share?" Laura placed a bowl of spaghetti on the table. "Wash up, I'll pour you a glass of wine, maybe I can loosen your tongue."

When the sheriff returned to the table, a candle provided the only light. Laura smiled, "I was thinking if the pasta doesn't do the trick I might just have one more ace up my sleeve."

"I wish I could say I was above being bribed Laura but that candle has already got me thinking it's time to fess up, and I promise I'll go peacefully," he chuckled.

❀

It was Thursday March 26, 1964. I was studying my lines for the lead in the senior play. In the play I would be the Japanese interpreter trying to convince my countrymen to work with the Americans who were now occupying our country. I was starting to think my role in real life was taking on some of the same responsibilities. Sheila had finally opened up to me. Earlier this afternoon she had a meeting with Sheriff McManus, Anna, and Gregg Croteau. I was seriously in love with Sheila and it seemed she cared for me as well. She called immediately upon leaving the meeting. I wrangled the family car, (I hadn't inherited the beast at Christmas as I thought I would but no one else used it— so one more mystery in my house. I picked Sheila up at the Gray residence. I had a hundred questions and Sheila answered them all. "Gregg is fine. Your job is to warn Rebecca that Joe Gambino was involved in that fire. I am going to have to go into protective custody tomorrow morning as well."

I was shocked. "What do you have to do with any of it?"

"Gregg shared with me what Joe had offered him if he'd go along with the scheme. I am what's called a material witness."

"Where will you be? Can I see you?"

"Can't tell you where I'll be, but I've been told this is all coming to a head very soon. I can call you once a week." Sheila waited for this to settle. "Anna has a message for Paul as well. Tell him she is truly sorry for any trouble she has caused him and she hopes she will be able to explain everything in time."

❀

I tried to focus on the script. Lying on my bed a single lamp yellowing the pages, real people I cared about kept coming on stage and interrupting my concentration. *Lovely ladies kind gentlemen, please to introduce myself, Sakini by name interpreter by profession, education by ancient dictionary.* When those lines reached the edge of the stage with my mind gazing into the footlights, Sheila was sitting there in the first row with Gregg, Anna, Paul, and Rebecca. Sitting directly behind them was sheriff McManus and another row back was Joe and Eddie Gambino. They weren't sitting though— they were standing, pointing— as if directing the way this would all go.

I shuddered closed the script and turned out the light.

• APRIL CRIED

The Beatles were dominating the airways. They had the top five hits on Billboard's top 40. The Beatle invasion had begun in earnest.

In Maine mud time had begun in earnest.

Skowhegan's older residents–that would be anyone over thirty-five— found themselves constantly changing radio stations with the same regularity as dodging pot holes. '*Those damn Beatles,*' and '*those damn pot holes*' left the lips of the working man as their hands gripped first the steering wheel and when safe the radio knob.

❁

The warming sun and greening of the landscape— both which brought smiles— had to compete with April rain which closed roads and caused unemployment while the earth healed. Arguments and debates took place over coffee at the area's restaurants— the lunch room at the factories,— even in the bars where idle woods workers and truck drivers found themselves by early afternoon. It was as if a heated political debate were taking place, the old chicken or the egg argument took center stage where weather was concerned.

At the high school we were between seasons too.

The basketball season had been a forgettable one. Our gym was the smallest in the conference and even that echoed with emptiness as one loss followed another.

The upcoming Baseball season offered promise though with a veteran team returning— some talented underclassmen sure to help.

With runners from a fairly successful Cross- Country season signed up for Spring Track we were anxious for the fields to dry out.

On the positive side, what mud time did do was slow things down. Discussion of the weather and for that matter the uproar over the Beatle's brand of music, helped make the toothache the town still felt regarding the fire at the fairgrounds recede slightly. It was still there and we knew it had to be removed but it was not center stage at the moment.

❁

Roxanne had found a rhythm in her life that had her whistling on her way down French Street. She was making good money in the stitching room, and Norma Gray, her boss was showing her patterns she had created herself. Roxanne asked if she could bring in some drawings she had done as well. The two had agreed to meet in Norma's office tomorrow to look at them.

Just as Roxanne began to enter Mill Street a voice reached her coming from the railroad bridge that crossed the Kennebec at the foot of Mt Pleasant Avenue. Now changed to a foot bridge that spanned the Kennebec River connecting downtown Skowhegan to the Eastern half of the town, it was a popular crossing. Delbert hollered, "W-w-waait up I- i-i have a sandwich for you."

Roxanne walked to the edge of the bridge and waited. She looked to her left and saw the back of Central Maine Power Company with white water gushing from the turbines used to make electricity.

She could just make out a corner of the junior High school that sat across the street from the power company. She studied the water flowing with gusto sending spring melt from a hundred little rivulets that found their way to this river downstream. An occasional four foot piece of pulp wood that had been hung up over the summer and had found freedom in the spring high water surfaced— temporary freedom. Most of the pulp would make its way to Winslow and be hauled up a conveyer belt and added to the mix that created paper.

Roxanne smiled to herself. She was beginning to have feelings for Delbert. Their relationship hinged on becoming friends first. Roxanne had experienced enough half-truths and outright lies when it came to the opposite sex.

Delbert didn't seem intent on moving the relationship any faster than Roxanne. This was the first girl that had ever listened to a complete sentence from Delbert and the time it took him to utter it— without either chuckling to herself or just walking away.

They followed Roxanne's usual route and managed not to knock into one another on the Swinging Bridge. The squeaking cables protesting all progress.

Delbert realizing Roxanne was not going to be satisfied hearing about John Wayne all the time, had gone to the library. Hell he walked these streets every day, he was going to find out who created them and why. He told Roxanne the history of the swinging Bridge and his words were beginning to come together in bunches. Oh sure he stumbled still, but for the first time he didn't feel like he had to rush his words before he was tuned out. That mindset had helped. Roxanne had helped too. By the time they reached Bridge Street Roxanne knew the span had originally been created for a farmer, to connect his property to the island. Delbert shut up as they walked the hill. He knew a lot about Skowhegan's island now but it seemed there would be plenty of time. When they reached Turner Avenue and Delbert realized he would be taking lunch with Miss Roxanne in her basement apartment he began to whistle— no stutter coming from his lips— *She loves me yah yah.*

Roxanne just smiled.

• MAY WAS FILLED WITH PROMISES

Sheriff McManus stood before his entire force of officers and asked for help. "I have enough evidence to bring in the individual or individuals I believe caused this mess. One piece still missing— someone, actually I believe two someone's— pulled Mr.

Croteau out of that fire. If we can locate those individuals I'm betting they saw one or both of our suspects. That gives us eye witnesses. One of those suspects is currently out of state. Everything we have is too circumstantial to even name names as of yet.

He paused and took a drink from the coffee cup he had inherited from his father. He looked deep into the cup, "My father was a woodsman and something he told me seems to fit most problems I've faced in my lifetime. *If everything seems to be working against you then you're probably approaching it in the wrong way.'*

"So let's go back to our original idea of a fair worker or a visitor who might have lingered at the fair that night. Maybe someone local who had become friendly with a fair worker."

Delbert shifted in his seat, said nothing but his wheels were turning.

"When you men are on patrol today revisit anyone and everyone local who does business with the fair. French fry stand, Hotdog and Hamburger joints, Cotton candy, ice Cream. Detective Fitzmaurice has the complete list he will be handing out with specific people to call on for each of you."

Delbert walked toward lower Water Street, the Redington Memorial home on his left. Delbert always wondered what went on in there. *Beautiful building,* Delbert decided. He walked to Coburn Park on the right and entered. Delbert did some of his best thinking there. It was deserted except for the squirrels scampering about. Two crows seemed to be arguing over something, but left when the law arrived. Delbert found a bench overlooking the mighty Kennebec, the water was beginning to recede. *I walk these streets everyday it should be me who solves this.* Delbert stretched his five foot nine inch frame to its limit, the warming sun energizing him body and mind. *Who do I know, do I know, do I know?*

Delbert's thoughts were interrupted when he spotted a wild flower that had clawed its way to visibility, just daring him to notice. Roxanne came to mind. To Delbert Roxanne was that rare flower that had passed unnoticed to everyone but himself.

Suddenly both his on the job musing and his new found flower, Roxanne, comingled. *Holy shit that's the thing Roxanne has been holding back but wanting to tell me, she knows something about the fire.*

Delbert stood, saluted the brave little wild flower and hurried back to town. Roxanne would be working. Delbert was going to plan and execute a wonderful dinner for Roxanne. He would have the groceries in hand while he waited for her near the end of the railroad bridge. Watching the water pass by under him might just help him plan his lines. He had to find a way to get Roxanne to open up.

❀

Sheriff McManus sat by himself in his office. Though he kept Chief Henry up to speed, he was pretty much handling this thing himself these days. Scoop Plummer was waiting for him in the outer office and the sheriff was not really looking forward to that. *Can't really tell him anything new which certainly makes me look ineffective at best. The election in the fall is starting to enter people's heads. If this is not over by fall I don't stand a chance for re-election. If the Somerset Reporter chooses to endorse that jack ass opponent, it's over Rover.*

"Send him in."

❀

Gregg, Anna, and Sheila sat on the small porch of the bungalow that Gregg was calling home these days. Anna was rocking baby Layla while Sheila's little boy Jeffery played with a little toy logging truck and skidder and several small pieces of wood he was busy maneuvering onto the truck. Sheriff McManus had given the toys to Sheila when he escorted her to her new home. Sheila thought the boy too young to understand the toys but he had surprised her.

Gregg left his chair and sat on the edge of the porch, leaning down to play with Jeffery. The sounds of pretend engine noises muffled the conversation Anna and Sheila were having. "We can't stay here forever, before you know it we'll be starting a new community up here."

Sheila spoke, "The sheriff seems to think this will all be over by the time this year's fair rolls around."

Anna had to chuckle, "What a difference a year can make."

"Welcome to my world, a short time ago I was just a kid, now I'm a kid with a kid and I suppose a price on my head, go figure."

Gregg looked up from his logging operation, "look at it from the positive side, we're here together, the sheriff obviously cares about us, and we're safe. Give him a little more time, I'm beginning to like it here. Room to run, read, and relax." he bent back to his workday.

"So Myron is going to warn Rebecca, right?"

"That's what I told him to do, he's going to tell her I will call her if she wants me to."

❀

I was sitting on the edge of the stage, Rebecca walked past on the floor below. "Lovely lady," I spoke in my broken Japanese accent, "come, join me" I motioned, "outside the tea house."

Rebecca hopped up beside me and I gave her an affectionate hug. "You are going to be a hit as Lotus Blossom, you have that slightly oriental look about you— mysterious eyes."

Rebecca laughed, "And you Sakini will convince us all to welcome these warriors from America as friends I have no doubt."

I laughed at that, "seriously though Rebecca I need to share something with you, something you may not want to hear."

Rebecca looked at me oddly, "Don't tell me the wars not over, Sakini, I already have my new life planned," then she laughed again.

I put a hand on each shoulder. The warmth she radiated without trying made me a little uneasy but a promise is a promise so I forged ahead. "Rebecca the boy you are seeing, Eddie's brother, is involved in the fire from last summer. They both are. Sheila asked me to warn you."

Rebecca began to protest.

"They asked Gregg to take part in destroying several race horse's their father owns. Gregg told Sheila, he had said he was going to refuse. Now he's missing and another man is dead. Sheila has been taken into protective custody, Anna too."

Rebecca sat there stock still, absorbing all this. Then she spoke, without committing herself to acceptance or denial, "I liked it better when you were interpreting for the whole country not me personally, Myron."

She slid off the stage landing lightly three feet below. She looked back once as she walked the incline toward the back of the auditorium.

I sat there thinking, *I obviously need to work on my lines, that didn't seem to go well at all.*

❁

A short walk from the high school, Delbert and Roxanne were busy working on the lasagna and garlic bread dinner Delbert had shopped for. Delbert opened a red wine that had been recommended by a clerk at Sampson's Super Mkt. Delbert was not a wine drinker by nature but this occasion called for more than a Dawson Ale. He was whistling as usual and the tune was clear and recognizable. Roxanne looked back at him from the stove and her recent research suddenly took voice. "How about singing that Beatle's tune to me Delbert."

"I-I-I do-don't sing Roh-Roxanne."

"Maybe you should Delbert, try it— I'll sing along— seriously."

What emerged was a tentative but surprisingly smooth rendition of, *I want to hold your hand.* When they finished Roxanne took Delbert by the hand and led him into her bedroom. She sat him down took both his hands in hers and looked him directly in the eye. "I know everyone in town just sees me as Rox- easy, not Roxanne."

Delbert started to open his mouth, Roxanne schussed him. "They kid among themselves when they think I can't hear them. To this town I'm the last girl in the bar at closing time when any old easy will do." She squeezed his hands, "But Delbert that's not me, I have dreams too. I read, I write, I can draw, I have feelings." She teared up, "So why am I telling you all this?" She gave Delbert a kiss on the forehead. "Because I am you Delbert, wearing a skirt." Delbert's eyes widened. "Everyone in town see's you as good old simple stuttering Delbert, wouldn't hurt a fly— hells bells, couldn't hurt a fly— but that's not you."

She took a book off her dresser, "I've been reading about you Delbert, well not you, but the affliction you were cursed with. That little song we just did that was our first lesson Delbert. We're gonna let this town see a brand new version of what's been a sad old song."

Delbert was thinking, *I have no idea of where this is going but I think John Wayne might just get the girl in the end,* he chuckled.

"Get your head out of those movies Delbert, we have work to do."

Delbert didn't get to ask Roxanne what she knew about the fire he was too busy singing songs and listening to Roxanne explain how she was going to help turn his stutter into stardom. Later, well later, he was just too busy.

❀

• A CABIN ON A LAKE SOMEWHERE IN SPENCER MASSACHUSETTS.

Joe Gambino Sr. was dealing a hand of five card stud to five fishing buddies. A fireplace in the corner sending out bursts of light added loud cracks of sound to the wise cracks that emerged from around the table. "You shoulda seen her mother," the punch line thrown out and a roar of laughter followed. Grizzled grimaces of game-on followed as the men studied their cards. Five fishermen came together three times a year. Hunting season, ice fishing weather, and early in the fishing season. Each was assigned a chair. If they were invited to return for the next adventure they sat in the same chair unless directed otherwise. Over the years new faces emerged. If you didn't occupy a chair that within a reasonable period of time moved you closer to Joe

Gambino Sr. you would find yourself disinvited to the party— so to speak.

Tonight Joe would be choosing one of the men sitting here to carry out an assignment that was of the utmost importance.

Joe Gambino Sr. was a smart man and as a businessman— just like the ivory soap commercial— he kept his private business out of the family business 99&44/100ths% of the time. Those damn horses, though; Nags— he just couldn't help himself. Joe didn't lose well, whether it was business or pleasure. He let his emotions guide his actions last summer and now his boys were involved— and his own bosses were not pleased.

• SO BACK TO THE GAME AT HAND.

Joe made a decision. He was going to be a gracious loser tonight. The last man standing in tonight's poker game would be rewarded with an assignment. Joe had watched this group of fishermen over the last three days and nights. He had a pretty good idea who would be emerging as tonight's winner.

Maine would be flowering nicely by now. Joe's brother who directed the horse racing in New England had kept his ear to the ground over the winter. There were rumblings that this fire mess might reach back to Joe in a bad way. He had already been denied his insurance claim. And the company in a ballsy move had dropped him as a client. Joe was a major player but he too had people to answer to. "Fix it!" He had been told.

The game slowly eliminated contenders even as the fire softened its comments— the fires' roar slowly diminishing along with the flashes of red and blue, yellow and green. The last deal found Joseph Gambino Sr. facing off with a brash thirty-three year old Irishman, Danny Walsh— just a flicker of life left in the stove.

The young man was respectful but fearless. He had moved quickly up the organizational ladder with bold but well thought out actions. He didn't flinch as he read the first three cards dealt. He checked when Joe checked.

As the fourth card was dealt face up Joe found himself with three tens. A very good hand in most circumstances. He let his mind wander to the fishing that had been going on the past few days. *An Irishman casting his lot with four Italians; he chuckled to himself. This had been the first fishing trip for Danny Walsh. Joe had watched the dynamics play out. Testing by the others— teasing, prodding— trying to raise some emotion from the **KID,** as everyone in Joe's group called him. A winter green icy stare was the best they could* elicit. *None of the group quite dared to move to the actual laying on of hands. For some reason it just didn't seem like a good idea.*

Joe Gambino Sr. chuckled to himself again. He checked his three tens.

Danny Walsh went fishing. "I'll bet two-hundred on this pair I'm holding," he offered.

"I'll raise that to five hundred Kid, I think you are playing that child's card game what's it called? Oh yeah, *Go Fish.*"

Danny Walsh didn't bat an eye. He plunked the three hundred in the pot.

The game they were playing has variations, in this version the fifth card was dealt face down. Joe Gambino Sr. couldn't believe his eyes. His triple tens now had a pair of threes serving up what is called a full boat. He remained stoic. The pair of Jacks that Danny had called with, stood as a pair of sentries guarding a six, an ace and a nine.

Joe raised five hundred, Danny never flinched. He raised it three hundred more. Joe studied his cards, he knew he had a winner. He sighed, resigned to what he must do.

"I fold. You got me kid."

Danny looked at him strangely but raked in the pot.

The fire was nearly out and the other men had gone to bed a half hour ago.

"Well let's call it a night shall we, we have an early start tomorrow morning."

"I'm just going to sit here a few more minutes," Danny pointed at his glass, "it would be a shame for Mr. Jameson to give up the night to an ice cube."

Joe toasted him, got up and walked to his room.

Danny sat there in the half-light mulling what had happened. He looked at the table where the folded hand sat, he couldn't help himself he turned over the hand Joe had held. He nodded to his glass, *I have a feeling I'm going to earn that pot in more ways than I can count.* He rose and toasted himself while looking at himself in the mirror over the kitchen sink. He drained the half inch of liquid then rinsed out his glass studying his five day growth; he looked downright sinister. Danny turned out the light on his way down the hall and gazed at the closed door where Joe Gambino Sr. slept. *It will all be made clear in the morning I suppose,* he sighed. In his room he snapped on the little lamp, rubbing his grizzled visage he sat down on the bed. He turned out the light but continued to sit for five minutes or more still thinking, still tasting Mr. Jameson, still trying to guess his assignment. Unstrapping his so called fishing knife he placed it under his pillow. A deep sigh from his lips echoed the air leaving the mattress as his six-foot- three inch body— still fully clothed— completely dissolved and eliminated the bed below him from view.

❁

• ONE LESS THAN ENCHANTED MONTH

The prom was a bust. The band was late getting there and it was a rainy night to boot. As we entered the Gym, (excuse me the night club) the mirrored ball hanging in space was being struck by spotlights sending little flicks of light dancing through the darkened room. The theme, *One Enchanted Evening* was going to need a comb over if it was going to make it to the memory book. I'll give the photographer credit, he was doing his best to keep that frozen smile on our faces after the flashbulb popped by cracking jokes and offering the girls the nicest compliments they would be getting all evening. We were all in a better mood than when we had entered.

Rebecca and I had come together alone. We were just two friends who didn't have a date for the prom. We had gone to Gene's restaurant for dinner.

Rebecca kept her hair short and her dress simple so she didn't have to join the herd in the ladies room trying to re-assemble and re-glue their hair and gowns. While we waited for the band to set up we table hopped. I made note of who was with who. Lots of underclassmen attending their first gala event. I could see the wheels turning, little smirks that indicated they weren't overly impressed with our enchanted evening— everybody is a critic.

It was nine-fifteen before the first song filled the night. The band thought they were being funny I suppose. Rebecca and I did see the humor but it was lost on the crowd. *Rainy Night In Georgia,* was met with a chorus of boos, started by the ladies who had spent big money on their doo that now didn't. Of course their dates hoping to make this a memorable— if not an enchanted— evening, weren't about to argue and joined in the chorus of discontent.

I swear the band had it in for us all night long. The boys wanted waltzes. Hell we had forked out good money for this opportunity. Even the most casual couple would be expected to offer a little more in the affection department tonight. The slow waltzes would be a warm up to this but the damn band kept playing music they liked to play. Jitter bug music and even wilder stuff. It was too noisy to talk in the gym but I did manage to catch Paul in the men's room and found out we would be attending the same after prom party. He and Ethel were there as just friends. Paul still had feelings for Anna and Ethel just wanted to see what the hoopla was all about. When we left which was early, the Beatles top five songs were being played in the order of their stature on billboard. Don't quit your day job guys.

❀

Paul took me aside in the little camp where a classmate Jack Davis was hosting the after prom party. It was still, a rainy night in Georgia, and had turned Maine cold. It seemed even colder when Paul told me he thought he was being followed on his way to school and on his way home. He had seen the same car parked outside Whittemores restaurant as well. Once, he was sure the car had been on his camp road. "Have you told the Sheriff?"

"No, I told my Dad though and he's going to call them if it happens again, probably just a coincidence he says."

"Well I would tell the Sheriff. This whole year has been upside down if you ask me."

"Myron you're my best friend so I am going tell you, I'm scared. If our friends are still in hiding, this thing is far from over and I am a witness."

❀

Danny Walsh had entered Maine one week ago. He met with Joe Gambino Jr. in Bangor and had the lay of the land. Joe's contact in Skowhegan still didn't know where most of the witnesses were, if in fact they were even in the county. One name had surfaced though, a boy who had seen someone making a call from the fairgrounds on that night in question. The boy had been interviewed and supposedly identified a picture. "That can only be me he saw. He might be worth talking to."

"Joe are you sure about this, I'm not up here to just talk to people I'm up here to make sure that fire doesn't re-ignite"

"Well, I'm sure I made a phone call and I'm sure that kid saw me make that phone call. That puts me at the scene. I've tried to get information from my girlfriend down there but she either doesn't know anything or she's not saying."

"This other guy, Gregg Croteau, you told him you planned to kill those horses?"

Joe nodded his head.

"Maybe it's time you left the state too Joe, I have a feeling this is going to get ugly."

"My classes end in a week, so that would be a natural I guess. Should I tell my girlfriend I'm leaving?"

The icy flash that entered Danny's eyes sent a cold shiver that made it all the way to Joe's spine. Joe who thought he was a tough guy had just met the **KID.** He had been told stories— and in that single look— he now believed them.

❈

Sheriff McManus once again sat across the table from Chief Henry, the two lead detectives— Fitzmaurice and Noonan— and the county

Prosecutor Richard Boardman. "I called you all here to assist me in laying out our case against the Gambino boys in the matter of the Fairgrounds murder and fire. We need to convince this gentleman that we have enough evidence to secure a conviction. If I miss anything feel free to chime in."

The case was laid out in a chronological manner beginning with what would be the testimony of Gregg Croteau and Sheila Thompson who would corroborate what Gregg had been offered by Joe Gambino Jr.

Paul Leland's testimony will place one of the suspects on the fairgrounds that night after the fair closed. He can also testify to words he heard that at least appear to be giving the go ahead to start that fire.

After the half hour presentation of pictures, reports from the fire marshal, autopsy results, and what would be critical testimony the Sheriff stood and walked to his desk. He stretched his giant frame widening his arms so they grasped both sides of his desk. It looked to the men still sitting at the table as though he was about to raise the desk and heave it to the heavens.

A half minute passed, no one spoke, and then the Sheriff turned. "This town is waiting, the citizens who know we're trying to solve this mess don't know how to voice their anger and those who think we're incompetent are having a field day."

Prosecutor Boardman spoke, "In my opinion we have enough to charge, I believe to convict we still need one more boot to drop. We need that person or persons who pulled Gregg Croteau to safety. I believe they witnessed the assault and the setting of at least one of the fires."

Detective Fitzmaurice cleared his throat, "We have interviewed anybody and everybody we can find associated with the fair who might have been there and seen something. Nobody has stepped forward with any new information."

County Prosecutor Boardman, stood. "We don't have enough to convict. Those boys will have the best lawyers money can buy. Everything we have is circumstantial. Sitting here we can make it all seem logical, a sparkling clean stream of evidence. At trial that stream— in a defense lawyers hands— will be turned into the Kennebec during mud season. Debris of doubt surfacing in roiling waves of tumultuous testimony." The prosecutor had to chuckle, "Did I just say all that?"

The men all chuckled in response.

Sheriff McManus ended the meeting with a one week deadline and a challenge. You go back and check your notes, and revisit every interview you have conducted. I want the name of an eye witness on this table when we meet one week from today."

Eyes made contact, heads nodded and chairs scraped. Not another word was spoken.

❀

May 21st and 22nd were the scheduled nights for our senior play, *Tea House of the August Moon.* We had been holding afternoon practices for the past week.

In a Sakini aside I will sum up what the play was trying to convey for those of you not familiar with it. World War two is over. Americans are occupying Okinawa and trying to teach the native population all things American. The natives' balk, not ready to give up their culture. The play is a comedy of confusion which allows for humorous misunderstandings. An export product— brandy— is created much to the delight of the villagers who drink as much as they sell. In the end the play promotes compromise and respect for different cultures.

That being said, the boys cast as local citizens were having a ball pretending to get drunk on stage. The audience laughed when they were supposed to and no one forgot any lines. One performance down, one to go.

Thursday afternoon the cast all sat together in the auditorium. Our Director, Mrs. Merrill asked for every one's attention. "After the play tonight I would like to host a cast party at my cottage on the lake. No alcohol obviously, but pizza from Barry's and you will get to see yourself on stage. A friend of mine is filming the play. So if you don't have a better offer, I've written the directions to my cottage on these little cards. You all did a great job last night so let's hold it together for a few more hours. Be here by six- thirty in costume and make-up please. With that we were dismissed.

❄

One of cast members was not in costume or make-up or even in the building at six-thirty. Paul was missing. By the time the play started he had still not arrived. Fortunately he had a minor role as a villager, and who would miss one less drunk? That wasn't like Paul though, and I was concerned. Oh well, the show must go on.

We didn't know until later the Sheriff had arranged his own little costume ball. Anna, Sheila and Gregg, all in disguise, got to enjoy our senior play.

❄

While our little village in Okinawa was commanding center stage Paul was hiding in the woods in his. After leaving the afternoon rehearsal Paul drove towards East Madison. He loved his car and with the windows open he was singing along with the radio to the strains of the Chiffons, *One fine day.* He pulled into his camp road and the dust had him putting his window up. The camp road was lined with hardwood trees wearing the seasons' new finery, the evergreens merely window dressing. His home sat in a little clearing with a lawn that spread out toward the lake. He went around a corner and the sun reached his eyes blinding him momentarily. He lowered the sunshade and his driveway a hundred yards ahead appeared. There was a car he had never seen before parked behind his dads. No one else lived on this fire lane so you had to have a reason to be in here. Suddenly Paul was nervous. In the blink of an eye he pulled into a little cut away designed to let a car pass if two cars should meet on the way in or out. He left his car sitting there and entered the woods. The pine trees that surrounded his home provided cover and quiet. He saw nothing out of place at first glance. He reached the cottage wall and got on his hands and knees. He put his ear just below the window in the living room. He could hear his mother sobbing, begging someone not to hurt them.

Inside, Danny Walsh was promising to do just that if they didn't tell him where their son was in the next two minutes. Paul risked a peek and saw a face obscured with a bandana but sounding menacing. "We don't know where our son is, he hasn't come home from school yet. He hasn't called so I imagine he's on his way. Please don't hurt my wife."

"I am not a patient man, if your son isn't here in five more minutes I will have to find him and I won't be leaving you in any condition to warn him."

"What do you want with him he's just a kid, what's this about?"

Outside Paul made a decision, he couldn't risk his parents getting hurt. He would lure this guy away and let his legs and the knowledge of the woods he had run for years keep him safe.

He stood up, looked straight through the glass and hollered, "You want me, catch me asshole." Then he ran.

Inside, in a flash Danny Walsh cut the telephone wires, issued a warning and slashed the tires on the family car on his way out. He wasn't about to run the woods he would find a place to hide his car and wait for the boy to emerge. No one could recognize him and he had removed his plates when he entered the yard. "You're not out of the woods just yet young man, Danny Walsh leaves no stone to gather moss," he shouted. The last word returned in an echo from the lake.

❖

The Sheriff arrived at Mrs. Merrill's cottage at 10:35pm. He didn't mince words. "Paul Leland is missing, if he contacts any of you, you need to convince him to call the sheriff's office. If he refuses then you need to call me, his life may be in danger. Further if you see a stranger in town that doesn't look like he fits, call me."

The party kind of fizzled after that and when we were all gone Mrs. Merrill looked around the room strewed with boxes of half-eaten pizza. This had certainly been a night to remember and now it would all be for the wrong reason. This class seemed to always find ways to get in the last word.

❀

Danny Walsh watched all the kids leave. He decided to have a word with the teacher. He had arrived back in Skowhegan just in time to catch the last act of the play and he had to admit he had laughed out loud a couple of times. He hung around in the parking lot wondering if the Paul might show up. He had a picture of the boy that had been taken by one of Joe Jr.'s contacts. When the kids all left in a caravan he followed. When the Sheriff's car arrived at the cottage and everyone left a short time later he decided to wait and have a little talk with the host. When the taillights had all disappeared he walked from his hiding place.

He knocked politely. Mrs. Merrill came to the door. Danny Walsh introduced himself as an investigator following up on the Sheriff's visit earlier.

The Sheriff thought maybe you could give us some direction on this. Any of these kids say anything when the Sheriff left. Mrs. Merrill asked him to sit. "Would you like a piece of pizza, there's plenty left?"

"Don't mind if I do."

She brought an RC Cola to the table and opened it. She sat opposite and studied this young investigator. "No one gave me any explanation of what is going on. They all huddled and mumbled and left."

"Wow this is good pizza, is it local?"

Mrs. Merrill a good actress in her own right, didn't even flinch. "No idea, one of the kids ordered it."

"Did this Paul we are trying to find have a best friend that maybe I could appeal to?"

Mrs. Merrill in full performance mode now, offered, "He's new here this year he hasn't really found his niche. I would say he's a loner, from my observation of the boy."

Danny stuffed one more piece of pizza in his mouth, washed it down with his cola and rose to go.

"Well it was worth a try, the Sheriff said see if one of the kids had let down their guard." He smiled tipped his ball cap and left.

Mrs. Merrill closed the door and leaned back against it. She didn't know what was going on but she did know this, any local person—detective or not— would recognize the taste of Barry's Pizza. She immediately tried calling the Sheriff's office, the line was busy. She had known Sheriff McManus since he was a student in her class staying after school for throwing spitballs. She would catch up to him.

❦

Friday morning all the officers were brought in and challenged to find a witness. Call in any favors you have out there— from pimp to parolee, from drunk to degenerate—promise them anything we need help here.

Delbert sat there quietly reviewing who he knew that might know even a little bit. *Got to talk with Roxanne, she knows something I just don't know what.* He left the Sheriff's office walked past the

Strand Theatre where *Donovan's Reef* was playing. John Wayne was starring. Delbert did a double take. *Whoa there little horsey,* his mind was racing, this film was not a war movie or an oater. Maybe he could coax Roxanne into going with him. He waved hey to people on the street, turned right intending to circle the block of businesses that had entrances on two sides. He stopped at Russakoff Jewelers and checked his features in the window glass. He took stock. Average height, all my hair and teeth. Not over weight. Nervous tics disappearing under the tutelage of Miss Roxanne. He smiled then. He looked down and saw a beautiful ring smiling back at him. There was no price listed. *They want me to come in and horse-trade. Well you know, this is the kind of morning where I just might do that.* Delbert entered a jewelry store for the first time in his life.

Delbert finished his rounds whistling and when he was not near any buildings or people he tried out his new singing voice. He did not stutter as the lyrics of

Zippedy-A-Dee-Doo-Dah left his lips and for the life of him he could not imagine a better morning. *My oh my, what a wonderful day.* Any one observing would have seen that Delbert was no longer staggering with stutter but rather sashaying with song— a small square protrusion giving definition to his right pants pocket.

Sheriff McManus sat with his three witnesses and told them in one week or less the ax was going to fall, and warrants would be going out for the arrest of Joseph and Eddie Gambino. "This is going to end one way or another. We can't keep you kids locked away forever." He cleared his throat, "You need to know there are people who have been sent here to keep you from testifying. For the time being a deputy will be posted on the property around the clock. You are not to stray. That means no long runs off the property Gregg."

Gregg looked like he was ready to respond.

The Sheriff held up his hand. "Paul Leeland and his family were targeted. No one was hurt but Paul has disappeared and we can't find him. His parents are in a panic." He let that sink in. "Who is Paul closest to?" Anna spoke up, "I was seeing him but we broke up in the winter. I would say Myron is his best friend—Myron Therrian."

I live on Milburn Street in a house that was built in the late 1800's. My mom and dad are really old. I have a brother and a sister who are ten and twelve years older than me. They both live out of state. I was a mid-life mistake. I pretty much do my own thing which includes feeding and clothing myself. My father spends his days reading the bible and Mom she spends her days watching my father read the bible. This is a big house, the upstairs has four bedrooms. There's no heat up here but there are vent openings in the ceilings downstairs that when open, allow some heat to enter the rooms above. There is a back hall way door and stairway that I use to either enter the kitchen or climb to my room on the second floor. Mom and dad sleep downstairs—I live alone up here.

Not at the moment though, I'm not alone, Paul is hiding in the room next to mine. I'm meeting later with John and Larry at Barry's pizza. Someone is messing with a member of the guardians of the midway. We need to be involved.

Danny Walsh entered Whittemore's and was directed to a booth. The smells of various menu items were wafting from the kitchen. Danny was hungry, it all smelled good.

Rebecca approached with a glass of water and a menu. "Hello, my name is Rebecca, what can I get you on such a beautiful Saturday afternoon?"

Danny looked up, directly into the eyes of Joe

Gambino's girlfriend but had no idea. Rebecca looked directly back into the eyes of the man who was here to hurt her friends— she had no idea.

"You live here in town Miss?"

"I do", a pause then, "Have you decided or would you like me to give you some time?"

"Let's just say a decision has been made," a tight smile accenting that decision. "But for now I'll have that meatloaf sandwich and some fries, and a Pepsi if you have it. All I have been able to find is Coke and RC."

"I think I can find one, though Coke claims that, *things go better with coke,*" she laughed. Rebecca an avid reader of magazines was up on the latest marketing war between the two beverage giants. She raised her hand in mock surrender— Danny was taking all this in smiling.

"On the other Hand sir, Pepsi says their drink is, *for those who think young.* Would that be you sir."?

Danny Walsh laughed out loud.

"How about we do the taste test bring me one of each and an extra glass?"

"Are you trying to buy me a drink sir? Rebecca's eyes twinkled.

"Just offering to maybe expand your horizons, how old are you anyway?" He took a long drink of his water.

"I'm a seasoned senior sir, eighteen soon to be nineteen."

Danny looked shocked. "Holy moley you are mature beyond your years. Maybe we should cancel that extra glass."

"That won't be necessary, I kind of like to experiment myself, new horizons and all that."

Danny was fifteen years older than this girl but she had started a heartbeat he couldn't deny.

Rebecca walked away wondering what had just happened. This guy looked like a huskier young John Kennedy and he had an Irish accent to boot.

When Rebecca got off work at three. Danny Walsh was still sitting in the booth, seemingly lost in thought. She walked over to say goodbye.

Their eyes met once again, this time it was as if miles had been traveled, books shared and life stories swapped.

He simply rose, took her hand and they left the restaurant together.

Police Chief George Henry was at the counter having his usual afternoon coffee. He was a little surprised Rebecca didn't acknowledge him as she left. He studied his coffee. *And who is this guy, never seen him before. Christ this town is changing, I'm getting too old.* He shook his head mumbling to himself.

The waitress at the counter asked the chief if he needed something.

"Hell no, yes, oh I don't know." The chief slid off his stool and left in a huff.

❀

Delbert was at the pinball machine. He was finding a direct correlation between his new verbal and physical control and his declining scores on this damn machine. While the important part of his life was improving daily, the skill and high scores that had his name posted on the wall were diminishing at the same rate. The boys were watching.#TILT#, Delbert had just killed the gatekeeper. Delbert walked to the counter in a smooth manner and ordered a pizza. The boys took over the machine.

Barry nodded to Delbert, "You seem different Delbert— in a good way I might add— what's going on?"

Delbert motioned Barry to the back room.

Delbert took a deep breath, wondering himself what was going to leave his mouth and in what form. Barry had always been kind to him though, so this is a good test. He set his shoulders like Roxanne had showed him. *'Don't slouch and slump Delbert,'* she had said, *'give your words a chance.'*

"Buh-Barry," he started, then the training kicked in, he pretended he was singing the words. "I have a girl now, her name is Roxanne. She's the love of my life."

Barry could hardly believe his ears. Delbert was standing taller and his whole countenance had morphed into a different person. Delbert told Barry he probably wouldn't be in as often, he was going to give up on the pinball machines. He had set his sights on a different goal. He finished with, "If she says yes, will you be my best man?"

Barry had tears in his eyes, "I certainly will Delbert, I certainly will. And I didn't just stutter." They both laughed and Barry gave him a bear hug.

Delbert walked to the pin ball machine to offer the last five pieces of pizza to the boys who were talking loud enough for Delbert to overhear.

He heard the names Gregg Croteau, Paul, Anna, Sheila, and then the boys clammed up.

Delbert cleared his throat re-set his hat, his words came out in exactly the way he imagined they should. "You see that score up there on the wall. If you need any help with this boys just look at that name up there and give me a shout. He looked each boy dead in the eye handed them the pizza, tipped his hat and left.

❁

Roxanne looked to her right, Delbert wasn't standing there on the Railroad Bridge. Ever since she had helped him with his speech and confidence, she had sensed he had something on his mind. *Hope he's not thinking he doesn't need me anymore,* passed through her mind. *Well I've got something he needs to hear too, got to get this off my chest.*

Delbert was waiting on her cellar steps when she got home. She joined him and for the longest time neither spoke just gazed at the maple trees dressed in their newest fashion statement. The gentle breeze moved the leaves seeming to mesmerize them. Finally Delbert spoke, "Roxanne," he started.

Roxanne stood suddenly grabbed Delbert's hand and put it on her heart. "You're in there Delbert, whatever it is you are going to tell me just remember, you're in there."

Delbert studied the hand that now wore the ring he had bought at Russakoff's.

"Actually there are two things I have been wrestling with. Both have to do with one another." He stood then and gazed into Roxanne's eyes.

"One, I would like you to be my wife, and two I need your help with this damn fire case."

Roxanne sighed, first she seemed to deflate as the burden she carried would finally find a resting place, and then she raised herself to her tiptoes and kissed Delbert full on the mouth.

"I can agree to the first part in a heartbeat." She then whispered, "I'm not sure if what I know will help you with the second— but I'm guessing it will."

"Tell me what you know."

A half hour later the concrete steps were making their presence felt to their backsides, and Roxanne had just helped crack this case wide open.

❀

Danny had driven Rebecca to her home and then proceeded to Keyes Motel on West Front Street where he was renting a room. They planned to meet later. Rebecca had mentioned the Drive In Theatre where the psychological thriller, *The Haunting,* was playing. "I love scary movies don't you?"

Danny Walsh had just smiled.

• JUNE IS BUSTING OUT ALL OVER

If this doesn't end soon I'm going to need a bigger place. Sheriff McManus looked out over the room full of people assembled in the little apartment housing Gregg Croteau. Anna, Sheila, and Paul, (who had been located at Myron's house and was now bunking with Gregg.) Roxanne and Delbert sat closely together on the little sofa. Police Chief George Henry stood shoulder to shoulder with the Sheriff.

Detective Fitzmaurice and Detective Noonan anchored a side wall.

The windows were open and the sweet smell of impending summer wafted through the screens. It had rained over-night, a cleansing rain that left little droplets of water clinging to every blade of grass and clover top. Inside, the young people looked just plain tired. Sheila's little boy Jeffery and Anna's infant baby, Layla Ray, seemed to understand the seriousness of the moment and sat quietly in their mother's arms. The morning sun dared to poke a finger of light through the clouds and found a window pane—curious too as to how this was all going to end.

"As we speak, State Troopers in Massachusetts are serving warrants for the arrest and extradition of Joseph Gambino Jr. and Eddie Gambino on charges of Arson, Second Degree Murder, Attempted Murder, Animal Cruelty and Destruction of Property."

Everyone in the room clapped.

"Now this isn't over yet, their family has resources that will fight this tooth and nail. But your help and cooperation has brought us to this day." The Sheriff smiled, "think of it this way, the woods been cut, it's been yarded out, now we just need to get it to market."

"How long is this going to take?" Asked Gregg.

"I spoke with the county attorney who has apprised the Attorney General for the State of Maine of what we're doing here. So we are bringing the big guns to this thing. Honestly, from what he told me it could take six months to a year to be done and through with it."

"So we have to stay here, in hiding, for maybe another year?" asked Anna.

"That's what we're here to discuss. For each of you it's going to be your decision. I'm going to lay out what we can do, what we can't do, and the possible risks involved. Then it's your call."

❈

Friday June twelfth, was our big day. Last day of school for the underclassmen and tonight the graduating class of 1964 would be ushered into the gym in cap and gown. An awards assembly was held at 1:30 pm with letters for sports and academics for both seniors and underclassmen handed out. Mrs. Gray was there, her younger daughter Ethel was receiving an award for highest academic average in the sophomore class and had been selected to the National Honor Society.

Sheila and little Jeffery sat with Norma Gray.

Paul's parents were there to watch their son march in to the sound of, *Pomp and Circumstance.* Mr. Leeland a lover of music especially Instrumental music remembered marching to the same music years ago. He had written an essay on the piece for a college class. As he sat there the baton rising and falling, the senior boys in their black and girls in white walking forward in measured steps he recalled the words that could be interpreted as either a celebration of accomplishment or a march to war. Suddenly his son appeared, marching with Anna Gray at his side. He closed his eyes. *What a year it had been. What had started out on such a positive note was ending with what he now deemed as a battle yet to be fought. Our lives have been threatened, there is a trial to get through and Paul is hopelessly in love with a girl with a child. Pomp and Circumstance— my ass. If we get through today we're leaving the state on an extended vacation.* He opened his eyes just as Paul passed his aisle seat. Mother Leeland was leaning over taking a picture. Paul had a tight little smile on his face but his eyes revealed the stress he had been under in recent weeks.

We had a kinda cool way of entering the gym. Just as we entered the vision of the student body sitting in the bleachers, we formed a line just behind the rear row of parents and friends seated on the gym floor. Then we were announced—kinda like at a wedding. Anyway my name *Myron Therrian, marching with Rebecca Tully* left the loudspeaker and we stepped forward. I had my own thoughts about what this day was all about and though it was way too early to put perspective to it I knew, we the class of 1964 had been part of our nation's history that would forever be revisited.

Rebecca's dad was actually sitting there and she waved. Another man was sitting with Mr. Tully but I didn't know him. He waved at Rebecca and she gave him a big smile and a head nod that indicated that she knew him and appreciated his being there. *Maybe he's an uncle*, I thought.

I saw the Sheriff and the Police Chief sitting With Jerome Barry. Jerome had donated pizza for our after graduation party tonight. He nodded. I nodded.

✿

Paul disappeared with his parents shortly after we graduated. Gregg came to live in the room Paul had stayed in. We were doing regular runs of five miles in the evenings. My parents were oblivious to it all.

They hadn't even figured out that Paul had been upstairs for a month and now Gregg had taken his place. That bible sure must hold good reading. Anna and Sheila were back in the Gray household. I was still seeing Sheila though we both knew I would be leaving in the fall, so we were taking it slow. Gregg seemed interested in getting to know Rebecca better but she had been strangely absent from the social scene.

This very Saturday morning, Gregg and I went in to Whittemores and sat in her section. Rebecca her usual sunny self, approached in her kidding way. "Well guys do I need to sell the menu specials or do you know what a couple of runners need for nutrition."

"We are both seasoned coffee drinkers now, so let's start with that."

"Gregg how are you? It's good to see you again." Gregg nodded, "you too Rebecca are you going to school in the fall?"

"I thought I was, but I might just wait a year. I could save enough for my first two years and hope for scholarship money after that. What are your plans?" She saw her boss beckoning her.

"Hold that thought. Let me get your coffee and check on my other customers, I'll be right back."

We watched her work her magic, offering a reason for a smile to appear at every table, she refilled a cup or put a hand on a shoulder.

She sighed as she poured our coffee, placing little creamers in the center of the table. "It's been quite a year for all of us. So Gregg as I was asking, any plans?"

"I will have a diploma by fall. After that who knows? Maybe a year in the shoe shop, I have learned to be a hand-sewer and can make good money." His face fell as he added, I've got a trial to get through too, not looking forward to that."

There was nothing left to add to that so Rebecca took their order and went about her business.

"Why don't you ask her out Gregg, we can double date."

"Maybe a little later in the summer, let's make this our watering hole, take it slow, see if we connect."

❀

The legal process was doing its thing and both Joe Gambino Jr. and younger brother Eddie were out on bond but as of yet had not crossed the Kittery Bridge. Their father's lawyers had managed for all the proceedings to be done without the boys being brought back to Maine

This morning they sat with their father and one of a team of lawyers who would defend them, at a table in a restaurant in Worcester, Massachusetts.

"The more ties these two have to Massachusetts the better. When they go in front of a grand Jury we want these two good looking all American Catholic boys to be actively engaged in their education."

Mr. Gambino took a sip of his coffee, "So this morning you both will be signed up for summer classes at Holy Cross and fully enrolled for the fall."

The boys began to protest.

"The oldest catholic college in New England, and you will stay in a dorm, no more apartment living for you two."

The boys once more wanted to argue.

"It's safe to say it's either a dorm room or a cell, wouldn't you agree Winston?"

"We are doing everything we can do to keep you from having to go back to Maine. If however you do go to trial everything you do from this moment on will have an impact, either positive or negative."

"What's Danny doing for us up there?"

"Never you-mind what anybody else is doing, you just mind your p's and q's down here." He paused, "But I will say, Danny is on top of the situation and has embedded himself in a way that will keep us apprised and ready if we do have to act."

Joe wanted more, "Dad can I at least be in touch with a girl I met up there, I really liked her."

Joe Gambino Sr. didn't feel it would be prudent to tell his son that Danny Walsh was minding that particular store now. "No contact understand? End of story."

❁

Danny Walsh had left Kyes Motel and was now renting a two room apartment over Carpenter's insurance Agency. He had reinvented himself as an aspiring writer complete with beard, gathering material for a book he planned to write. Rebecca had asked him why he was in town and it had been the first thought to cross his mind. Now with the new orders from Joe Gambino Sr. to watch and wait that first thought provided the perfect cover.

"So all those people in cars going by and these businesses down there are all possible characters and scenes for your story?"

"Rebecca, this is going to be a small town murder mystery I'm writing so I won't know how it's going to unfold until I get a feel for the town and the people. Want to help?"

"How can I help?"

"You be my tour guide, show me the town, give me some background, point out some oddball characters, I'll interview your friends and neighbors."

"Have you written a book before?"

"Nope, first one, I've written a bunch of articles though, how hard can it be?"

"So help me out here, first book, and you choose Skowhegan, why is that?"

"Honestly, your little fire last year made all the papers out of state. I was a cub reporter for a twice weekly paper in Delaware. We have quite a horse racing industry down there and the story of race horses dying in a fire struck a chord with me. My father owns the paper actually, and I sold him on the idea of me writing a book. I think he was glad to get rid of me." Danny laughed out loud. "He said I questioned everything he did— go ask somebody else questions, you're really good at that."

"So what have you written up to now, for this book I mean?"

I'm still gathering material. I have all the articles from the Waterville Sentinel, the Bangor Daily, and the Somerset Reporter— now I need interviews with local people. How were they affected, their emotions, their suspicions. Then I create my characters. Then, the who, the what, the why, the when."

"I'm impressed, I've never met a writer—so what's my first assignment?"

"Your first assignment is to give me the credibility I need to ask questions. People aren't going to talk to me unless they trust me. You can help create that."

Rebecca nodded, that made sense.

"So I'm an uncle on your mother's side. You told me she was originally from another state anyway, right? I'm her youngest brother, moved here to be closer." He smiled, "Let's face it, I'm too old to be your boyfriend." He let that sink in. "Know when I realized that?"

Rebecca, who was confused about what she felt for Danny had wondered what he was feeling.

"It was that damn horror movie at the Drive-In Rebecca, you bought into the story and was scared at all the right places," He laughed loudly. "Me, I was just bored as hell, too old, and the popcorn had way to much salt. I knew right then." He laughed once more.

Rebecca laughed too. She looked at Danny, "So an uncle you'll be and it's kind of cool to have a male friend who isn't trying to use me for his own personal satisfaction, not used to that."

❊

All the Sheriff could do was wait. He took a two week vacation and rented a little cottage on Embden Pond. His wife Laura joined him for the second week. The first week had been all about the fishing and late night poker games with Jerome Barry, Doc Berry a local dentist, and Fire Chief Russell Clement. Police Chief George Henry who had come to like the Sheriff had even spent one night.

Laura spent her first morning sweeping out the remnants of last weeks' visitors. All the windows were open and a breeze sweeping down the mountains from the west moved across the always frigid waters of Embden Pond—the cool air a sharp contrast to the already blinding sun peeking in those same windows. Both seemed to be competing for Laura's attention.

Sheriff McManus had no problem declaring the winner as he suddenly shivered at the kitchen table. "Close at least one of those damn windows will you, Laura, you're killing me here."

Laura who was well warmed from pushing a broom, cut her man no slack when it wasn't official business they were discussing. "You won't freeze honey, you have a weeks' worth of alcohol protecting your pores."

Sheriff Mac took a sip of his coffee and gave her the look.

Laura closed the window, not all the way though— last word and all that.

Sheriff Mac noticed that last word. *Oh it should be such a fun week matching wits with this woman.*

• WHILE THE CATS AWAY

Rebecca introduced Danny to Myron and Gregg one morning at Whittemore's Restaurant.

"So you worked at the fair parking cars and generally kept an eye on things in the evening, Myron. Would you be willing to jot down what you remember from last summer? This is going to be fictional but accurate as well. Details that help the reader imagine being there will make for a richer story." Danny turned his head.

And you Gregg, Rebecca tells me you were actually injured, would you be able to tell your story?

Gregg wasn't sure Rebecca should be sharing anything about this, he paused. "I don't really remember much. I was there, I got hurt, now I'm here." He dove into his eggs and home-fries.

Danny spoke, "they say lack of memory sometimes is the brains way of protecting a person from an ugly truth." He paused. "Nothing wrong with that Gregg, might even be a good idea, who knows?"

Rebecca, thought that last comment odd, but Gregg didn't react so she let it go.

"Are you going to use the name of the town and peoples' real names?" I asked.

"Nah, different names, different location, just real facts or as close to real facts as I can get."

When Danny was left sitting there at the table alone, nursing a final cup of coffee he realized he had created exactly what Joe Gambino Sr. requested— the eyes and ears of what would be needed if his boys were brought back to this town for trial. He toasted himself. Rebecca watching him as she served another table wondered to herself what that was all about.

❦

Delbert and Roxanne sat across the table from one another in Roxanne's basement apartment. Delbert was just finishing up two pancakes that he had slathered in syrup.

"You don't even give those guy's a chance to tread water Delbert, you drown them immediately," Roxanne kidded.

Delbert smiled. "So I've bah-been thinking, Lets move in together." He kind of cringed waiting for a shoot down. When

Roxanne simply set her cup down and looked directly at him he raised up and continued. *The visual of creeping out on the ice to check whether you should be there this early in the season crossed Delbert's mind, but he took another step,* "We could save a lot of money." Still nothing, *the ice wasn't cracking at least.* "Let's rent a little place downtown. I was even thinking of getting my license and a car." *No way back from out here, tread lightly.*

Finally Roxanne spoke, "Wow you have been thinking. Why do we need a car?"

Delbert chuckled, *ready to pull that little ice fishing shack right out to the middle.* "So that's a yes to the first three questions?" Roxanne smirked. Delbert sitting a little taller now, *the fish were biting,* "Since I was thinking of maybe a honeymoon on the coast, that would be a long walk don't'cha know?"

"And when were you thinking all this might happen?"

"This fall, when the leaves begin turning and the summer tourists have gone. I was reading an article about Camden, in *Down East* Magazine. Sure looks like a beautiful place."

"What about this trial, that might, maybe, probably won't happen— when is that scheduled for?"

"November is what I'm hearing. Just a waiting game for us. We have our witnesses. The other side is just trying to delay."

"You know Delbert, what I saw, what I'm going to be testifying to. I'm a little worried that someone might leak what Sheriff McManus is calling his absolute most important key witness— me."

"That's why you have me Roxanne, to keep you safe."

Roxanne studied her protector. Delbert had indeed grown almost before her eyes into a confident and capable lawman. She walked to the sink and looked up at the tree trunks that offered her only view from down here. "Yeah let's get a room with a view of the sky, shall we Delbert?"

❦

The remainder of the summer was pretty calm.

People working, taking their summer vacations. Kids enjoying their summer break. The date for the trial had been announced. November 9th in County

Superior Court in Skowhegan, the murder arson trial of Joseph Jr. and Eddie Gambino would commence. There was a brief buzz in town about that. A one day revisit of the painful memories, then like a summer wind that kicks up a mini dust storm everything settled back down.

❦

This year's version of the fair will be taking place in two weeks. The Fair has a special theme this year. The flyers, bulletins, and media both written and radio have billed it, *From The Ashes*. Several of the buildings that have been replaced will be showcasing the latest features and equipment. All the buildings have a fresh coat of paint. The new Grand stands have easier access for the handicapped and a state of the art sound system won't change how often you rip up a race ticket in despair— but you will be able to follow your failure in stereo.

How can I say this in a way that will help you understand just how oblivious we were in this little town— the only word that I can come up with is, <u>lulled</u>.

Webster defines the word lull as—to put to sleep or rest; to soothe or quiet; to give a false sense of security; cause to be less alert, aware or watchful.

I blame the damn weather for part of it. Every day that summer was delicious. We breathed it in, held it in our lungs for hours at a time. Swallowing, then digesting the sweet smells of summer, the smiles on our friends and neighbors faces as endless blue skies and star filled evenings. The summer formed a pattern— we just held it in— breathing out only after we finally closed our eyes on the day. We would wake in the morning to find that a gentle rain had arrived overnight washing the palette clean of all but green and blue—another do over day.

❀

Norma Gray was charged once again to create the flower garden under part of the new grandstand. This year she had help in the form of daughter Anna and new friend Roxanne. The new Grandstand was larger and the space beneath offered even more of a show case for the flowers. Sheila, who was still living with the family was caring for her son Jeffery and Anna's little girl Layla.

Anna had been re-hired at the drapery factory for at least the summer and perhaps beyond. She couldn't bring herself to return to the Sheriff's office.

The garden club met monthly from February on, discussing ways they could beautify the town during the spring summer and fall.

They invited town officials in to plan where their efforts could be placed. Over the early spring when they weren't plowing or sanding roads when a late storm landed, or filling a pot hole, the town crew had been busy building wooden tubs that were now filled with blooming bouquets of flowers. Placed at every intersection that yielded a stop sign it would appear the eight-sided protrusion was simply a taller flower emerging from the mass of color below. The message, **Stop! Smell the flowers.**

Roxanne had been invited by Norma to attend the first garden club meeting of the year. She was as nervous as Norma had been, thinking and worrying rejection and ridicule. Norma remembering her own trepidation decided to let Roxanne's creativity speak for itself. She introduced her by showing some of the wonderful patterns Roxanne had created. After seeing the beautiful and creative ways Roxanne saw the natural world she was asked how she envisioned what the organization should be doing. Roxanne took the pedestrian approach—quite literally. "I don't have a license to drive. Everywhere I go in this town is on foot. I see the work you have done in Coburn Park. It's beautiful. At the fair the flower garden is beautiful. Little pockets of color. Please don't take this as a criticism but what I don't see is color for the everyday person."

Eyebrows rose, body language became uncomfortable.

Roxanne, not used to speaking to a group— but a pro at reading impending hostility, shut her mouth.

Norma came to the rescue. She cleared her throat, stood and distributed copies of the vision Roxanne had presented to her. Beauty cannot be denied and as each club member in turn received their copy and saw the town as Roxanne did, the hard lines of winter freeze on their faces melted, till collectively they softened their countenance. Roxanne's vision was now on full display on nearly every corner in town.

And so it was that in the summer of 1964, window boxes appeared just under the windows of down town merchants. The before mentioned tubs of flowers at every stop sign in city limits, from Main Street to Madison Avenue. Every intersection of every side street sported color. The bridges had pots of color hanging from their railings. Roxanne had stood then and said simply, "This is the Skowhegan I know, this is where the people live."

❁

Danny Walsh became a fixture in town as well. The only person who had seen his face in his natural role had been the English teacher. Thankfully— for her sake— she summered at a cottage on the lake in East Madison. She had never followed up that call. This morning Danny was interviewing the Sheriff for his book. He sat in the outer office and leafed through a copy of the town report. Very dry reading he thought till he got to a report on the cost to the town from the fire the summer before. The damage went beyond buildings, to plumbing and electrical damage, to fencing and clean up, to police costs of protecting the fire scene from vandals and possible evidence contamination. It seemed nearly every report, from assessors, to the Women's garden club indicated loss from the raging inferno.

Danny sat there thinking, *what a stupid idea all that was and what a mess. And I'm supposed to bury the ashes.*

Danny stood as Sheriff McManus entered the room and signaled him to come on in. *He's a bruiser,* his first thought on seeing the Sheriff up close and personal. When he observed and read the warning signs posted in the Sheriff's office he realized this man was not your typical county hick-hack.

❁

The fair came and went. The people came and went.

The new buildings and extra effort that had gone into re-introducing the annual Skowhegan State Fair was deemed a success. It seemed the very air breathed peace and tranquility in the little town.

Below the surface however— like a fissure in the earth's crust— problems were puddling, gases were gurgling. Nothing you could put your finger on but like that first twinge of a muscle pull— an ache— had the populace stretching their torsos, cricking their necks.

For the town the ache was loss of another major manufacturer. One of the Industries that employed over a hundred citizens was closing its doors after Labor Day. Obviously for the hundred citizens dealing with this, it was very personal. Shock, blame, complaint all hit the airways— competing with those constant pleasant days that seemed a little tiresome suddenly.

Unconsciously people were seeking a new pattern. Some ugly thunder and lightning storms that matched their own mood were called for. Let the storm drains run full, let the streets flood a little, let the world feel their pain, cry their tears. A diversion that allowed for a venting of anger. Point that coffee cup to the gods on high— swear a little.

The industry affected was Skowhegan Drapery. Norma who had been promoted within the last year sat at the kitchen table wondering what she would do now. Her own cup of anger had re-filled three times and witnessed the dead dark of three am slowly soften allowing the bleak light of a constant drizzle to shape the morning. She looked out the window, *finally some damn rain, bring it on.*

Anna wandered down with little Layla in her arms. Sleep walking, Norma called it. Mechanical mothering, her hair looking like it got caught in a haybailer. Even her attempt at a good morning was a muffled malapropism that left Norma chuckling to herself.

"What are you laughing at Mom? I know my hairs a mess but Layla is hungry."

"Hand me that child and go back up and fix yourself, you look a fright." She smiled, "Good morning daughter we need to talk. I have some ideas I want to run by you. Roxanne is coming over this morning and the three of us might just start a little business, interested?" she hugged Layla, "sorry little Layla I meant the four of us."

❀

• AN EARLY AUTUMN

Scoop Plummer got the scoop. He hung around the court house, trading witty barbs with attorneys in the hallways during what were now the dog days of summer. Thankfully— at least in his mind— the rain had stopped but a week of humidity had everyone's tongue dragging. He was the only media guy present when a black car pulled up outside the Superior Courthouse. Four nattily dressed men emerged and when they entered the courthouse they were greeted not only by the county attorney but also Maine's Attorney General.

What the hell is this? Scoop licked the end of his pencil and slipped in a side door. Scoop had contacts that ran the gamut— from Janitors to Judges.

Three hours later he had this weeks' headline.

He would offer a morsel to the Sentinel— with his name attached of course. The Bangor Daily would get just enough to raise interest. Both papers would have to concede in print that the Somerset Reporter, the weekly paper for the county, would be devoting a full page to the story. Scoop could imagine the headline and the beginning sentences of the article.

• MURDER, ARSON, TRIAL MOVED UP TO OCTOBER.

Scoop Plummer, out scooped the daily newspapers in digging into why the most anticipated trial in recent memory is being re-scheduled to October, a full month earlier than the November date set in the spring.

When the full article was published and available, the paper had to run an extra printing to satisfy the county populace.

Scoop seemed to be two inches taller as he entered the Sheriff's office.

He sat in front of Sheriff McManus with the ever present tablet on his lap and the wet end of a pencil in his hand.

"So Sheriff, all the ducks in a row here? Does this change anything from your end?"

"Scoop you just finished making headlines, you looking for a Pulitzer in journalism or what? Sheriff McManus pointed to his ever-present sign. "Don't get picked up for carrying over the road limit, Scoop," he kidded.

"What can you tell me?"

"I can tell you it's all out of my hands now. This department along with Chief Henry and his officers have collected what we believe is enough evidence to convict. The rest is up to the county prosecutor. Not that I'm trying to put pressure on him, but that's the reality. It's his woods operation now."

"I never seem to get much worth printing from you Sheriff, how about something?"

Sheriff McManus sat back, thought to himself then decided. "As you know there has been public support for me to run again for this office. I have even agreed to have my name placed on the ballot but I have said repeatedly and publicly I'm still not positive

I will serve a full term if elected." The Sheriff rose ushered Scoop to the door as if dismissing him empty handed once again. Just as Scoop turned to beg for a morsel, the Sheriff smiled, "Here's your scoop, Scoop. Sheriff Arthur McManus revealed to you today he will in fact complete a full term in office if re-elected." The door closed on that topic.

❀

Most of the rest of this story took place with me out of town. I started my college career at a small college in North Carolina. But even as I crossed the Island Bridge headed out of town my thoughts were of my friends and the town I love. We had gathered one last time over the weekend at what had been the two most important social places in our young lives— Barry's Pizza and Ma Beane's. We kidded one another and made promises we would not keep. At Barry's it was one more pin-ball challenge fueled by pepperoni pizza. Barry wished us well and two hours later we were on the other side of town gathered around the Jukebox sitting on picnic tables listening to the latest Beatle's song. Here smells of hot dogs, hamburgers, french-fries and fried clams fought over air space. Even the thoughts of goodbyes and good luck seemed muted as some of our group had bigger worries.

Paul who was also going to be running for a college out of state would have to return to testify. He had called me and wasn't excited about that. Anna would have to divulge the ugly details of that night at the Drive-In. Gregg and Sheila would have to swear that they had heard of the plan. We all wondered aloud about a witness that the general public was just becoming aware of— this mystery witness the only eye witness— the prosecutions' star witness— who would guarantee a guilty verdict. We group hugged and suddenly we were all going our separate ways. As the wheels on the bus went round and round, round and round I was mentally trying to figure out who that witness could be.

❀

Danny Walsh was summoned back to Massachusetts. He sat in a small coffee shop in a small suburb of Worcester, Mass. Joe Gambino Sr. and both his sons filled the other three chairs. Inside, smells of pastries filled the small room. Coffee aromas tried but the pastries were the clear winner. Danny realized he really was using his five senses in a very overt way to spark his writing. Small talk was taking place as the waitress took the breakfast orders which allowed Danny to reflect on the trip down. *He had noticed on his drive along Route Two out of Maine the leaves changing color. The wood smoke silently becoming part of the landscape. He had his windows open and at times smelled apples. He saw several deer at the edge of a wood. Geese flying in formation. When did this all happen? Danny was beginning to think maybe he could be a writer, could set scene to word.*

The coffee aroma, still fighting to be top dog, circled the small café and landed smack in the middle of their table. Four steaming cups raised in unison, saluted the reunion of father and sons. Danny's cup joined in the toast.

After ordering breakfast Joe Sr. began, "I know you might have heard some of what I'm going to say but let me put all this into some kind of chronology. So bear with me here." He studied Danny briefly, "You ok Danny, you look distracted."

"I'm fine, long trip and all that, sorry."

Joe Sr. closed his eyes briefly as if reviewing the script typed into his brain. "For over a year now the smoldering sparks and smoke of that fire has hung over our family. We have tried to clear the air in a number of ways, through the legal system and also using other methods." He looked directly at Danny Walsh. "None of that has worked. You boys are scheduled to go on trial in that backward little town next month."

Eddie started to interrupt.

Joe Sr. simply ignored him and continued, "They have only one eye witness. We still don't know who that is." He looked again to Danny to explain.

Danny took a quick sip, swallowed the black flavorful bitterness and sat up straight. "I have settled into that town and set myself up as an author looking to write a story about the fire. People have begun to trust me and even step forward hoping they have something to add to the dialogue. Every bit of gossip that has seeped from the sewers over the last twenty years has reached my ears. I know who was sleeping with who on the night of the fire. I know who wanted to be sleeping with who, and I know what the testimony will be from every witness on their list— except one."

Danny scraped his chair back, "Mr. Gambino I need to use the men's room but when I come back I have some further news that could affect one of your sons, that doesn't directly involve the fairgrounds."

While Danny was in the men's room Joe Sr. looked at each of his boys in turn, shaking his head like he was offering up a silent meany-meany-miny-mo and sighing deeply.

The boys threw up their hands in innocence.

Danny returned and signaled the waitress over for a refill. When she had left the table, Danny repeated his coffee ritual. The cup hit the table a little more harshly than intended but it got their attention.

Danny didn't sugar coat what followed, it was served up black bitter and brutal. "Eddie you are being accused of rape. You are also the recent father of a little girl named Layla, both results from the same act."

Eddie jumped up, "What the hell are you saying, I didn't rape anyone? Dad this is total bull-shit."

Joe Sr. looked at his son and told him to sit down and quiet down, just listen.

"The facts as I have heard them involve a night at the Drive-In after a party at your camp. You drove a girl who had been drinking heavily back to town. You took her to the Drive-In theatre which had emptied earlier, parked near the woods and raped her. This girl was seventeen at the time so in the eyes of the law— in Maine anyway— that is statutory rape. By the way, all the tests they conduct to determine paternity, match. That's what you have to look forward to if you go back to Maine."

Danny took an extra-long pull of coffee.

Joe Sr. lit a cigarette and took an extra-long drag.

"This changes everything, neither of you boys is going back to that one-horse town. I have contacts out of the country."

Joe Jr. spoke up, who told you all this anyway it still sounds like crap to me?"

"I developed a source who you might recognize Joe. She swore me to secrecy until the trial. So you are all the first to know. Remember Rebecca, Joe she speaks highly of you— but your brother Eddie here— not so much."

Joe Jr. got all red in the face, "are you messing with my girl Danny, I'll kick your ass?"

Danny just smiled, "Out of respect for you Mr. Gambino I'll let that pass. See Joe, you and your brother are both like raw nerves, that's why you're in this mess to begin with. You are right Mr. Gambino these boys should not go back to Maine under any circumstances."

"So will the trial go on without them? Can they do that?"

"I have no idea, I would suggest you talk to your lawyers, they would know a lot more than we do."

❀

In fact the Gambino lawyers even without knowing what Eddie was going to be accused of had planned a strategy of absentia that would keep the trial from going forward. They studied the Maine law. They had continually made excuses why the accused could not be in Maine for any pre- trial motions. Then they successfully got the trial date moved up. The prosecution agreed immediately, eager to have a victory under their belt before Election Day. The boys would be deposed the day before the trial began— once more all agreed.

In the end politics trumped the legal process. The Maine State District Attorney, in a tough campaign for re-election high fived his staff on this political wind-fall.

❀

They didn't go back and read the fine print of the law. Always read the fine print. The accurate reading of the law and the result was this: if in fact the men did not show up for trial, the trial could not go on. Warrants could be issued and if and when the men were found they could be extradited and returned. Then a trial could be held. *Quite the process. Quite the mess.*

Simply stated the law in 1964 did not allow a defendant to be tried in absence unless the absence was considered voluntary. The voluntary part meant the defendant had stood before the court when the date for the trial was announced. Then if the defendant didn't show up for the trial their absence was considered voluntary. The boys (through their counsel) had signed off on the original date. Since the new trial date constituted a need for the boys to be there or agree to it once again, and they hadn't been returned for that hearing or signed off, the trial could not go on in their absence.

Leaves were gathered on the lawns and sides of the streets. Crisp brown and auburn reminders of summer past. Raked, jumped in, and eventually burned or collected by the town. For Roxanne who had learned to live in the moment with never a future guarantee, it was simply a beautiful day to get through. She watched children taking turns leaping into a pile on a lawn on Bridge Street. The screams of delight making her smile. She had a lot to smile about these days. The sun warmed her face and she paused on the swinging bridge on her way to meet with the Sheriff and who knows who else. She had not attended what was supposed to be the first day of the trial. Roxanne was to be the last witness called, on the final day of the State's case. She looked around, still a little wary of the unknown that had framed this drama from the beginning. The Sheriff didn't explain why he needed to talk with her but Delbert had come home last night with what he was hearing on the street. Roxanne wasn't a bit surprised at what Delbert told her. Nothing ever surprised Roxanne.

She was unemployed and she wasn't surprised. The reason for the factory closing was coming to light. A cheaper source of labor out of the country was becoming more and more attractive to owners, and she wasn't surprised. Within a decade the Shoe Industry would suffer a mortal blow as well. Roxanne's entire adult life—right up till she discovered Delbert that is— she wasn't surprised by anything or anyone who crossed her path. Someone was always seeking instant gratification and it seemed Industry owners were donning that mantle as well.

She passed the fire station and returned a greeting with a wave of her hand. She looked down at the mighty Kennebec from the bridge that was anchored south of Stern's department store on the left.

Roxanne nodded to the mannequins just beyond the glass, dressed in long coats, scarves and mittens. One good looking male sporting a tweed overcoat and fedora seemed to wink as she passed. Roxanne smiled. *Guess you have competition Delbert, better mind your p's and q's.* She looked in the darkened window of Barry's Pizza struggling to read the plaque on the wall that still honored Delbert's high score. She had lots of things running through her head this morning, some of it exciting. Norma had contacted her with an idea and the folder she carried tucked under her arm was for a meeting with her following her trip to the sheriff's office.

Sheriff McManus ushered Roxanne into his office.

He offered coffee but Roxanne was coffee'd out. Sheriff McManus not one to enter the woods without a plan got right to the nub of it.

"This trial is not going to happen any time soon. The powers that be have dropped the ball. What that means for my witnesses is a state of limbo is in effect. As for you, Roxanne we had stalled on releasing your name to the defense lawyers. Thinking the trial was to start this week we were about to put you into witness protection. The defense has your name now."

Roxanne wasn't sure what all this meant. The quizzical look she offered prompted the Sheriff to continue.

"You are our key witness, you actually saw Eddie Gambino at the fire scene. I don't think the Gambino family really thought we had an eye witness."

"Ok, I understand that but you are saying the trial isn't going to happen anyway, so what's the big deal?"

Sheriff McManus set his face like he was approaching a windblown widow-maker snarled in a bunch of other trees. "This is what I believe is going to happen. Joe Gambino Jr. and younger brother Eddie are going to leave the Country for a while. I also believe now that your name is known to them, that you are in danger. If the only eye witness is eliminated, this trial will never happen even if they can be found and brought back here."

"Well I'm not going to go into hiding Sheriff, I can tell you that."

"I know Roxanne, and I'm sorry. All I can do is warn you to be careful. If you need us we'll try to be there. This whole thing sucks a box full of donuts."

Roxanne rose, "You know, Delbert is a lot more capable than you give him credit for." With that said she left the office.

❀

Danny Walsh was still in Massachusetts. A different town a similar café. Only two chairs pulled up to the table this morning. Joe Gambino senior sat across the small table with menu in hand. "I think a gourmet breakfast is in order don't you Danny, for once those damn lawyers got it right." He raised his cup.

Danny sat quietly. He knew he was not asked to breakfast to toast the end of anything.

"The boys are safely out of the Country, already complaining about the heat and mosquitoes. I think about six months of penance should suffice— call it a short term sentence for stupidity."

Danny smiled tightly.

"Two things Danny. The boys can't come back until that eyewitness is eliminated—that's number one."

He paused for effect, "Number two, I would really like to get to know my new Granddaughter."

Danny raised his eyes at this. "So I understand how to solve the first thing, but the second?"

The kid has two parents. One on the scene, the other living it up in the Caribbean. What if we reverse that picture? Eddie might have to pay a small price for his actions. My lawyers don't think it would go beyond probation actually. We never had a girl, the wife, she thinks we should be responsible Grand Parents." He shrugged. "So we're going to send a representative up there, talk with the girl, help her understand how much we could do for her daughter's future; play nice. If that doesn't work you have two jobs to do— capiche?"

Danny nodded to his cup, "I'm heading back up there today, need to be there in my research mode for the book I'm supposed to be writing."

"Well eat a good breakfast first, I'm celebrating this morning."

• SEASON ENDING INJURIES

• OCTOBER 20, 1964

• WAKE COUNTY NORTH CAROLINA

Sheila had called me the night before all upset and nervous. She told me the trial was postponed late last week and now was maybe never going to happen unless the Gambino brothers could be found. She said Gregg is leaving just as soon as he can pack his bags. She went on and on which was not like the tough minded Sheila I had come to know and love.

I tried to calm her down by asking about Jeffery.

"He's fine, just an innocent little boy," Sheila calmed as the talk turned to Jeffery discovering a pile of leaves that had him laughing out loud as he dove and hid and re-emerged shouting **boo** Mama, over and over.

From nine hundred miles away I managed to calm Sheila's fears. "I'm sure this is all over, Sheila and the bad guys won. They aren't stupid enough to come back to Skowhegan Maine, there is no reason to now. I miss you."

"I miss you too, Myron, I'm sorry, I just wanted this over and probably you're right but it all seems like a permanent dark cloud has settled over the whole town. Mrs. Gray's company closed, Gregg's leaving." Sheila paused, she suddenly realized that part of her funk was that she really cared for me and I was a long way from home. "Some good news, Ethel has been named Captain of the Soccer team and I'm starting on the varsity as well. I wasn't sure about going back to school but it's working out. How about your season?"

"We actually have a big meet tomorrow for the conference championship. I'm running as third man and my times are getting better and better so who knows?"

"Well I'll let you get to your studies, I have to get Jeffery to bed then do my own homework. I'm sorry for laying all that crap on you Myron, run with the wind tomorrow," she paused as if she wanted to say something else, the line was open I could almost feel the unspoken words then she hung up.

❁

I was into the second mile climbing a long straight uphill when I spotted the uniform color of our number one runner. This ascent had a seven percent pitch to it and every one was gearing down for the grind. He was near the front of a long line of runners maybe twenty, strung out like power poles, I decided if I was going to finish in the top ten I needed to make my move now. I found a determined grinder gear and set my game face. As I passed what my mind pictured as stationary telephone poles my stride became effortless. In the length of that half mile climb I passed all but the top five runners. I looked at my team mate and he glanced back and winked. My lungs dragged in great mouthfuls of air when for a brief instant the trail leveled off. After cresting the hill an even steeper descent had us running with our heads down through a stretch of woods. Tight little s turns with heavy woods on both sides sprouted roots barely visible but each a little mine that if struck would end your day in a heartbeat. I had never run this fast before. I removed myself from the effort and allowed my body to soar. Coming out of the woods I was a hundred yards behind the leader, I had passed my teammate. Three quarters of a mile to go. Two runners separated us and I bore down like a fox determined to catch the hare. With half a mile to the finish line I could just make out his number, a gold number ten moving up and down but growing slightly larger.

With a quarter mile to go, he disappeared around the last turn of woods. It was flat from here on and I made my move. He was about twelve seconds ahead at his pace. I broke into a sprint that would cover the distance in just under a minute. I had guessed right, he had no sprint left— just pace. My lungs were exploding and my legs began to scream. With fifty yards to go I caught him. He had nothing left and suddenly I had nothing left. It seemed those last fifty yards were traveled in slow motion. Even the cheering was muffled and distorted as if coming through a time warp. We hit the finish line in a dead tie. My knee snapped suddenly as I pulled up and I fell to the ground as if struck by a stone.

Our team won the conference title. I finished tied for first and the cartilage in my right knee had been torn badly. I sat on the bus in a seat by myself, my leg raised and wrapped in a towel with ice packs cooling the heat and ache. Team mates kept moving back to where I sat patting my back and singing my praises. All good— except my season was over.

Actually we all knew any chance for a division title disappeared with my injury. Our sixth runner who would now move up to number five wasn't yet capable of giving the finish we would need.

Only the first five finishers on a team figure into the scoring in Cross-Country.

I was operated on two days after the injury. Rehab would be a year or more. I was going to be allowed to finish the first semester courses at home. I had decided to go back home on crutches to face a Maine Winter. I could see Sheila and Jeffery while following the rehab protocols. I needed some comforting. When I called my mom to tell her I was coming home, she sounded like she didn't know I had gone. Well at least nobody's moved into my room—but wait who knows. Certainly my parents would be the last to know.

❀

Delbert and Roxanne got married in the home of Roxanne's grandmother who actually navigated the steps to her granddaughter's apt. on a late Saturday afternoon in early November. In attendance was Norma Gray, Roxanne's new business partner and Jerome Barry, the one man who had stood by Delbert for years.

Outside, the wind was howling and a naked branch kept tapping the window as the late day sun found its way through the small window just before settling in for the night. The burst of light struck the golden iris of Roxanne's slightly weepy eyes. "I Do," she offered to the question that would link this man at her side, his hands firmly grasping her gloved hands. Delbert heard the tapping of the branch as a last S.O.S. from John Wayne.

Even as the question was repeated for his own response Delbert realized the tapping was not a distress signal at all but rather an announcement of a future he thought he would never have. "I Do," left his lips then Roxanne's lips sealed the deal.

Somewhere out there in picture land the Duke was smiling.

❋

Danny had been back in town for several weeks. He had little to do but write until Joe Gambino's representative reported back with a thumbs up or reported the effort as a— not going to happen.

He sat in his room overlooking the down town. He put down his pen and walked to the window it was an entirely different view today. Snow had fallen overnight. Not the staying kind— he had been told at the restaurant by a native with a need to talk— just a reminder to get the damn wood cut, split and stacked. Danny recorded all these new scenes eager to incorporate them into his story.

Thanksgiving on Thursday should be enlightening. Rebecca had indeed stayed at home this semester while commuting to classes at Colby College in Waterville. She had received money in the form of a scholarship from her employer at Whittemore's. "You are not going to waste a year Rebecca," he had said when he handed her the envelope, "however this offer is only good for Colby and you have to work weekends for me." He had laughed then, indicating her college choice was her own but Rebecca responded by doing just what he suggested, commuting to a campus twenty miles down the road.

She had invited Danny to Thanksgiving dinner. Rebecca worked the two weekend nights at Whittemores. Danny ate there often so the two still touched base but there was no time for any conversation. He intended to show her the rough draft of the story he was writing. He also wanted to use her as a conduit for a conversation about Anna. Get her take on anything she might have heard.

❋

The eyewitness Roxanne— now that served up an interesting dilemma. Danny had never eliminated a woman before. He found out she was recently married to a deputy sheriff who from all he had heard was the town buffoon. She was working out of the home of Norma Gray, Anna's mother. If he could sit and interview Anna for his story perhaps he could also lower the defenses of a key witness.

❀

Sheriff McManus sat at the kitchen table, a small light over the stove casting enough light to make a pot of coffee. When he heard the first perk he went to the door and looked to the end of his driveway. The paperboy had been here. Good. Still in his flannel pajamas he threw a winter coat over his shoulders slipped on a pair of boots with no socks and shuffled out the door. It was still dark and the newly fallen snow glistened in the moon light. Wood smoke filled his nostrils. *Getting cold* he said to himself as he bent to pick up his next thirty minutes of entertainment. Even in the dark without unfolding the paper he knew what the local headlines would be. *Oh well* he thought to himself as he closed the door. The smell of fresh perked coffee welcomed him back into the kitchen "Well somebody loves me," he said quietly as he stirred his cup. He spread the paper out and separated each section. Laura liked the paper neat when she read it. Sheriff McManus went to the local section first this morning. **A Clean Sweep** the headline shouted. Every county official from County District Attorney to Sheriff had been thrown out of office in the recent election. The State Attorney General was gone as well. The newly elected, were touting their victories as a change in direction for the county that was sorely needed. The truth of the election lay in the town of the county seat, Skowhegan. The trial to settle the murder and arson case that had hung over the town for more than a year had turned into one more fiasco. **Kick em out, all of them** had actually been written on campaign posters that dotted every intersection. It seemed Ethel Gray's mantra using her soccer ball as a weapon was all the rage. The tubs of flowers that had delivered a very different message up until a month ago had been put into storage. Now those who had held office while those flowers were blooming were being put into storage as well.

Sheriff McManus wasn't bitter about it. Reflective this morning, his only regret— he hadn't been able to deliver the load. The woods business so paralleled the ups and downs of nearly any profession you could name. Find a lot worth cutting, pay a fair price to the owner, develop a plan, and build what infrastructure you need. Hire a good crew and arrange for transportation of the wood. Oversee it all by being hands on and finally get the load delivered. Sheriff McManus sipped on his second cup. Those political hacks in the prosecutor's office hadn't even looked for an obstruction. *Oh well* he had mentally already moved on and was going to be walking a wood lot later in the morning.

Laura snapped on the kitchen light, "What are you doing here sitting in the dark, feeling sorry for yourself?"

"Laura you know better than that, in fact I think I'd like my third cup of coffee down at Whittemore's, care to join me?"

❀

Danny Walsh was sitting at the counter half way through the two egg special with an added scoop of baked beans that he was wiping his toast through when the Sheriff, and a woman he had never seen before entered and walked to a booth at the back. The Sheriff was not in uniform. Having followed the election Danny was surprised the Sheriff was in street clothes, there's a transition time he thought he had read. The Sheriff had given a nod in his direction. To Danny's mind this guy didn't miss much, glad he won't be in the way down the line. He raised his cup in recognition.

When he finished his meal he walked back to where the Sheriff sat. Sheriff McManus introduced his wife. Danny offered a polite comment on the recent defeat and turned to leave.

"That book is going to be missing some chapters now isn't it or are you going to maybe turn it into a thriller and write your own ending?" The Sheriff smiled.

"You know Sheriff you didn't give me a lot of material to use. I'm not sure the readers are too interested in Maine's logging past as it relates to crime in the street," he laughed at his own witty comment.

The Sheriff laughed too, "You're probably right though up till now it has served me well."

Danny was ready to leave. "As far as that ending, I'm going to finish the few interviews I haven't done and go back home. Write it all up and if I need to change the ending— I actually have some ideas about that."

When Danny left the table Laura spoke up for the first time. "You realize you just danced the dance, don't you?"

"Oh yessiree I do and I hope the new Sheriff knows when to lead and when to follow."

❁

The new Sheriff while not officially aboard just yet was busily assembling his team. He had made a decision that any one in any elevated position in the sheriff's office would have to go through an interview with him personally. The detectives and sergeants who had served through several Sheriffs, had gone through this before. Usually it was perfunctory and maybe one or two new Sheriff's picks usually came aboard or were promoted. This time was different. The new Sheriff put the blame for the length of time it had taken to investigate and still not solve the Skowhegan Fair fire squarely on the shoulders of the men most directly involved. A new group of detectives and sergeants would be serving the newly elected Sheriff. "I need fresh eyes, this town is changing."

❀

Danny Walsh sized the new Sheriff up in the first two minutes of meeting him.

"You can use my name if you want. That's Wainwright, Edward J. My dad always said the J. was for justice.

Now I'm living his dream."

Danny barely managed to squelch a giggle. "The man sitting in front of him was maybe a buck forty on a six foot frame. *He won't have any problem figuring the direction of the political wind,* thought Danny.

"So you will give me access to all the files on this case for my book?"

"I don't see why not, the case is in the hands of the lawyers now. It's all public. Have at it. You might mention how the new Sheriff assisted in getting the facts straight in this case."

"You got it Sheriff. Well I'll just request those files then. Have a good day."

❀

Norma sat at the kitchen table with sketches of potential designs laid out in front of her. Roxanne was looking over her shoulder offering the back story to her sketches.

"I remember every toy I ever had and how it made me feel. These designs for the patterns on kids clothing will appeal to the nostalgia of the Mothers who buy them."

"I've never seen anything like them before. I remember that spinning top, I had one just like it. And the little red wagon, these are incredible, Roxanne."

Roxanne broke into a rare smile, "From what I'm observing Mothers are changing how they dress their kids. It's becoming a game of making their kid look special, not just throwing clothes on them."

She closed her eyes for a moment, "My mother focused on something clean she could pull out of the laundry basket, not folded, not ironed but clean and that was all that mattered. Everyone in my grade school was pretty much dressed the same. Didn't have to match and most of the time it would have looked the same on a boy."

Norma stood, tapped her drawing pencil on the table and signaled Roxanne to sit down." Let me get us some coffee and holler up to Anna, we got us a business to start." She looked around, "Right out of this kitchen. I have some contacts in the fabric business, what we need to do is develop a business plan." She turned before shouting up the stairs. "Do you take sugar? By the way that writer fella called and wants to interview Anna for his book. So we need to be done by 10:00. I want to be there when he speaks with Anna. You never know about those writers."

❦

It was Sunday, November 22, 1964. I was reading the weekend paper. The front page was plastered with the tragedy of one year ago. I would be seeing Rebecca later in the day. This wouldn't be a good day for her. After each article I did another set of leg lifts. My knee surgery had gone as planned I was told. Tell my knee that. All I know is it aches like hell and I'm still a month away from attempting to bend it. I do leg lifts to keep the muscles above the knee strong. Atrophy they told me, don't let your leg atrophy. I kidded the first time I heard that word, the surgeon had used the word when he visited me after surgery. A southerner, it sounded like he was saying <u>a-trophy</u>. I dead panned, "I don't see me collecting <u>a trophy </u>anytime soon Doc, so know worries." Now I know what he meant.

I was into my third set of lifts when the phone rang. My parents agreed to have an extension put up in my room after putting up with me sleeping in the living room my first two weeks home. I pretty much stay up here twenty-four seven now. *'The only time the phone rings it's for you any way,'* my mother had said. There is a half bath up here with an old tin shower stall and I clean up with me sitting on a wooden stool. The call is from Rebecca.

"Can I bring you anything Myron, like food for instance?"

Nah I'm good, Sheila has been great, she's trying to fatten me up. I lost ten pounds since the surgery. So now I'm reliving my past, eating Italian sandwiches and pizza from Barry's on a regular basis. Why do you need to see me? I mean beyond the fact that we are good friends. You sounded a little strange when you called before, all mysterious like."

"I'll explain when I see you. Maybe this idea that's floating out there about a conspiracy to kill President Kennedy has got me looking around corners. Any way I need someone to talk to. Sheriff McManus is gone you know."

"I read the election results, not surprised he's not waiting till coronation day for that stick man to take over. The new sheriff's kid ran with me for a year. His father mentally beat on him every time he finished a race. Leonard wasn't much of a runner but still. I wouldn't stick around either if it was me." I looked down at the black headlines, "Yeah I'm reading the paper right now and on page six a columnist is summarizing the confusion and suspicion a whole year later. Not going to go away anytime soon either." A silence then, "Say you can bring me something, an RC Cola, ice cold from Barry's."

"I'll see you at two pm. then"

I hadn't been around to hear all that had happened since I left at the end of August. My parents didn't communicate with me. Sheila had given me the Reader's Digest version of events along with her fears but that was all I knew. I didn't even know Sheriff McManus had lost the election till I read it in the papers" Rebecca that afternoon shared all that she knew— from Joe Gambino Jr. and his brother leaving the country to what she had heard from the customers at work including police Chief Henry shared. Oh yeah and what she was being told by new friend and writer— Danny Walsh.

❀

Mrs. Merrill our English teacher and Drama coach for the senior play had finally made it down to the Sheriff's office. She waited nearly a half hour to get to speak with the new sheriff. When she was seated she tried to explain why she was here. "I believe I met a very dangerous man earlier in the spring. I'll never forget his face and I would be glad to have someone create a sketch from my description. Sheriff McManus had asked me to come in before but I kept putting it off, correcting papers and all that. Anyway I'd like to help."

The new sheriff unfolded his frame from the new cushioned chairs like Gumby in a comic strip. "Well Mrs. Merrill that ship has sailed, and the reason to find this guy you mentioned has shipped out as well, but thank you for coming in."

"Well then, I'll be off to correct another batch of papers. A three day week this week and I'll hardly find the opportunity to dress the bird. Sorry for taking up your time sheriff, I'm sure you are busy." This lady could act.

Mrs. Merrill opened the Sheriff's office door just as Danny Walsh entered the outer office. Their eyes met, Danny revealed not the slightest recognition. Mrs. Merrill remained neutral as well. She did hear the sheriff ask the man if there was another file he needed to see.

"Mrs. Merrill thought to herself, *must have been a round trip ticket on that boat.*

❀

Sheriff McManus was in his shed sharpening up his chainsaw when Detective Fitzmaurice pulled into his driveway. It was Thanksgiving morning and the

Sheriff planned to hunt a little— later in the afternoon. He would hunt for an hour or two on his woodlot up in Solon and if he got lucky he would be filling the bed of his pickup with more than a load of firewood.

It was cold this morning and his efforts to ready all his gear had vapor starting to emerge from his flannel shirt. Pat Fitzmaurice about the same age as the Sheriff, North side of forty but fit, moved with a purpose. *He walks like he talks, no wasted motion,* thought Sheriff Mac as his former detective and still good friend approached.

"I'm putting in my paper work Mac. This new Sheriff is an idiot."

"I only saw him on the campaign trail and just once in my office after the election—said he thought the signs I had up were cute— he said that."

"He's reassigning all personnel— after we go through a personal interview–with him of course. Four of the other guys are moving on as well. You going to restart that woods business, I'll work for you?"

"Not sure right now, I had six weeks of vacation time stored up so, I'm going to cut a little firewood, do a little hunting, maybe get down to Florida in February for a week or two— Laura would like that."

"You realize this murder and fire are never going to be pursued don't you?"

"From our end we did all we can do. My worry is that the father of those two boys is going to want to bring them home at some point, that means shutting some people up, permanently."

"So what can we do, we're about to be private citizens?"

Sheriff McManus picked up the chainsaw he'd been sharpening earlier and studied the gleaming edges of the chain. "I've come to know and like that Gray girl, Anna, and Delbert he's part of what was our law enforcement family. Now he's got a wife, our star witness. I still believe they are in danger. I'm beginning to think we might have to approach this like that story I told you guys about the men who were stealing our fuel and equipment."

The driveway squeaked as Sergeant Sylvain pulled in behind Pat.

"I think we should do a little hunting this afternoon and you boys can help me get in some firewood, that's what I think." Then the Sheriff winked.

❀

Danny Walsh was convinced there was no danger left here to squelch. He was on a payphone that was located just off the railroad bridge on the corner of Water Street and Russell. "There's a new Sheriff up here, numb as a fence post. He's all excited I might include him in this book. He's given me every file they have. I'm telling you boss there's no need to take this any further. New State and County Attorney's too. They are not going to take a potential loser to trial."

Joe Gambino listened, "I don't like loose ends. Best I can do is say forget about the girl with the kid. My wife is having second thoughts anyway. She remembers the two boys as being little jerks right up till they became big jerks," He chuckled then. Then he became serous. "The eye witness, she's got to disappear."

"This is going to cause us problems boss, this is a small town, and everyone knows one another's business. It's not my place to contradict you and I'll do as I'm told but I don't think it's necessary."

"Danny, you can't see my face right now but feel my words, **I want that witness gone from this earth, capiche?"**

The phone booth had steamed up and as Danny emerged he was blinded by the late morning sun. The wind had kicked up causing him to shiver. He sighed deeply, this was going to be a mistake he could just feel it. Thanksgiving Day, alone in a small town, the street deserted, Danny looked at himself as he passed various storefronts. He was thirty- four years old now, his last birthday passing unnoticed by anyone but himself. A hired enforcer, about to climb the stairs to a two room apartment. The one thing he was looking forward to was continuing to write a story that could never be read or printed. Oh well, Rebecca had promised a nice dinner, *there's that at least.*

The little bit of positive thought, *there's that at least* disappeared shortly after arriving at Rebecca's home. Danny had not had the good fortune to meet Mr. Tully, Rebecca's dad. Danny pulled into the driveway and exited his vehicle. He knocked and the door opened to a shot gun leveled at his torso.

"Who are you and what do you want?"

"Ah, ah um, a friend of your daughter's sir, can you put that down?"

Mr. Tully kept the gun in place. He was a little man beaten down by life but right now standing there like that, he loomed large. "You sure you're not one of them?"

Danny thought, *what response is going to work here?* He had his mouth open when Rebecca came down the stairs.

"DAD! For god sakes what are you doing? Put down that gun."

"You sure he's not one of them?"

"No dad he's not one of them."

Later as Danny and Rebecca did up the Thanksgiving dishes, Rebecca added to the little bit that had calmed the situation enough to allow Mr. Tully to go to his room and shut the door. He was mumbling well below understanding when he wandered off.

"It's that damn shop. First they send him home because he's too injured to work, then when he tries to collect worker's compensation they send people around to see if they can catch him active enough to deny his claim. He's a nervous wreck."

"That gun looked pretty steady, he had a good bead on my belly," Danny smiled.

"Well that gun was not loaded. He's so nervous he couldn't load a shell if there was one in the house. I went in to his *place of employment* that's what he calls it— and asked if maybe he could be given a different job—hourly so he didn't have to depend on pure speed and accuracy. The boss took me right onto the floor where my dad worked, played all sympathetic like but shook his head no— tried to take my arm. It was hotter than hades in there and nobody looked up, kept their eyes on the machine they were running. The noise had the man hollering his lines and racks of shoes were flying by like a kid on roller-skates. He took me to the machine my father normally operated. A guy was grabbing each shoe one at a time like his life depended on it and I guess at some level it did. Each shoe was attached to a foot shaped piece of wood. He placed the rough edges of the bottom of the shoe to this grinding wheel and in one motion flipped from toe to heel. Any miscalculation could wreck the shoe—or your fingers. The guy never raised his head but the sweat was dripping off his nose and he didn't even stop to wipe it away. "Piece Work" the boss shouted over the din, "that's the only way we work here except for a couple of jobs."

"I saw more in that short visit about the way the world works than all the days in my classes hearing about the, **Captains of Industry** and how they made this country great. The men and women running those machines and millions of others in a thousand different places are what made this country great, thank you very much." She shifted gears, "Now you have me started. The damn car business runs the same way. That's why there's no car in the yard. We used to have one, a nice one but old. When my father went to trade they offered nothing. He ended up selling it to a friend for just a little more than that nothing. Ok so now he has no trade right, good position to be in he was told. Goes back to buy a good used car, they want an arm and a leg. He leaves shaking his head knowing just how many little shoes would have to turn their heads to pay for it. That good position he was told he'd be in— it's called bend over. Hence no car in the yard."

Danny looked at Rebecca, "Whoa, you are on fire there girl. I think I'm glad it wasn't you holding that gun."

Rebecca snapped him playfully with the wet dish towel, "Be very glad Mr. Author that I'm not disposed to violence, I'm just like those workers— yes sir, no sir, can I help you ma'am, are you ready to order, would you like a menu or a minute?"

"Yeah, I think that's why I freelance, not real good at taking orders from people."

"You pitched right in with those dishes though," she kidded.

"I guess you bring out the domestic in me young lady, I'll have to write you in as a calming influence in the story.

"When am I going to get to read this tome anyway?"

" I was going to share a rough draft today but it will all be written soon, just got to come up with an ending I can live with; like I said I'm not good with taking orders, it has to be my ending.

Rebecca frowned, "Well who else's would it be, if not yours?"

❀

Roxanne agreed to meet the writer Danny Walsh.

"This is all going to be written as fiction so no names will be used. I just want to get a feel for that night. The emotions, the actions, what you smelled even."

Roxanne was sitting at the kitchen table in Norma

Gray's home. Norma had agreed to sit with her as she talked with this writer fella.

"So what have you written down about that night so far?" Asked Roxanne.

"I just have the bones— you know the basic facts I got from the fire department, the hospital, witnesses that saw the flames, the aftermath really. Now I'm trying to recreate the drama of that moment, how and why you reacted the way you did. Why you didn't come forward immediately, things like that. The case is dead, but it will still make a great book I hope."

"So you don't see any harm in Roxanne giving you the details of something she still might have to testify to if those boys are ever brought to justice?" asked Norma Gray.

"As I said this will be a work of fiction so no, I don't see the harm."

Norma sat back crossed her arms then she spoke, "I don't want to tell you what to do Roxanne, this is your decision but if it were me, I wouldn't say anything to this man."

Danny Walsh raised his eyebrows quizzically.

Norma who had experienced more than her share of bull crap followed up. "You say this is going to be a work of fiction. So use your imagination Mr. Walsh. A lot of us got hurt in all this mess and I'm not sure we're ready to be read about."

Danny turned his head, "Roxanne, it's up to you, I would love to hear your story."

Roxanne sat quietly, she had actually been thinking about what she would say since Rebecca brought the request through Norma.

She studied Danny Walsh, looking for a pattern maybe. "I 'm somewhere near your age I would guess Mr. Walsh, and up to now nobody has ever given a fig about my life story. Now because of something I supposedly saw or did, I'm worth interviewing and writing about," she sipped her coffee.

"My husband is with the Sheriff's office. He says in his experience most people get into trouble by running their mouth." She let that sit for a moment like a cup too hot to sip. "People at the top are going to do what they are going to do whether you add your two cents worth or not." Roxanne had to smile at the effort it had taken Delbert to hold a conversation in their early days. "He told me if they put you under **the light**, that's what he called it, **the light** just imagine yourself at the beach on a sunny day. Answer their questions but don't offer any of your own little anecdotes or your humor, don't try to be funny, they don't like that he said. Half the time they don't get the punch line anyway." She stood then and walked to Norma's kitchen window. She stood there for nearly a minute studying the world that lay just beyond this room. Then she turned but did not rejoin Danny at the table. "I'll pass on filling in the dots Mr. Walsh. Thank you for the opportunity but in this little town it's best to keep a low profile. We're just beginning a new business and we don't need to get people upset any more than they are."

"Would you like another cup of coffee Mr. Walsh?" offered Norma Gray.

Danny Walsh smiled tightly, "good with the coffee," he rose, "I guess I need to get back to using my imagination as you suggested." He placed his cup on the table, "no idea how this story is going to end." He left thinking, *this is a tight knit little town, it seems these people will go to the mat for one another.*

◈

Delbert loved the cold. He loved anything that put people back on their heels a little. His whole life had been an awkward moment— that little hesitation he could sense in people before allowing Delbert to enter their lives— even if only briefly. Cold and wind and snow changed people's daily routine. They had to add layers and cover body parts that embraced obscurity. They walked differently— awkward like Delbert, the original poster boy for obscurity.

This morning there was no snow but the cold and wind had people bundled up and anonymous. He walked twenty yards behind someone who was going in the same direction. Delbert chuckled as the wind nudged the person to the left then the right. *You don't suppose they have been drinking,* he kidded to himself silently not trying to catch up as he headed down Mt. Pleasant Avenue headed to the Sheriff's office. When he reached the bottom of the avenue another man crossed his path. Their eyes met, possibly a head nod— nope— but recognition in the man's eyes. The man had come from his left, Railroad Street maybe or Ash or Cedar St.

Delbert knew immediately this guy was not a native Mainer. He had his collar up but his ears were exposed. Delbert let him move ahead. Delbert stopped. He looked briefly down at the water exiting the dam behind Central Maine Power. In that moment Delbert viewed all that Roxanne had brought into his life. Why that thought passed through his mind at that moment Delbert couldn't say but his instincts told him this stranger knew Roxanne and knew of Delbert as well. It's a good distance across the railroad bridge and in that time Delbert experienced a John Wayne moment. He remained far enough behind not to raise suspicion but give him a clear view of where this guy was headed. It was a walk that consumed maybe five minutes. Delbert stood on the sidewalk of Madison Avenue, looking north. He lingered at the corner where the Baptist Church stood sentinel. The man a hundred yards ahead now, crossed Madison Avenue and entered Whittemore's restaurant. Delbert nodded his head and crossed the avenue headed for the Sheriff's office.

He had gone a short way when the picture cleared up for him, *Whittemore's* he had never seen this guy by himself— but he had seen him— with Rebecca.

• SNOW OR IS THAT WHITE NOISE

During the first two weeks of December it looked like perhaps it was going to be an open winter. Colder than normal temperatures but no snow on the ground as yet.

Danny Walsh had still not decided how to get rid of Roxanne. Honestly he didn't relish the idea either. He was being forced to come to a decision however after getting the call from a representative of the Gambino family late last night. He was to find a phone booth and call a number this morning at exactly 9:22 am.

It was now 10:15 and the joyous news had reached Danny's ears. The boys were coming back home for Christmas and Joe Senior wanted to know that the best Christmas present ever had been delivered. "You'll see to that won't you Danny," he had said.

"Neither, snow nor sleet will keep me from my appointed rounds," he had answered.

Just as he hung up and exited the phone booth the first flake hit him right in the eye. Omen maybe.

• DELBERT FINDS A PATTERN

Former Sheriff McManus heard the knock on his door. He rose from the recliner placed the paper to the side and looked out through the curtain. Delbert was standing there facing the door at full attention looking like he would salute whoever opened the door. Laura was at work, he checked the watch the men had given him when he was defeated in the latest election. 8:35 am and the date December 19th. Delbert accepted the cup of perked coffee but declined the offer of a biscuit with molasses.

"Roxanne fed me good this morning before she left for her new job."

"Laura said she heard Norma Gray was starting a business of some sort and that Roxanne was going to be working for her."

"Yep they are designing kids' clothes with toys and bears and stuff on em."

"Well good for them, seems like all the factories around here are either slowing down or closing down altogether."

"Yeah I'm seeing a lot more people walking these streets than I did just a year ago in the middle of a workday." Delbert hadn't stuttered even once.

Delbert started to fidget with his hat, obviously small talk was over.

"So what brings you here this morning Delbert, I realize I haven't sent you a Christmas card yet, but it's in the mail," the Sheriff winked.

Delbert never cracked a smile but began, "You know Roxanne is the only eyewitness to what happened at the fair. I-I I'm worried something is going to happen to her, soon."

The Sheriff scraped his chair up to the table a little closer, he was about to speak but Delbert beat him to it.

"Roxanne cured me Sheriff, all of me, my speech, my confidence— everything really. I know people laughed at me my whole life but I'm not that same man. And Roxanne too, people laughed at her, but I'll tell you she is a smart lady— talented too."

The Sheriff leaned in a little closer, "So what's making you feel like she's in danger?"

"I can't put my finger on it exactly, but even you always agreed I was a good watcher for the town.

Anyway, I've been watching and talking with Roxanne at night and the only new piece to the puzzle that we can come up with is this writer fella."

Sheriff McManus sat back and the brief interview with Danny Walsh flitted through his mind. Now that he thought of it the guy hadn't seemed all that upset when denied access to any files. A sudden thought, *maybe he got just what he had come for, a chance to size up the man who might be hunting him down someday, and that little verbal dance he had experienced in the restaurant with Laura there— Hmm.*

Delbert had begun to speak but Sheriff Mac interrupted. "You know Delbert I haven't let this go either. I've been meeting with the lead detectives every week going over what we might have missed in all this. We all agree Roxanne is the only certainty that these boys could ever be tried and convicted. Has Roxanne ever met this man?"

"Actually he tried to interview her at Norma's house but Norma encouraged her not to talk with him and she shut him down."

"Do you believe he could be out to hurt Roxanne?"

"I only met him once and that was just in passing on the railroad bridge. He gave me a bad feeling Sheriff. I didn't recognize him then but I followed him to Whittemore's, and that triggered where I had seen him before— with Rebecca."

The Sheriff got up and went to the kitchen window.

The day was grey it looked like it might begin snowing again any minute. A squirrel was scampering across the driveway with something in his mouth. He disappeared around the shed.

The Sheriff turned, "let's say you are right about all this Delbert, how do we smoke him out before he acts?"

Delbert spoke up, "Roxanne makes patterns, and she sees stuff in her brain most people don't see. That's why she and Norma are going to have a good business. Their kids clothing is going to be like nobody else's."

Sheriff Mac began but this time Delbert spoke over him, "I see patterns too Sheriff Mac— have all my life. How people always take the exact same route to the store, start shopping by getting their groceries in the same aisle. Choose the same items week after week— unless somethings on sale of course," He smiled. "But more than that, how people approach their weekends, carrying that brown bag with a pint or the Ballantine ale from the same place week after week. Knowing at some level that there will be the same fighting and crying and slamming of doors or physical violence even. I got to know whose picture is sitting on which little table in a lot of places sheriff. I didn't even realize it till Roxanne started telling me how her brain works. I have made it my professional life's work, seeing patterns." He paused, "I will have that biscuit now sheriff if you're still offering, all this newfangled talking I do now has got me hungry."

Sheriff McManus realized he had missed the transition in Delbert. He was actually enjoying this conversation, the man made sense too. He spooned molasses on a cut biscuit and served it up.

Delbert hardly missed a beat, "I figure if I know Roxanne's travel pattern, this guy does too by now. Here's what I know. No matter where she is coming from or going to— day or night— she crosses that little swinging bridge on the island. Perfect place to ambush her would be on that bridge. A man could hide back there and either shoot, kidnap, or whatever the plan— hit her over the head and toss her off that bridge maybe."

Sheriff Mac looked again at his watch. The date hadn't changed. He closed his eyes briefly. If pattern was what he was hearing then it was time to change the pattern, add a little confusion or anxiety. He thought aloud, "What if we somehow made it known that Roxanne was going to have to leave, go out of state maybe," he paused, "stay with me here." He paused again, "a sick relative possibly, no idea when she'll be back, leaving three days from now." The sheriff imagined the men he had been conversing with weekly— trusted men. "She would go through her regular routine and we would have our team in place and ready to intervene. I know the fire chief would be glad to have a little help at the fire station on the island. And I think I know the perfect conduit to plant the seed. I just need to get in touch with Chief Henry."

Delbert asked what he could do to help.

"You have the toughest job of all Delbert, you have to sell this idea to Roxanne, then make sure she follows her regular pattern to a t."

Sheriff Mac walked Delbert to the door. It had started to snow. "More snow Delbert, you ready for it?"

"I love snow Sheriff," he smiled, "makes it easier to see the patterns— if you follow me."

The sheriff nodded and watched Delbert exit his driveway. The foot pattern clear distinct and in a straight line. As he watched this deputy he had never fully appreciated trudge back onto the roadway the snow piling up, he spotted that same squirrel again, this time he was coming out of his shed with something in his mouth, it was colored. *Oh Shit, that's the little rubber gasket I was going to replace in my chainsaw.* "Hey you drop that"

• FOUR MORE SHOPPING DAYS

Chief Henry sat at the bar in Whittemore's. It was Sunday night December 20th Rebecca was working. College was closed for the holidays and the first semester had ended. Outside, the snow continued to pile up, the wind was moving it around— nasty night it was going to be. A puddle of water glistened at the entrance. Rebecca was behind the bar reaching for a pot of coffee. Chief Henry spoke to her back. "When you get a chance I'd like a word with you."

Rebecca turned, "sure thing Chief, just let me get this coffee back to that table, pretty quiet right now. I'll be right back."

When she returned she sat down and sighed, looking a little tired actually. He took one of her hands, "You have known me a long time Rebecca, do you trust me?"

Rebecca looked at the hand covering hers. Age spots had begun their journey, mapping all the experiences these hands had endured. They were strong hands.

"Actually I do Chief, the kids I grew up with in this town feel like you always gave them a fair shake. So with the endorsement of my former classmates, the class of 1964 at least, yes I trust you." She smiled.

Chief Henry smiled in return. "I don't know if I ever told you how sorry I was when you lost your hero. A lot of us older folks liked him too. I know you planned to follow a path he created. I hope you still do that." He cleared his throat seemingly stalling for time to gather himself— how to begin. "So here it is," He continued to hold her hand as if his thoughts needed an ally, "we think that writer fella may be here to hurt people." The thought was airborne now and he released her hand. "Gregg, Sheila, Anna, Roxanne maybe all of em, but we are betting its Roxanne."

Rebecca stood, she went to the back of the bar and poured herself a coffee, she made a motion inviting the Chief to continue as she added cream and sugar.

He waited till she sat back down. "As you are well aware just like about everybody else in this town she's the only eye witness to that fire fiasco."

Rebecca's eyes widened. "Are you sure about this, he seems like a really nice guy. He's never come onto me in any way." She chuckled remembering the discussion of the horror movie. "And he does seem to know a thing or two about writing." She saw the serious look in the Chief's eyes. "Wow I'm blown away."

"Are we positive— no we aren't— but if he's who we suspicion him to be, he's working for those boys' father? We have a plan to smoke him out. If he doesn't take the bait then he's in the clear. This is how you can help."

When he had finished Rebecca set her game face and nodded in the affirmative.

❀

It was on the 21ˢᵗ that Danny chose to take care of business. A slip from Rebecca this morning at breakfast was forcing the issue. He had hoped to at least let Christmas pass. Sure he'd been given a Christmas deadline but a day or two wasn't going to matter, nobody works over Christmas anyway he had reasoned. *So be it,* he thought. He spent the morning putting the finishing touches on his book. No one would ever read what he had written but the process had convinced him he had the interest and the creative talent to take up this new profession. He had decided this would be his final mission for those damn Gambino's. In his book he took them to task for their foolish actions, this past one and other mistakes he had cleaned up. He was especially proud of the colorful descriptions he was using. He reread the final scene looking for any holes in his thinking. He would have to change the names later obviously if he became a real writer, then maybe he could use at least parts of this story. But for now the image of Roxanne filled his head and he had to use her name to visualize the actions he was soon to take.

He put his writing away, checked the time. He was surprised at how long he had sat there. Hungry once more, he made himself a bologna and cheese sandwich washed down with a Dawson Ale. He relieved himself and slipped on his parka and after nearly freezing his ears off recently he added a stocking cap. Darkness was just beginning to claim ownership as he closed the door to his two room apartment. He shook his head. Damn, he didn't want to do this.

If he had eaten more slowly or perhaps had another Dawson ale things might have turned out differently. A scant two minutes after the door closed the telephone rang— incessantly. Just a minute longer— oh well.

Danny stepped into a pre-Christmas scene, one without the downtown shoppers. The downtown had called it a day what with all the snow that had fallen throughout the day. Christmas lights hadn't given up though, twinkling in the darkened windows. Danny looked into the window of the one business still open, Barry's Pizza. He could see a lone customer navigating his way through a pinball labyrinth. He couldn't recognize who it might be from this distance through the still lightly falling snow, which meant the player couldn't identify him either if he did manage to drag his attention away from his challenge. He began walking the route he had earlier described in his journal. His steps were guided by the words he had written. He crossed the railroad bridge and for the last time stared down into the icy cold waters of the Kennebec River. An ever repeating scene below, always slightly different and yet the same. Turning right onto Mill Street, trees hid the view of the torrent of water coming over the dam. He could hear it though and that brought an image already documented in his story. I think I described that sound well, he silently congratulated himself. The stark lifeless limbs watching him pass wore their own white jackets tonight. The snow had stopped falling but had dumped another inch in the past hour making the roadway very very slippery. He descended the slight pitch watching his footing. As he reached the end of Mill Street he was climbing again. The stop sign actually brought him to a halt. For a moment he remembered all the stop signs in town disguised as part of a flower pot and thought that clever and creative. He looked up, the skies would not allow a moon to offer a viewing this evening. Good sign. Briefly Danny's mind left his mission and did an inventory. All was packed and a rental car waiting in Waterville, tomorrow. One more night spent in town then the 10:00 am bus in the morning. He had taken this roundabout route rather than risk being viewed on the main road. He would be visible but just briefly as he crossed from Mill Street onto a short stretch of the main road. He would enter the parking lot behind the Jr. High. *It's Just like I wrote this,* he mused. His journal was again guiding his footsteps. He walked towards the little swinging bridge behind the Jr. High. He stood briefly under the dim light and began crossing to the other side. He had a hard time keeping his footing as the bridge moved in two directions with every step, the bridge complaining aloud like a senior with arthritic knees. The footing was treacherous as well. He got to the other side and found himself out of breath. *I wouldn't want to have to navigate that twice a day.*

❀

When Roxanne appeared as she did every evening just as darkness settled on the town she would be wearing a red ski jacket and a sky blue hat. Danny had watched her often enough so he would recognize that outfit even in a crowd. The plan was a simple one. Wait until she appeared in the one dim light at the entrance to the bridge then begin his own re-crossing. The bridge would squeak and squawk and move and shake with every step taken. It was at least eighty yards across. In the middle, the darkest spot he would let her pass then strike her hard from behind. Toss her over the side and continue on his way. She would either succumb to the blow or drown. With any luck at all she would pass through the dam behind the power company and not be found until spring. He recalled the sound of that water a short time ago and in his mind watched a red jacket bobbing in the waves. He waited.

❀

At 4:47 pm on a dark and dismal evening on the 21st of December in the little town of Skowhegan a red jacket and blue hat appeared beneath the small incandescent light at the entrance to what was locally known as the swinging bridge. The bridge announced the crossing by adding its own motion complete with groans and whispers. The three inches of snow covering the wooden planking muffled footfall but added challenge. Face covered with a scarf, gait unsteady the bridge dictated pace. Danny Walsh moved. Suddenly they were two checker pieces moving laterally then diagonally toward one another. The lurching of the bridge defied a straight forward movement. When they were twenty yards from one another the figure in the red parka appeared to slip and grip the railing and struggled to regain their balance. By then Danny had closed the gap. The figure in red was trying to gather their balance, arms flailing. Danny was at their shoulder. He couldn't help himself he had to say it. "Merry Christmas," he uttered as he raised the black jack over his head. The figure in the red jacket slipped even further just then, as if startled— to a sitting position. Twisting, trying to regain their balance, they hit the snow covered planking, sighing in apparent frustration. Danny Walsh brandished the blackjack looking for an opportunity to strike.

A much deeper voice than the one in Danny's writing and his memory spoke then. This voice was holding a revolver pointed directly at Danny's midsection. At that moment darkness turned to midday as lights at both ends of the bridge lit the scene. Danny responded to the lawful order and dropped the blackjack. The bridge came alive with movement as if struck by a violent wind storm.

Delbert who had seen every escape attempt in the book both on screen and off didn't attempt to get up, he simply sat there holding Danny Walsh at gun point waiting for the troops to arrive.

If Delbert had known the Gambino boy— Eddie—he would have done him proud just now, not falling for those tricks the boy constantly had commented on in his cowboy books.

Chief Henry with two deputies trailing him arrived, out of breath himself. He put the cuffs on and walked Danny Walsh to the Island end of the bridge staying ten feet behind, his gun leveled at the man's back. Delbert remained sitting with his head resting on a lower railing. He had a lot cross his mind but one thought stuck. If he got his name on a plaque or on a wall he wouldn't mind. Since his association and education by Roxanne he couldn't do squat with those damn pinball machines.

In fact his name on the wall of pinball fame had been replaced by a young man with lots of time on his hands and a wounded wing to boot. Delbert had noticed it just earlier this evening— before he changed clothes— just when he observed Danny Walsh appear to try to see into the window at Barry's Pizza. Myron Therrian was the new leader in the pinball world. A new sudden thought, *Hurt Roxanne would yuh, I don't think so*!

Sheriff McManus watched the capture from his truck on the Bridge Street side. Pat Fitzmaurice sat in his vehicle on the island side, both unofficial witnesses and contributors to the plan they had put in place with Chief George Henry. The new County Sheriff would be coming to this party late and would never live it down.

EPiLOGUE

I sat in the courtroom for the entire trial of Danny Walsh. It lasted just two days. Police Chief Henry had issued a search warrant for Danny's apartment and found Danny's journal, a complete transcript. It began with the fire, his own knowledge of it, what witnesses had told him as well as his orders and plans to silent witnesses. Notes had been turned into dialogue. Excerpts of the finished book were read to the judge. Danny didn't request a jury trial, he was smarter than that. He had already made a deal with the States Attorney, though it would be up to the judge to go along with it. Something about testifying against his old boss. Though it seemed maybe Joe Gambino Sr. had been punished enough as of late.

Sheila sat with me, as well as Anna and Rebecca. My knee was healing slowly, I was just beginning to walk without a crutch— running would have to wait. I was new king of pin ball though— name right up there on the wall.

Anna waved to Sheriff McManus who was sitting with Delbert and Roxanne on one side and Jerome Barry on the other.

Chief Henry sat by himself but nodded his head when Sheriff Mac got his attention.

❋

Oh yeah about that phone call. Two minutes— if that long— after Danny left his apartment. That was a call from one of Joe Gambino Sr.'s attorney's. It seems that at 12:30pm on the 21st of December 1964 a small airplane flying from an airfield in the Caribbean headed to Miami crashed into the Atlantic, killing all six aboard. Two of those killed were the sons of Joe Gambino Sr. Joe Jr. and Eddie. The reason for the call— to tell Danny his own mission was to be aborted.

• THE END

Sheila and I married four years to the day from when we first met at Ma Beane's. Jeffery ended up becoming a teacher, having two siblings a boy and a girl. We all still live in North Carolina. I never did run competitively again. Happy though.

Paul became a lawyer who tried to make a difference. He worked representing the poor and downtrodden. He never married. He passed away in the summer of 2009. The Cancer got him. One trial he couldn't win.

Gregg Croteau, he did leave the State of Maine just before the shit hit the fan. He never returned. We sent out fliers trying to get him back for a reunion even though he didn't graduate with us. No luck.

Rebecca, she did join the Peace Corp and is retired and living in Florida. She never came back for a reunion either.

Anna and her mother Norma along with Roxanne opened a children's clothing business that is still running— though on line—even today. Anna never married. Her mother Norma remained single too. They still live in Skowhegan. Norma turns ninety this year but still tends to her flowers. Daughter Ethel played Soccer for The University of Maine and went on to a very successful coaching career. Anna's daughter, Layla Ray went in to nursing. She lives in Waterville, MaineSheriff Mac and his wife moved to Florida after that first February vacation. I have no idea where they are or if they are still with us.

Jerome Barry sold his business and bought a farm if you can believe it. Somewhere in the western part of the state.

Delbert and Roxanne ended up adopting three children, all handicapped in some way. They continue to be the true heroes of that year and all the years that followed.

There that's it.

OH OH! I just got a letter in the mail. It's addressed to me but has no return address. Oh my god it's from Danny Walsh, somewhere in witness protection.

Here, I'll just let you read it.

Hey there Myron,

I heard you were writing my story. That is, the story I would have written if I wasn't in such a damn hurry to get out that damn door all those years ago. Yeah I'm still alive. I turn eighty-five next week. I thought maybe I could get my two cents worth in and if you think it worthy of print—well there you go my fifteen minutes of fame finally published. Ha ha.

I served five years in Thomaston prison in Maine, all in solitary for my safety they said. Anyway, I bet I wrote four different drafts of this book you have written. Rebecca has stayed in touch after I reached out to her. She forgave me my transgressions and we still communicate. No one is after me anymore, they are all dead. I just wanted you to know that your town and the people in it changed my life. I never wanted to hurt Roxanne, the whole plan didn't make sense to me. I went straight after those five years in prison. I got a job in a little weekly paper down in Florida and sold advertising for thirty years. I became part of the story I concocted, go figure. And so, I live on a boat somewhere in the keys and fish every morning. I still have a Jameson in the late afternoon and am still trying to read all the great books of our time.

One final thought. If you ever need some material for a new story, well, it's too late for me but if you're interested I have kept a journal for all these years. Lots of good stuff in there, hell you could write a book— ha ha. I will stay in touch.

Yours in writing, Danny Walsh.

PEOPLE I WISH TO THANK:

- My brother Zane for sharing coffee and ideas many years ago when this story was first started.

- Tommy Quinn for graciously sending me historical data of Skowhegan.

- The Skowhegan Historical society for letting me view the past.

- The Hight family for allowing me to study Skowhegan Fair material.

- Nina Padilla who designed and painted the original cover.

- The class of 1964 of which I am a proud member.

- Finally, as always my family, I love you all.

AUTHOR PAGE

Robert Wesley Clement is a native of Central Maine where he spent his first 56 years. He now lives in Palm Coast Florida with his wife Carey.

Other books include: AS IT LIES, This Old House, Troubled Waters, Pebbles From The Pond,, The House that Jack built, Ghost Writer, and Rogue Wave.

Please visit my web site at rwesleyclement@gmail.com